Karma Neutral

Karma Neutral

Is it possible to make good all the mistakes of your life before it's too late?

T J Hobbs

Author of the outstanding spiritual novel
DAY TRIPS TO HEAVEN

A record of this publication is available from the British Library.

ISBN 978-1-910027-10-3

Typesetting by Wordzworth Ltd
www.wordzworth.com

Cover design by Titanium Design Ltd
www.titaniumdesign.co.uk

Printed by Lightning Source UK
www.lightningsource.com

Cover image © T J Hobbs

Published by Local Legend
www.local-legend.co.uk

The Author

T J Hobbs is a natural health care practitioner who has been working on her own spiritual development for well over twenty years. She is especially drawn to Native American and Celtic Shamanism. *Karma Neutral* is her second spiritual novel.

Several other novels, short stories and children's picture books are in progress; she also really loves science fiction and is working on a series of *Solar Star* novels.

Her other interests are horse riding, Tai-chi, travel and photography. She lives in Hampshire, England.

www.tjhobbs.co.uk

Other Publications

T J Hobbs is the author of the outstanding spiritual novel

DAY TRIPS TO HEAVEN

(ISBN 978-1-907203-99-2, also available as an eBook)

Trainee spirit guide Ethan is having a hard time learning the ropes. With angelic help, he is allowed to bring a few deserving souls from Earth for a preview of the afterlife to help them with critical decisions. This charming story is full of gentle humour, compassion and spiritual wisdom.

www.local-legend.co.uk

About This Book

We have all said things that should be left unsaid and not done things that needed to be done. Sometimes these things have hurt other people, either through our thoughtlessness or intention. Then, in moments of reflection, we begin to wish that we could make good our mistakes and wipe the slate clean. But that's not possible… is it?

Karma is the 'record' of all our thoughts and actions, both good and bad. Many believe that we carry karma with us from one lifetime to the next and that it affects our material circumstances here and our spiritual development hereafter. Whether this is true or not, surely we all wish to end our lives at peace with those we have wronged and with our own consciences.

James Wylie is a successful, self-made businessman who has given little thought to the effects of his relationships with others. But when he receives a devastating diagnosis, he begins to reassess his life and realises that he has to do something about it – fast. This powerful novel, full of surprises, is both a spiritual adventure and a love story, asking deeply important questions of every one of us.

One

"… an inoperable brain tumour."

I sit in my GP's office on a hot August morning and all I hear him say are those four words. From that point on, he and his small stuffy room recede far into the distance and, although I know he is still talking, all I hear over and over again is *'inoperable brain tumour'*.

"Mr Wylie… Mr Wylie!"

I blink and suddenly find myself staring back into his soulful eyes.

"Do you understand what I have told you?" he asks me. A rush of anger spurts up through my body.

"Yes, of course I understand, I'm not stupid," I hiss. "I understand that I'm a dead man." My reaction makes him blink a couple of times but he manages to retain his composure. I guess he's done this before but this time it's me and my life, damn it.

"Well, I wouldn't put it quite like that," he says softly. I raise an eyebrow.

"Oh? Then how, pray tell, would you put it?" I ask him.

"Um, well, you may have as much as a year of quality time left before you become sick."

"Oh goody, that's okay then," I say angrily.

"I'm sorry, Mr Wylie," he sighs. "I know this is a great shock and I think you need some time to take in what I've told you." He's not wrong there and we sit looking at each other in silence for a couple of minutes. I don't know what to do or say anymore and I'm not sure how I feel. There's a sort of emptiness in the middle of my stomach, like an open space that is icy cold. Finally I manage to engage some of what's left of my impaired brain.

"There's no treatment?"

He shakes his head. "No surgery, I'm afraid, because of where it is located, you see." I don't but I'm not ready for any further medical explanations, not today anyway, and he must sense this because he adds, "Come and see me again in a couple of days and we can talk more about other options." I frown, as I was under the impression that I didn't have any other options.

"What are they, then?"

"For helping you deal with the symptoms. And how you want to be treated." He didn't add "…at the end" but he didn't have to and I shudder. I don't want to end up in a hospice; I would rather die alone in my own bed than be surrounded by other dying people. It suddenly feels very claustrophobic in here. I need to breathe and I have to get out into the fresh air so I get up and head for the door.

"Okay, Doc, I'll do that," I tell him as I grab the door handle and turn it.

"Good, see you in a day or so," he says to my retreating back as I make my escape.

A barrier of heat hits me as I push open the glass door and stumble out onto the crowded and polluted London street. I turn right and begin to walk, totally baffled by what has just happened to me as I had gone in there thinking I may have something that the wonders of modern medicine would cure quite easily – and now I've been told I'm a dead man walking. It's… oh, my God, I just can't believe this. I stop suddenly.

"Oy mate, what're you doing?" a man behind me shouts as he swerves to avoid me. I mumble "Sorry" and he shakes his head at me.

So I just stand there looking about as two young, pretty girls in cotton sundresses walk by me laughing at something and looking so happy and carefree. How can the world carry on as if nothing has happened when my world has just fallen in on me? It all looks so bloody normal. The traffic is just about moving, the pigeons are hopping about under people's feet, businessmen are hurrying by looking stressed and women are still pushing prams with crying infants in them. All of these people going about their lives completely oblivious to what has just happened. Deep inside me I feel so angry at how unfair all this is and have a desire to yell at all of them, "Don't you understand? I've just been sentenced to death and I don't deserve it!" In just a few minutes everything has fundamentally changed for me but I know that, even if I told them, none of them would give a damn.

Turning left into my street, up ahead in the square is my town house and office but I can't face going in there just yet. Jenny, our receptionist and secretary, will be back from lunch by now and is bound to ask if everything is alright. She has been the one making all my appointments so she'll feel justified in asking me what has happened. I know she's worried about me and I know that if I see her now I'll break down and make a total fool of myself, which would be humiliating. I need a little time to get my head around this. God knows, I probably look as shell-shocked as I feel and I'm in no condition to fend off her enquires; the thought of losing it altogether and bursting into tears is too awful to contemplate.

Instead, I walk into the square and make for the small park behind it. This area is a survival from an earlier age and a peaceful haven with shady trees, some benches to sit on and, even in the city centre, teeming with wildlife. I make my way to one of the benches and sink down. The trees shade me from the heat and give me time to calm down and get my head sorted out. I feel shaky and nauseous, like the rug has been pulled out from under me.

How can a few headaches and dizzy spells end up killing me? It had all started as I was sitting at my desk on a bright March morning when a stab of pain hit me right between the eyes and made me cry out so loud that Jenny rushed in. That time painkillers helped, but it only got worse so I had to go to my GP. I tried to blame Jeremy, my business partner, as he had gone off 'to find himself' – whatever that means – and left me in the lurch for a year. When he'd told me his plans I had looked at him in amazement.

"You're what?"

"I know you don't understand, James, but I will be forty next year and I still haven't figured out what I want to do for the rest of my life." I snorted as I'd be forty then too but knew exactly what I wanted to do.

"Jeremy, all you need to do is get as rich as possible and then retire, like me," I'd told him but he wasn't amused. Instead he'd given me one of his looks, which was never a good sign and meant that he had made up his mind and nothing I could do or say would change it. He'd given me one of those looks when I'd almost backed out when we had decided to set up our own business and leave the safety of the firm we'd been with for fifteen years. I thank God we did it, though, as we've been more successful than we ever dreamed possible. So now I was faced with this look again and knew I was beaten. I'd smiled and through gritted teeth agreed to him taking a leave of absence. Little did I know at first who he was intending to bring in to handle his clients; if I had, I doubt I'd have let him go.

"Harry Granville? He is coming here?" I'd exclaimed, as I hate Jeremy's slimy brother-in-law.

"Yes, he is."

"Why? You know how I feel about that fat, over-bred pain-in-the-arse. And you're forcing him onto me?" Jeremy had closed his blue eyes, run a hand through his blond hair and taken a deep breath.

"I know you don't like him, James, but he is a good broker." I'd snorted at that as I had grave doubts that he could count let alone do anything else. "But he is Carol's brother, family, and I need someone I can trust looking after my interests."

That was when the penny dropped and I saw it all very clearly. This wasn't his idea, it was Carol's, and Carol and I don't get on at all. So this was her way of getting at me, putting her oafish brother here to keep an eye on the jumped-up commoner. She's a Lady and Harry is an Honourable, children of an Earl, whereas I come from a small Estate cottage in Berkshire, very common and vulgar. I bet she wanted me to object so that the partnership broke up, which I suspect has been her aim for years. Well, I wasn't going to give her that satisfaction; I wouldn't have to see Harry as he'd be in Jeremy's office so I would go with it, just to spite her. "Okay, I said, "he can come but he stays away from my clients and my office."

Jeremy had breathed a sigh of relief and smiled. "Of course, and thank you James, that's a great relief to me." I bet it was and I would have loved to have seen Carol's face when he'd told her of our agreement.

So here I am now, sentenced to death and all alone. I look at the house which is both my office and home and wonder if all the sacrifices I've made have been worth it. I haven't taken a holiday in five years and spent my hard-earned money on property so that I could retire early and live comfortably – and now I could die before the year is out. How's that for irony?

"Oh, bugger it! It's not bloody fair," I say to the wind, feeling a tear on my cheek. "God, I'm bloody crying now," I add and I can't remember the last time I cried. I have to try and gather some willpower to go in there and get on with my life, however short it might be, so I come out of my dazed state and look around to find that nothing has changed. But it's time to return to my world now so I get up and walk back to my office.

Two

I stop at the bottom of the five steps that lead up to the blue front door with its shining brass lion's head knocker and take a deep breath. Glancing down at the basement flat's window to look at my reflection, there I see a tall, athletic, dark-haired man with a pale oval face, high cheek bones and dark blue eyes staring back at me. Amazingly, I look calm and composed. Maybe I can bluff my way past Jenny and into the relative safety of my office, so I stride up the steps, twist the door handle and push open the heavy door, stepping into the cool Reception area. Jenny looks up from her computer, her titian red, shoulder-length hair bouncing as her head moves and her clear eyes search my face as I approach.

"Any messages?" I ask, surprised that my voice sounds so normal.

"Yes, your doctor's office `phoned," she says as she checks her watch, "twenty-five minutes ago." I raise an eyebrow at the enquiring tone in her voice.

"Oh, what did they want?" I am not going to tell her where I've been for the last twenty-five minutes.

"You didn't make another appointment," she says.

"Oh yes, I forgot. Well, I'll ring them back later."

"It's okay, I looked in your diary and booked you in for Friday morning at eleven-thirty."

"Aaah… did you? Okay, fine. Thank you, Jenny," I manage to say. She smiles up at me, pleased that I seem so happy. But, unknown to her, I am rueing the day I took on such an efficient and capable receptionist. She's the glue that keeps us together and on the rails but this is one time I wish she weren't quite so damn good. "Anything else?" I ask.

"No, James. I'll have those letters ready for your signature by the time Mr Scarlini leaves." For a second I can't think who she's talking about, then I remember the new client.

"Oh, good. Well, I'll be in my office so buzz me when he arrives." She nods and returns to her work, leaving me able to escape into my office.

The meeting goes well, I think, but it's hard for me to concentrate fully on him and his money when all I can see in my own future is darkness and death. I don't think he notices my distraction as he is like a lot of young men, totally focused on himself and his own importance. It hits me then, while listening to him droning on about how much money he makes and how he wants to make it work for him so he can retire by the time he is forty, that I'm looking at a younger version of myself. But now I might not reach my fortieth birthday next July. I try to put such thoughts away and concentrate on my latest hard-won client who is sitting in front of me.

"You do think it is possible, don't you?" He has a slightly accented Italian voice.

I nod although I'm not one hundred per cent sure what he's asking as I haven't been listening too carefully. But a nod seems to be the right response. I have a reputation for ruthlessness that is hard-earned as there's no room for sentimentality in business and I am dedicated to mine; I've had to be as there was no-one helping me up the ladder. I've had to work very hard to get to where I am now and this is the reason I get up in the morning and work seven days a week. For some reason I have always been able to see the patterns and understand the ebbs and flows of the markets, just like a surfer reads the waves. I can read my ocean and I have proved to be very good at it.

"Yes, Mr Scarlini, I'm sure we can get you the results you're looking for." He smiles and reminds me of a shark. I shiver and suddenly I have an almost overwhelming desire to get this meeting over with as soon as possible. "Now, have you read over our contract pack?" I ask him.

This had been sent out to him a few weeks ago, and in it our charges and conditions are spelled out clearly, legally binding.

"Yes," he nods, "I had my lawyer look at it and he was impressed." I smile a little tiredly as I've heard this many times before. When we first set up our business we spent a lot of time and money getting this very important piece of paper right, so I know it is excellent.

"Well, if you would like us to work for you, please sign it here… and here… and we can start work immediately." He nods again, taking a gold pen from his inside jacket pocket and, with a flourish, signs on the dotted line. I get up and walk around the desk to shake his hand. "Welcome aboard, Mr Scarlini."

"Mario," he says.

"Mario. Well then, let's get this to Jenny and start the ball rolling." He follows me into Reception where Jenny looks up and smiles as we approach. "Jenny, Mario has decided to join us," I say as I hand her the contract.

"Wonderful," she replies and gives him the full-blast smile that's reserved only for clients. As he returns it I know that she has conquered another male client, all of whom think she only smiles like that for them. The fools, she is a consummate professional, never mixing business with pleasure, but that doesn't stop her flirting and she nearly always goes home with a gift from one or other of our smitten clients. Sometimes the Reception area resembles a florist's shop. None of them know that she's in a long-term relationship with a plumber called Kevin, to whom she is devoted. He leaves the building and I turn to go back to my inner sanctum when Jenny stops me.

"James, I have those letters ready for your signature," she says in that reproving tone she uses when I've forgotten something. I've always had a lousy memory and I don't suppose a brain tumour is going to help.

"Right, let me do them now," I reply, trying to sound as normal as possible. I must sound convincing as she hands me the letters without further comment and I sign them without checking them as I know they will be as perfect as they always are. I sign the cheques too so that she can get them into the last post and then I'm free to return to my office to think. "There you go, all done. Now, I have some paperwork to catch up on so unless there's an emergency on the markets I need to know about, hold all my calls."

By five o'clock I have another thumping headache, an unhappy reminder of my own mortality. I can't see my computer screen anymore so I shut it down and sit in the quiet with my eyes closed. I never usually have time to reminisce but now I've been told I have little time left, so at this moment I have decided to start writing down my thoughts and feelings about what I am facing. This is my account. I used to do this as a kid when I was unhappy and it helped a lot; not that I expect anyone else will ever read it or even care.

Maybe, yes, it's time for me to reflect on how I have got to where I am now. I am the baby of the family, third child of Patrick and Mary Wylie. My father was an Irishman who came to Lambourn hoping to be a jockey but he never really made the grade. He then worked in almost every racing yard in the area over the following years, getting the sack from most of them for being drunk or for not turning up when he should have. Mr Reliable he was not, either in work or in regards to his family. The only thing he was good at was getting drunk. So it was left to Mam to keep us fed and stop us being evicted for non-payment of the rent; thankfully it wasn't too high as she worked three jobs for the local Lord so we qualified for an Estate cottage, but she was always tired and worn out. I can't remember a time when there was joy in our house and if Dad was there it became darn right dangerous as well. He took his frustrations out on anyone who was within range and he didn't care who that was. All of us – me, Mam, my older brother Terry and my sister Trisha – we all felt his fury and his fists at some point in our lives. So I didn't feel any sorrow when he finally drank himself to death aged fifty-two as he'd made it a miserable childhood for all three of us.

My only happy memories of home are when I roamed the surrounding fields and woods. I'm a natural loner but then having a dad like mine made me even more quiet; I don't trust people very much anyway because we had to keep so many family secrets. Still, I knew I had a brain and I was always determined to use it to find a way out of that situation and make a fresh start somewhere where no-one knew me. So I worked mucking out at the local racing yards at the weekends to earn the money I needed for my escape plan. Once I'd taken my GCSEs and got myself a position on the bottom run of a brokerage house, I made my getaway as I knew my father would hate the idea of me escaping his clutches. I worked hard and although I was the lowest of the low this had potential and I knew I could make something of myself in London. I had no hesitation in moving to begin my new life there. No longer would I let anyone call my Jimmy or Jim; in this new life I am James Wylie, stockbroker, and not the kid from the poor end of the village with a drunk for a father.

It was hard getting started and I have earned the reputation I have of being a cool, ruthless operator who stops at nothing to get what he wants. It is exactly what I had to do to survive. Now I have another survival battle on my hands and how I'm going to manage it I haven't worked out yet. I've had such tunnel vision in my determination to succeed that I've never thought about what I might have missed out on.

Sitting in the gathering gloom of my very modern and austere office, I am not sure if I really want to think about life and death even now. I sigh and feel leaden and defeated. The pain in my head has returned with a vengeance, perhaps it's all this thinking, so I pull myself upright and using the furniture I slowly make it to the door. The Reception area is dark as everyone has left for home by now. I usually like having the place to myself but now it just feels cold and lonely. I shiver though not from cold. No, today I crave some company and a shoulder to cry on but there is no-one like that in my life, no best friend or confidant to talk to. Until now I never needed one and opening up and talking about feelings has always sounded a bit weak and 'New Age' for me. I'm not a touchy-feely sort of person, not my thing at all.

I cross Reception and eventually make it up the stairs to my apartment, where I take some pain killers and fall onto my bed as oblivion is the best solution at the moment.

Sitting in her circle in the most peaceful, star-spangled summer night, Tara Kelsey tries to centre herself and relax. The familiar surroundings have always calmed her in the past but today she can't get comfortable; it isn't a physical need so much as emotional comfort she's seeking. She knows why as for the last five years all her energy has been ploughed into fulfilling her dream of a space where many spiritual and alternative therapists can practise together. And now 'Tranquillity' is up and running. It hadn't been easy and it took over her life, but it's now going from strength to strength, its reputation growing with new therapists and clients queuing up to use it. It is growing beyond her wildest dreams and now she has time again to start looking at her personal life and getting that sorted – which is scary. She knows what she wants, love and marriage and maybe a child, but the prospect of dating and trusting another terrifies her. Past disasters still haunt her and she worries that time is running out: she'll be thirty-four next birthday.

A familiar female voice interrupts her thoughts. "It is possible and closer than you think, little one," it says. Tara turns to find Juliette sitting next to her with a smile on her lips, her blue eyes twinkling and her auburn ringlets framing her pale, delicate features.

"Really? It's still possible? Sometimes I think I am meant to be alone."

Juliette laughs. "I know you do. But Harper is right when he says you will find love – though the time has to be right for you both. Remain open to it and he will come and turn your life upside down."

Tara shivers. "Is that a good thing?" she asks and Juliette raises an eyebrow.

"That's for you to find out. Just remember I'm only a whisper away if you need me. Blessed be." And with that she vanishes leaving Tara to wonder what the future will hold.

Three

For the next few days I operate on remote control, seeing to business between bouts of dizziness and nausea. Friday arrives and Jenny reminds me of my doctor's appointment. Her face looks up at me with worry lines on its usually smooth skin and I try to appear as though nothing is wrong with me; but she has caught me a couple of times clearly in pain and was there once as I nearly fell when a dizzy spell hit me. It's only a matter of time, I suppose, before my condition will start to really affect my work and I shall have to stop.

"Are you alright, James?" she asks.

I smile as brightly as I can manage and lie, "Yes, sure, I'll be fine. When is that appointment again?"

"Eleven-thirty."

It is already ten past so I turn slowly so as not to bring on another dizzy turn and make my way to the surgery. I only have to wait five minutes before my turn and Doctor Patel is waiting for me, reading my notes as I enter his room. He looks up and smiles.

"Ah James, how are you?" he asks. Somewhat tactless, I feel.

"Still dying, Doc," I reply flippantly. He doesn't react, probably used to my abrasive manner by now, and he doesn't even break eye contact with me.

"I've downloaded some information for you," he says and begins to gather up several sheets of paper from the printer. I don't want to take them as somehow that means accepting his verdict on what's wrong with me and I still haven't. When I don't take the papers he puts them down on the desk in front of me.

"I know you are angry at the moment."

Predictably, a flame of rage shoots though me at his words. "Oh really, how the hell would you know how I feel?" I almost shout at him. But he doesn't turn a hair and just sits there calmly.

"Because James, there is a process people in your situation go through, a form of grieving."

"I suppose someone has done a bloody study on it, have they?" I retort sarcastically but he just smiles, which only infuriates me more.

"Well yes, actually someone has, but the point here is that it is very natural to be angry – you have every right. Then this is often followed by a deep depression which some never come out of, although those who do and can come to terms with their prognosis move on into a state almost of, well, bliss." He obviously sees my disbelief as he adds, "Oh yes, James, it does happen and these people suffer a lot less pain and spend their last months calmly and happily. They find a peace they have never experienced before and it's beautiful to see."

I raise an eyebrow at him as he waxes lyrical on how nice it is to die and I'm sure he can see that I am not buying it, so he tells me that the information he's giving me is about palliative care and making your legal arrangements if you want someone you trust to have power of attorney over your affairs. I snort at that; someone else having the say on when I die, I think not.

"James, you must do these things or your family will have to make these painful decisions for you," he says in a reproachful tone of voice.

I glare at him and say, "I don't have any family to tell." It is a lie but I don't want him poking about in my affairs. He moves back into his chair.

"Oh, that is unfortunate. You will need help soon. Is there someone you can talk to, a friend perhaps?"

"Of course, I'll be fine," I lie again, hoping this will bring an end to this interrogation. "What about some different painkillers?" I ask as the ones I've been on aren't cutting the mustard anymore.

"Yes," he hands me a prescription with a name I have no idea how to pronounce. "Now, they are very strong so it is essential you take only the prescribed dose." He looks at me like my teachers used to when they were sure I was planning something. I bet he thinks I'm going to top myself, but I am not planning that, well, at least not yet. Ask me again in a few months and it might be a different story. If the pain gets too bad and can't be controlled then I might do something about it because I am a coward who hates pain. Until that time comes, however, I am going to stay in the game a little longer.

"I'll do that," I reply, then add, "Is there anything else I can do to help myself?"

"Well, there are many complementary therapies that help you with pain control and sleep and appetite…" He can see from my blank face that I have no knowledge of any complementary therapies or even what he means, so he continues, "…aromatherapy, reflexology, massage, things like that."

"Do they actually work?" I ask. "I mean, don't you doctors think they're useless and the people who practise them are con artists?"

He actually laughs at that and shakes his head. "No James, I don't think they are con artists. I am an acupuncturist myself and I've studied herbal remedies as well. There are many cures in nature and I believe that one day GPs like me will work with complementary therapies. In fact, a lot of hospices now use them and they're very much appreciated by both the staff and patients, especially in controlling pain and giving a sense of peace and wellbeing when you're entering the finally stages of life and getting ready to leave."

I don't want to think about that yet though I suspect there is something about hospices in the pile of papers I suppose I shall have to take with me. I have one more question. "How long will I be able to keep working?"

"That is up to you," he grimaces as he replies. "Everyone's symptoms are different and the tumours grow at different rates, so only you will know when you should give up work." He pauses and then adds, "Why do you want to keep working?" He knows I don't need the money but it's not about that, it's about who I am.

"My life is my work," I tell him. Unfortunately it is true as I have spent so much time and effort becoming successful that there has been none left to do anything else. I don't have any hobbies or interests. I suppose I had other dreams and ambitions once. I thought about learning to fly but never got around to it and over the years these dreams have got pushed into the background until I forgot them completely.

"Now might be the time to try new things," Doctor Patel suggests gently. "There must be something you have always wanted to do… think about it, maybe make a list?"

I suddenly feel embarrassed by my total lack of dreams.

Most of the following weekend is spent fretting and working when I can though not as much as I would normally. But nothing is normal anymore, nor will it ever be again, and I am still having trouble getting my head around that. Even concentrating on work is just not happening because it all seems so pointless now and for the first time in my life I have no purpose.

I get up from my computer and walk around the apartment but it feels claustrophobic. I need to get out of London and with the day stretching out in front of me like an eternity I grab my keys and jacket and head out of the front door. I still have a car though it is rarely used as this city is no place for driving, so I pay heavily to house it in an underground garage about a quarter of a mile from my house where it is looked after and secure. Using my card to access the dark, cavernous underground facility, I make my way via the stairs to Bay 27 where my dark grey Lexus sits waiting for me. It is very dusty but other than that it looks exactly the same as when I drove her last, nearly two months ago.

"I hope you'll start, old girl."

I insert the key and turn it and she coughs once as she opens her lungs then she fires and a healthy roar erupts from under the bonnet. It feels good to be back behind the wheel again with all that power at my disposal. Smiling for the first time in days, I reverse out of my garage space and turn for the exit. I automatically turn right although I don't have a clear destination in mind, yet I soon find myself on the M4 heading west. In a while I turn off the motorway at the Newbury junction and find my way onto the B4000 to Lambourn. It has been eight months since I came back home, although I've now lived more years in London than I did in Berkshire; still, I guess where you were born and grew up is always home, even if you weren't particularly happy there.

The sun is shining and the sky is cornflower blue over the fields of golden wheat that stretch into the distance. I have forgotten just how beautiful the Downs are especially in the summer so I pull over to the side of the road and climb rather wearily out of the car. It feels good to breathe in lungfuls of fresh country air after the stuffiness of the city as I lean against the car and look around me. There is no other human anywhere in sight, just me and a skylark whose sweet song fills the air around me. I always loved these tiny birds and I tilt back my head and screw up my eyes trying to find the singer; scanning the blue expanse above me, I finally find her fluttering away up to my right. Then as I lower my head the world suddenly spins, my stomach flips over and I stagger forward to lean heavily on the car to stop from falling. Slowly the world rights itself once more and I stop spinning, but I feel sick and take a deep breath, trying to regain my balance.

"Oh, God," I mumble. I feel weak and shaky and I hate this but unfortunately these sudden attacks are becoming more frequent. I take another deep breath and thankfully the world stays where it's supposed to be. "Okay, good. Now, James, take it easy," I tell myself as I ease myself back into the leather driver's seat with a sigh and close my eyes.

Immediately, I'm sure I hear someone calling my name. I sit up and open my eyes looking all around the car but there is no-one there. I'm alone but somehow I don't feel like I am. I shiver and say, "Hello?"

"James, look outside the box and you will find the solution to all your problems," a female voice replies. Is that an American accent? "Look and you will see the way. Don't give up."

Then before I can ask what the hell is going on, I am alone. Don't ask me how I know, I just do. I sit there in shock for minutes, but as I repeat the 'message' to myself I begin to feel lighter. Maybe there is hope for me yet? I smile and begin to feel better, so I start up the car and continue down the hill to my mother's house.

Four

As I pull up I'm struck by how good the house looks as the outside has been repainted and now the ugly pebbledash that for as long as I can remember had been a dirty brown colour is now pure brilliant white. I know my mother cannot afford to do this and, as it's a tied cottage owned by the local Lord, why would she? Taking a really good look around the rest of the cottages I notice that many of them are now smart too with only a few out of the twenty left as I remember them. They were lived in by people who worked on the Estate, such as my mother who still cleans for Her Ladyship. Over the years, as fewer people worked on the land and the need for ready money to pay off death duties arose, all but three had been sold off and Mam lives in one of these that the Estate still owns.

I get out of my car and walk up the garden path, noticing the other cars in newly-made driveways and a Ford pulling in next door. No-one on this estate had a car when I lived here as this was the poor end of the village and we were never allowed to forget it. I still have no idea why I am here and I haven't decided whether I'll tell her yet about the tumour. I'm not sure I can cope if she gets upset and I still haven't come to terms with it myself. As I wait for her to answer the bell, I take a deep breath to steady my nerves. I am always edgy when I came back here; even though Dad has been dead for over ten years I still half expect him to come around the corner and grab me by my hair. The door finally opens an inch or so.

"Who is it?" a quivery voice asks.

"Mam, it's me, James," I reply through the crack.

"Jimmy?" She opens the door a fraction wider to get a good look at me. I look down at her wizened face that looks a lot older than her sixty-four years; her once bright blue eyes are now red-rimmed and watery as if she has been crying. The shock of seeing her looking so worn out and old gives me a kick in the stomach.

"Mam, are you okay?"

"Oh Jimmy, it is really you?" she cries. The door is flung open and she bursts into tears and throws her skinny arms around me and hugs me tightly. I am very uncomfortable with outward displays of emotion – some have called me repressed – but I can't help how I feel as we were never a huggy-kissy family. The only time I got physical attention from my father was when he was hitting me in a drunken rage and now Mam, whom I can't remember ever hugging me, is distraught and clinging to me like a limpet. I feel the urge to break away and run to my car as fast as my legs will carry me, but I gulp and try to push down these emotions and stay calm. "Oh Jimmy, my baby boy," she says between sobs. A voice behind me makes me jump.

"Are you all right, Mrs Wylie?"

I turn my head and instantly recognise Arthur Beaton as he had been in my year at school though we had never been friends.

"Yes, Arthur," Mam smiles, "I am now my Jimmy has come to see me."

"Oh yes, I recognise you now. How are you, Jim?"

I hate anyone shortening my name, but I hold back the impulse to correct him and reply, "I'm fine, how are you doing? Do you live around here?" I couldn't resist that dig as he was one of a gang who liked to call kids like me who lived in this neighbourhood names.

"Yes," he says proudly, pointing at the house next door to the left.

"Oh, right," I reply dryly. He must have suddenly remembered the name-calling as he goes very red in the face. I turn my back on him.

"Arthur keeps an eye on me, Jimmy, and takes me to the shops," Mam says so I feel compelled to turn back and be nice to him.

"That's good of you," I say with half a smile.

"It's a pleasure," he says, then gets the message from my face that he should go now. "Well, nice to see you Jimmy, and I'll pick you up on Friday as normal, Mrs Wylie." Mam nods.

"How about a cup of tea, Mam?" I ask her and she smiles up at me. I follow her inside to the small kitchen and squeeze myself onto a stool by the table giving her room to get to the sink and fill the kettle. There are some official looking papers on the table and the letterhead catches my eye. It's from the Estate office.

"It's so good to see you, son. It has been a while." There's a mild reprimand in her tone which is deserved as I haven't been home since last Christmas. I don't come often and feel guilty about it, for which I blame my Catholic upbringing.

"I've been busy," I tell her as it's my stock answer to this question and the excuse I have been using for at least the last twenty years or more after I left for London. I quickly change the subject. "How are Trish and Terry?" I ask, not that I am the least bit interested in my siblings. They have never featured much in my life nor I in theirs; if they weren't family we would never have been friends. Both of them are older than me and they viewed me as an annoying younger brother. We don't have a thing in common anyway; all Trish ever wanted to be is a mother, so she married at eighteen and then produced five children in quick succession. Terry went from one dead-end job to another, getting drunk most weekends until finally he grew up a bit when he fell in love and married Lucy and got a regular job and now they have three children.

Mam is in her element now, talking about her grandchildren, which gives me an opportunity to look at the papers from the Estate. I scanned them quickly and I soon understood why Mam has been crying; they are increasing her rent again and I know she'll never afford it. I suddenly realise that she has stopped talking and look up to see her standing over me with the tray of tea things and that same distraught look back on her face. She looks like she is about to drop the tray so I grab it from her and place it safely on the table.

"Oh, Jimmy," she wails and starts crying again. "What am I going to do?" For a few seconds I'm embarrassed and confused – crying women do this to me – but then I get up and take her tiny body in my arms and hold her tight.

"It's going to be all right, Mam, I'll sort it out for you," and I feel good saying it because I mean it too. I know that since the Estate have been selling off unwanted cottages she has felt vulnerable, frightened they will throw her out; they can't do that but she is still worried and I hate to see her scared like this. Now with such a rent rise I am worried the stress will kill her. But maybe I can get them to sell me the cottage and then Mam can live in peace. It's worth a try and I do have the funds to do it.

"Are you all right, son?" she asks. She must have seen something in my face because she falters and looks at me hard while I try to look unconcerned.

"I'm fine Mam, just tired. It's been hard without Jeremy but he'll be back soon." I'm usually a very convincing liar; it's a gift I've used to my advantage all of my adult life. No-one really knows me – perhaps I don't either. But the mask I wear is my protection as well as my professional persona.

"But how can you help me, Jimmy?" she asks.

"Don't worry, Mam, I'll fix this, I promise you. Maybe they will be prepared to sell me the house," I tell her. She looks at me quizzically as if she doesn't know who I am. "I promise you that you whatever happens you will not have to move out of this house." She purses her lips and frowns and I think she is going to ask me how but she surprises me.

"Why?"

For a few seconds I am lost for words. "Why?" I ask her. She nods.

"Yes, Jimmy, why will you sort it out for me? I mean, I'd be over the moon if you could but you're…"

I nod and finish her sentence for her, "…not renowned for offering you any help."

"I don't blame you, Jimmy," she smiles. "I know you had a rough time growing up and we didn't help you when you went off to London." She sighs. "I would have if I could."

"I know, Mam, but I managed," I tell her. She doesn't have a clue just how hard it was but I'm not about to tell her. I lived for a long time in a hostel, a half-way house that helped youngsters like me who were working but didn't earn enough to rent a room or buy a flat. But it allowed me to work at the Exchange during the day and study in the evenings, then I worked at a pizza joint at the weekends. It was a hand-to-mouth existence for the first two years but I had the burning desire to make something of myself and not have to go home with my tail between my legs, which kept me going through the dark times. After two years I passed my first professional exams and was promoted and the wage increase finally got me a small place of my own. I was on my way.

"Well, I'm so proud of you, with your nice house and a good job." She hasn't quite got the idea that I actually own my own business but there's no point telling her again.

"Yes, I am fine," I lie.

"Now, if you could only find a nice young lady to share it with, I'd be so happy." I might have known this conversation was coming as every time I see her I get quizzed on my love life. I have even resorted to inventing non-existent relationships to keep her off my back but then sometimes I can't remember who I am supposed to be going out with. It's time to steer her away from this particular obsession onto another one.

"Now, Mam, you don't need any more grandchildren. Haven't you got enough already?" That did the trick, she settles into her chair with a smile on her face and for the next hour I only have to grunt occasionally just to show I am still awake as she talks about my nephews and nieces quite happily. As I haven't met them all, I do get a bit confused about who belongs to whom, but Mam thinks I know them like she does.

As she rambles on I sit back and relax, looking around the front room where we are having our tea. It is as depressing as I remember it, with the old-fashioned seventies wallpaper still hanging, now grubby and faded, and the dark furniture. I had hated it then and I loathe it even more now. Yet there is a market for this 'retro look' and some people are actually remaking and selling these awful designs. Maybe I could sell all this on eBay and buy Mam all new furniture to get her out of the past; the place definitely needs to be modernised inside to complement the spruced-up outside.

Eventually I manage to extract myself with the excuse of work to prepare for the morning and the M4 soon becoming a bottleneck. I take with me the letters from the Estate office and promise to let her know immediately what they say when I talk to them, then make my way out to the car. I recognise that I have another headache coming on, so I swallow a couple of painkillers before starting for London.

Just four Tube stops from James is the Tranquillity Healing Centre. Tara sits staring into the distance instead of writing up her last client's record card. She fiddles with a strand of her long blonde hair as she goes over again in her mind what happened the night before at the monthly development circle. For some reason she cannot get it out of her head, nor the images she had seen during her meditation. Although they were only flashes, she knows they are very important to her and her immediate future. On sharing this with the group, her spiritual mentor Harper Gordon had nodded and smiled. Then he had closed his eyes to tune into his own guidance to see what he could pick up for her. It seemed like an age before he opened his eyes again and looked at her.

"There is great change coming to you in the next three months. A man... his name has a 'J'... will bring this about." He had paused, then added something very strange indeed. "You will know he is the right man when he says, 'To your own self be true'."

She had suddenly felt cold and asked him for more information, but he had shaken his head, telling her to wait and see. So now, instead of concentrating on her work, she is wondering about this man and what might happen when they meet, as she is sure they will.

Five

I awake with a start next morning, feeling disorientated and foggy as I've being having some very weird dreams. I lie there and try to remember them before they slip away. There's a blonde woman and she is doing some sort of healing on me but the details are very fuzzy and the harder I try to focus the more they slip away. Perhaps I should look on the Internet today and find out a bit more about alternative healing; after all, the voice did say I can find solutions if I look for them so maybe that's what I should be doing. It takes me another few minutes to come round and look for the time. It's 8:02.

"What?" I exclaim as I sit up and reach for the clock. I miss it completely, managing to knock over the glass of water on my bedside cabinet in the process. "Bugger." Now there's water dripping all over the novel I'm half-way through and onto the ivory white carpet as well. I can't believe this, I never oversleep and am habitually awake at six every morning like clockwork; I'm so dammed habitual that I don't bother setting the alarm anymore. And I hate being late. With a groan I force myself out of bed, stepping onto the growing wet patch at my bedside.

I manage not to cut myself shaving and even get down a piece of toast, then check myself in the hall mirror before leaving the apartment. I had always been told by my mentor that first impressions really count. "Even if you can't really afford it, buy yourself a well-cut suit, some white shirts and expensive ties, add some dark socks and black polished shoes and you will make the right impression." I had taken his advice to heart and with my first proper pay cheque bought a good suit, two shirts, one tie, socks and shoes and now it's part of who I am. The person staring back at me from the mirror has black hair – with a touch of grey at the temples – and even teeth now very white after some expensive dentistry. The suit is dark blue Armani, the silk tie also dark blue and the black shoes shine impressively after years of polishing. I nod to my image as I look surprisingly good and then it hits me: how many more days will I be doing this? I shiver as I really don't want to know the answer to that. Then another even more unnerving thought crosses my mind.

"How much longer do I want to do this?" This shakes me to the core as I have never really thought about what I'd do when I stopped working, except that I planned to retire at forty-five and maybe go into property development full-time. I have the contacts and enjoy the design aspect. But all that has changed now as I have less than a year to live – so why am I still thinking of working? It's a question I can't answer yet.

I go downstairs and past an empty Reception desk, wondering where Jenny is. Then I notice my office door is open a crack so I enter to find Jenny with her back to me, oblivious of my arrival and reading something; my heart skips a beat as I realise what she has found, as stupidly I had left the pile of papers the doctor had given me on my desk. I had meant to take them up to the apartment but had forgotten. I am not sure what to do now, turn and run before she sees me or… too late, she turns around guiltily and when she sees me her face goes white.

"Oh, James!" she cries, rushing over to me with her arms open and enveloping me in a hug the like of which I have never had before. I am frozen to the spot and don't know what to do, so I just stand there rigidly, arms straight down by my sides while she hugs me, her warm, soft body pressing against me. After what seems like a lifetime she lets go and steps back to look me in the face.

"Why didn't you tell me, James?" she asks in an accusing tone. I open my mouth but my brain can't come up with any words to say. "Can they operate?" she continues. This time I have some.

"No, it's not in the right place apparently," I tell her. Looking down to avoid seeing her expression, I hastily move behind my desk and into my comfort zone, hoping to forestall any further gestures of sympathy.

"But…" she stammers.

"Yes, it means that I'm dying. But let's not get hysterical about it," I add quickly, trying to avoid eye contact. She stands there blinking, her mouth moving but with no sound, thankfully, coming out. "Look, I haven't told anyone about this yet because I'm still coming to terms with it myself. So please, can we just carry on as normal, at least for now?" I see her ready to jump in but raise my hand to stop her. "Just until I decide what I want to do."

From the expression on her face I can tell she thinks I'm taking this way too calmly and she is probably right; inside, I feel incredibly angry, confused, depressed and far from calm, but it isn't my way to get all emotional or wobbly. I need to deal with this in my own way and in my own time. I can see her mind turning and finally she works this out for herself and sighs.

"Okay, James, but do you mind if I read these?" she holds up the papers Dr Patel had thrust at me and which I still haven't looked at.

"Be my guest," I tell her and watch as she turns to leave my office, closing the door very gently behind her.

To take my mind off my own troubles, I get stuck into my mother's instead. I had been planning to go to a property auction on Friday so had already liquidated some of my stocks; there's a couple of hundred thousand just waiting to be spent. Reaching for the `phone I ring the Estate office and fortunately got hold of the person I need right away. He is surprised by my offer but interested and tells me he'll talk to the owner and get back to me; he doesn't seem to think he'll object as my offer is more than generous.

At the end of the day I ring Mam to tell her there may be light at the end of this particular tunnel.

"Oh hello, son, it's nice to hear from you again so soon."

"Well, I may have some good news for you. I've spoken to the Estate and they are going to consider selling the house." At first there's silence from the other end which is not what I expected.

"But I can't buy it Jimmy, you know that," she then wails and I can visualise her eyes filling up with tears; she obviously doesn't understand what I am saying, or maybe I could have put it better.

"No Mam, I'm buying it for you so you will never have to move."

"What?" she cries. "How can you manage that, Jimmy? It will cost such a lot of money…" and I immediately feel like a naughty child again. It's that tone of voice she had used on me whenever I did something wrong and it suddenly makes me very angry. I am trying to do her a favour and now she is implying that she doesn't trust me.

"Look, Mam, I earn a lot of money and I buy houses all the time," – this is a slight exaggeration but in the heat of the moment I feel completely justified – "and yours won't be all that expensive. So in a few days I hope to be able to tell you it will be yours to do what the hell you want with it."

"Don't swear, Jimmy," she replies, which only makes me angrier. I now feel like slamming the `phone down on her but somehow resist the temptation and try to calm down as getting angry only brings on the headaches. I take a couple of deep breaths as she says, "But I can't accept it, Jimmy, it wouldn't be right to take such a big gift." I had a feeling she would say this; after all, she hates taking charity even when she needs it, so I've already thought of a way round this.

"Look, if you like you can leave the house to me in your Will and that way I'll get it back but you can enjoy it in the meantime." There is silence while she thinks about this.

"It'll be sort of like I have it on loan?"

"Yes, I suppose so," I tell her. If that's the way she wants to see it then it's fine by me since I'll be dead before her anyway and she won't be able to tell me off for tricking her.

"Alright Jimmy, we will do that," she says quietly after a while, then adds, "So if you own it, will I pay you rent?"

"No, of course not. You will own it so there'll be more money left over at the end of the month."

"Oh, how lovely. I'll be able to treat the grandchildren."

I groan inwardly as both Trish and Terry earn a lot more than she does. This really annoys me but she isn't going to change and I no longer have the energy to argue the point with her. Life is too short and that's an understatement.

"Well, it's your money so you spend it how you wish," I say with resignation.

After the conversation, I press my palms to my temples as there is now a deep throbbing coming from behind them and even though I want to deny there is anything wrong with me, every day the symptoms seem to be increasing. The headaches and double vision now happen almost every day and the nausea is awful. I have not eaten a full meal for over a week and have no appetite at all, even thinking about food makes me feel sick. Yet however much I wish to bury my head in the sand and hope it will just clear up on its own, I know it is not going to so I have to start making plans... plans for my death and to get my house in order.

But the throbbing is too strong even to think straight at the moment so I reach for a couple of painkillers, swallow them and lean back in my comfortable black chair, closing my eyes. Gradually the pain eases and I slip into a dreamless sleep.

Six

Tuesday is a day when I feel under attack from all side and it starts with having to fend off questions from Jenny about my illness. I only manage to do this after I answer her torturous quiz on what it's like having a brain tumour; she must have memorised all those leaflets over the weekend. This is rapidly followed by two unwelcome 'phone calls from my siblings. Terry's call is mercifully short and to the point.

"Why are you trying to buy Mam's house?"

I explain and surprisingly he listens and then agrees that it's the best option. Then not two hours later I have Trish on the line bending my ear.

"Are you really buying Mam's house, James?" she asks accusingly. I sigh and I want to tell her to mind her own business and leave me alone; but she won't do that so I might as well talk to her now and get it over with.

"Yes, I am trying to."

"Why are you doing that?" This is code for, 'What are you really up to?'

"Because I can," I reply, knowing this obtuse reply will really annoy her. There follows a brief but welcome silence as she digests what I've said.

"Are you ill or something?" she then continues. My heart misses a beat – does she know? Then logic kicks in: no, she can't possibly know and if I keep calm she won't find out.

"Why, do I have to be ill to do something nice?" I reply dryly, trying to sound indifferent.

"Are you on the level, Jimmy? Tell me the truth for once in your life." What a bloody cheek! When has she ever been truthful to me? I have to take a deep breath to keep from exploding.

"Trish, I really don't give a damn what you or anyone else thinks. Quite frankly, you can all go to Hell but Mam is my Mam too and if I want to help her when she needs it I will – and I don't need your bloody permission to do it." The more she asks about my motives the more she is winding me up; Trish has always been able to push my buttons even when we were kids and she is trying to do it again. But I am older and wiser now, or I hope so. I am not going to tell her anything more. Still, I haven't yet put her off.

"So if you buy it, will you own it or will she?"

"That's between Mam and me."

"So you are up to something," she says triumphantly.

"Yes, Trish, I am. Goodbye," I reply and put the `phone down very gently before going into Reception. Jenny looks up from her work. "Jenny, if any more calls come through from my siblings, please tell them I am in a meeting."

"Yes, James. Is that just for today?" She smiles.

"No, it's until I tell you otherwise."

She nods her understanding; she might not like it but I know I can trust her to do as I ask. Jenny comes from a large and very close family who support one another, but mine isn't like that. The sad fact is that we loathe each other, except for Mam whom we all love and who loves us all in return.

I sigh to myself as there is something else I've thought of that I never got around to but has to be done now, which is to make a Will. I've made an appointment with my solicitor for tomorrow so now all I have to do is work out where I want my money to go when I'm gone. The properties I own also have to be put up for sale. There's so much to do – this dying lark is quite exhausting…

At ten the next morning I am shown into my solicitor's office and Craig stands up to greet me and shake hands. I have known him now for over fifteen years and he has handled all the legal details of my various property purchases, lettings and sales and is the architect of our airtight client's contract. He is a short, stocky man with freckles and a shock of sandy-coloured hair. I always feel that he is very uncomfortable in a shirt and tie and would be happier on a rugby field than in an office. Strangely, just recently I have found out that this is exactly where he spends his Saturdays in the winter. I tell him about buying my Mam's house and he says he will do any paperwork needed in double-quick time, which I am grateful for, and then we get onto the real reason I have come to see him.

"I also want to make my Will," I tell him and see a look of surprise, followed by delight.

"My God, have you finally got around to writing one?" I have to smile as this has been a thorny subject for many years with him nagging and me procrastinating.

"Yes, I have," I answer. "Well, I have the bare bones of it here." I take out the sheet of paper I worked on last evening and hand it over to him. As he opens it up and begins to read, his eyes go up and down a few times but he makes no comment. When he's finished he puts it down and looks across at me.

"Are you sure this is what you want?"

I know what he is referring to as I have left my family out of it entirely. Mam will have the house of course and I expect she will leave that to her grandchildren so in a way I am giving it to them. It will probably be worth quite a bit more by then. As for my siblings, well, he should know how I feel about them. I have worked hard to make my money and I am damned if they are going to benefit from that; so instead my estate will be divided up between the six charities I have supported for many years.

"Yes, Craig, I want it just like that, so at least my money can do some good in the world." I didn't add that if I left it to my family it would be squandered and wasted.

"Yes, I see that. But your family… you have nieces and nephews don't you?"

"Yes, but I've not even met some of them so this is what I want." He nods but he still isn't happy. "And maybe I could add a hand-written note on the Will saying why I'm not leaving them anything – or they could challenge it? At least, Trish would."

"Alright, that's not a problem though it's not really necessary. When I've drawn it up you can add your reasons at the bottom. Can I ask what has made you finally change your mind?" I know what he means, as every time we've met he has asked me when I'm going to do this and now I am doing it without provocation. I guess he has a right to know.

"I'm dying, inoperable brain tumour," I tell him.

The colour drains from his face and his mouth drops open in shock. "Oh, my God, James, that's…"

"…a bummer, yes," I finish for him.

"It's more than that. I'm so sorry."

"Well, that's life," I reply, looking down so I don't get all embarrassed by his sympathy as I can't handle that. Fortunately, Craig is a true professional and he quickly pulls himself together, promising to give the work top priority. I move on to tell him that I want all my properties sold too, but giving tenants some time to buy their homes before they go on the open market. "…and twenty per cent below market price for good tenants who have been in their properties for over three years," I tell him, enjoying watching his eyebrows shoot skyward again.

It is a day of shocking news for Craig as I am not known for my generous nature, usually conducting business in an aggressive manner and going for the best deal possible all the time. But that was then and this is now. Being told you have only a short time left does tend to make you sit up and smell the roses. Anyway, on the whole I've had good tenants and if they are now about to be told they could lose their homes, a bit of good news may make it easier to bear. They should, I think, at least get a chance that I never had.

Am I going soft? Perhaps I've just realised that money is not the be all and end all that we are told it is. I surprise myself by this thought, as up until now it has been all I have wanted and chased throughout my life – but what has it got me? Yes, I am very rich but I am alone. Is that being a success? Or am I a complete failure in the living stakes? I don't know but I want to find out before the grim reaper comes calling.

Craig, bless him, promises to get on with things right away. "What about your house and office? Will you be selling that as well?" he asks.

"God no, I'm not going to make myself homeless."

"No, but I suppose you will be giving up work now?"

"Yes," I sigh and nod, "but I haven't set a date yet and I still have some time before that will be necessary. Even so, I will not be selling it so I'm afraid you will have to deal with that when I am gone."

He gulps and looks down and I know he is finding this as difficult as I am, so it's time for me to get out of here before we both lose it. If this is how it is going to be, telling people, then I don't what to do it again; there are very few people who actually need to know anyway so I will limit this news to as few as possible.

On returning to my office, Jenny looks up and grins at me.

"James, are you doing anything straight after work today?" she asks with a mischievous glint in her eye that immediately rings alarm bells somewhere inside my head. I'm not sure what I should say but since she knows how limited my social life is now I guess there's no point lying.

"Aaah ... no. Why?"

"Oh, you'll see," she says with that look on her face that I have grown to know all too well. It means that short of torture she is not going to say anything else and it will be a waste of breath trying to prise another word out of her. A clam has nothing on her.

The best thing to do is retreat so I turn and hurry back inside the sanctuary of my office and close the door. This is where I have always felt safe from the world but I can no longer ignore the fact that the world is not going to stay on the other side of the door. I have to start working out how and when to give up work. Jenny has already cancelled prospective new clients at my request, but that still leaves the existing clients. And then there is Jeremy. There's a meeting arranged with him already but that was going to be about his return to work after a year's break, not my forthcoming permanent retirement.

I have still not got used to the idea that I am dying. I'm among the ninety per cent of the population who tend to think we are immortal;

most people get older and suddenly realise they are not. But I haven't got to that stage yet, I am still at the almost immortal one and defiantly not the dying one. I'm not even sure how I feel about death, which may seem a strange thing to say… but is there life after death? Reincarnation? Somehow I have always believed there is, but why I do I don't know.

Harper looks at Tara. He has asked her what she thinks of the photograph he likes for the front cover of their book about their new healing techniques but she is in another world.

"Tara!" he says loudly, which finally gets her attention and she looks at him in surprise. "Where are you, girl?" he asks and she sighs heavily.

"Sorry, Harper. It's just that I've been getting more messages from Juliette about some man."

"Nice messages, I hope?" he says with a smirk and a hint of innuendo. She smiles but ignores him as his humour is often a bit near the mark and she's known him long enough not to be upset by it.

"Stop what you're thinking Harper, it's not like that at all. Well, I don't think it is. It's weird. I feel he is coming into my future but he's already been in my past, a long time ago. On the Isle of Skye. You know I've done a lot of past life work with soul retrieval before but he never came up then."

"Interesting," he says. Then something pops into his head. "Maybe he is this 'J' bloke I told you about. Anyway, until he does turn up let's go back to choosing a cover or this book will be published in a brown wrapper. And it isn't even that sort of book."

Seven

Five o'clock finally comes around. I still don't know what Jenny is planning for me and it's making me nervous, but a knock on my door signals that I am about to find out. She opens the door and is followed in by a young women I have never seen before, carrying what looks at first glance to be a reclining garden chair. She isn't as tall as Jenny, only about five feet four inches, and has a more womanly figure than my slim assistant. Her hair is light brown and cut short, framing her oval face and large eyes. I smile at her apprehensively.

"James, this is Katrina, a good friend of mine. She's a reflexologist."

"A what?" I have to ask. She sighs, seeing from my face that I am completely baffled.

"She is a healer and she is going to give you a relaxing treatment."

"A treatment?" I squeak, eyeing her nervously. Now I am worried.

"Yes, it's wonderful. I have one every month and no, you big scaredy cat," she forestalls my next question perfectly, "it won't hurt a bit."

"Oh, right," I reply quietly as I am far from sure that I want a treatment even if it doesn't hurt. Katrina smiles at me.

"Try it," she offers, "and if you hate it I promise I will stop, okay?"

I feel cornered but she doesn't look dangerous so I decide to give in gracefully, more because I don't wish to embarrass Jenny or myself by making a fuss. Katrina begins to set up her green chair and check that it's safe before turning back to me.

"You sit on this and take your shoes and socks off. I'll do the rest." For a moment I'm not sure I heard her correctly but then Jenny starts to attack my shoelaces.

"Hey, I can do that myself," I tell her. "I'm not senile yet."

She gets to her feet with a big grin on her face. "I was just checking," she says cheekily, then adds, "Anyway, I have to go. Kevin's taking me out for a meal tonight so I've got to go and get dolled up."

"You're not leaving me?" I cry as she heads for the door.

"Yes, I am. Sorry James, but you'll be fine. Katrina won't eat you." And with that parting comment she is gone, leaving me with a strange women who has designs on my feet. I smile weakly and quickly get on with removing my shoes and socks.

"James, I need to make a client record and tell you a little about this treatment before we start," she says, taking some paperwork from her large bag. She begins asking a lot of questions which takes up the next several minutes until finally she is satisfied and hands it over to me to sign. "Okay, James, now let me tell you about reflexology and how it might help you now."

I lean back in my chair and hear about pressure being applied to areas of the feet that correspond with areas of the body, a bit like acupuncture. Katrina promises that it's very effective in rebalancing the body so it can heal itself.

"…and it's been proven to be a gentle method of pain relief for people with term… conditions like yours." She looks shyly at me to see if I'm upset by her words. But how can I be as it is the truth? "So I hope this brings you relief from the headaches and helps you feel like eating again."

To my surprise, it is a very comfortable chair. She settles herself at my feet and from her bag produces towels, moist wipes and a pot of cream. She begins to work and her hands are so gentle and warm that I think I might enjoy this after all. I have never had anyone caress my foot before – I think I could get used to it – as she goes on to talk about yin and yang and chi, laughing at the complete incomprehension on my face.

"You've never heard of chi, have you, James? The ancient Chinese believed that all energy, that's chi, is either male or female and we are all a combination of both. We become sick when our chi is unbalanced and we can restore good health by restoring the balance. Unfortunately we live in a very unbalanced world where a lot of men seem to go overboard on the macho energy and suppress their yin. But it's happening the other way around too, with women getting more aggressive and violent. Is this all right?"

"It is surprisingly pleasant," I have to admit as I begin to feel a lot more relaxed than at any time since being told about the tumour. Then as she turns my right foot slightly and starts to move her thumb in a caterpillar-like motion from under my ankle to my big toe, I feel a tingling around the back of my head that gets stronger as she works. "Aaah… I can feel something," I exclaim.

"What do you feel, James? Do you want me to stop?"

"No, it's all right, a sort of tingling and burning but it doesn't really hurt. At least, nothing like the headaches I get."

"Well, that may be because of the tumour," she says and looks up at me, though not with the pity as I saw on Craig's face but with professional interest. Then Katrina stops talking, sensitive to my need for some quiet time now and I close my eyes, gently drifting off into beautifully coloured clouds that I seem to be floating through. This is very peaceful and it is as if I am being caressed and cleansed by these colours and I don't want it to stop. Slowly I move into a purple patch and a word enters my mind, a word I have heard before but have no idea what it means. It repeats over and over again, getting louder all the time, and I feel the peace around me slipping away with no way to stop it. Suddenly I have the sensation of falling and as I hurtle downwards I jerk myself awake and the word slips from my mouth.

"Karma!"

As I open my eyes Katrina is looking at me with concern. "Are you okay?" she asks.

"Yes, I must have fallen asleep and begun dreaming."

"What were you dreaming about?"

"Oh, well it was lovely at first. I was floating among bright, coloured clouds, not like any I have ever seen before, then it changed and I kept hearing that one word repeated over and over again. Karma."

"Do you know anything about karma and what it is?"

"No," I shake my head, "I mean, I've heard the word before but I have no idea what it means."

"You and most of the population," she says with an edge to her voice. "Many people use it but don't have a clue what it really means and its implications."

"I'm afraid I am one of them," I admit, "so perhaps you can enlighten me?"

"How long have you got?"

"About a year, if I'm lucky."

Katrina goes red in the face and I feel bad about making her embarrassed, but then I find myself wanting to laugh and in the end can't stop a chuckle from escaping. She looks up and can see that I am not in the least offended – I've had far worse things said to me in my life – and slowly a smile appears on her face too so I tell her I'd still like to learn about karma.

The usual explanation, she says, is that it's a universal law of cause and effect. We have to suffer the consequences of our actions, a sort of justice. But then it gets more complicated because this is the tip of the iceberg: families have their own karma as do tribes, races, religions, countries, companies, organisations and so on it goes. "Anyway," she says, "don't worry about all that. If I were you I'd only look at my personal karma – after all, it was your mind that came up with the word. That means taking responsibility for your own choices and your actions. Then it's about how you react to things that happen to you, rather than the event itself. It is not as simple as, say, you stole £50 from a chap so you give him £50 back."

"It's not?"

"If only it were that simple. No, a karmic debt is a debt of the soul and not just a material one. Let me give you an example…" She carries on with the treatment while thinking. "Right, let's try this. In the Falklands war there was a young Welsh guardsman who was badly burned when the ship he was on got bombed by the Argentineans."

"Yes, I remember it."

"Well, he went through Hell with the burns and the mental scars yet in the end he emerged as an example to us all of forgiveness and compassion. He could have become bitter and twisted, blaming the pilot of the bomber for his injuries and making everyone's life a misery. But instead he chose to forgive and move on with his life. He let go of the 'Why me?' syndrome and the endless blame game so many people indulge in and decided to release the anger and cope with his new life. He even met the pilot of that bomber. He's a hero of mine," she says with a grin.

"So how is that karma?" I ask.

"There are always reasons for things happening to us even if they're hard for us to understand or accept. They may be opportunities for getting rid of some of our karmic debts, since none of us come into the world karma neutral," she goes on. "Think of it as being overdrawn at the bank – I believe we have all lived before and that is where the debts and credits come from."

Suddenly I get a picture in my mind of an angel holding a huge account book with my name on it and he is counting up the pluses and minuses. I have a feeling that I am deeply in the red and it's not a nice thought. "So you're saying that the things we've done, not just in this lifetime but in past lives, are still on our karmic records?"

"Yep. And we can't go bankrupt and get those debts wiped out. We've got to do it the hard way and pay it all back."

"How do we do that?"

She rolls her eyes. "That, my friend, is the million dollar question. The answer will be different for each of us." I sigh with resignation and she laughs again. "Your face is a picture," she says between giggles. "Really James, if you're interested in this you should go and see a friend of mine, Tara. She has the knack of helping people with karmic issues – and she is also a wonderful spiritual healer. Honestly, she's a lovely person and not at all scary."

"I believe you," I reply without conviction, not at all sure I'm ready for more therapy just yet.

At last, she wraps the towels around my feet and leans back in her chair. "Well, that's it. You have survived your very first reflexology treatment. See, it wasn't as awful as you thought it was going to be, was it?" Yes, I am surprised by how much I have enjoyed it and a little sad it is over.

"Thank you, Katrina, that was great."

She looks to see if I am just saying that to please her but I think she knows I am not because a grin appears on her face. "And if you want to see Tara, I'll give you her card and one of mine, just in case you'd like to risk having another treatment." She rummages in her cavernous bag and finally comes out with not just two business cards but a few pieces of paper too. "Oh good," she says, "I thought I'd lost these but they had fallen to the bottom as usual – it's my book list." She hands me a copy and I read the first line.

"For students?"

"Yes, I teach reflexology and aromatherapy evening classes and get a lot of questions about which books I'd recommend students to read, so I decided to make a list. A lot of them are more about spiritual development – look, there's one on karma and reincarnation."

"And where would I get hold of these books?"

"Er, a library?" she teases. "There's one a couple of streets from here and they have a large section of weird and wonderful books. Most of these are among them. I know that because I was the one who requested them and once a book's requested they have to buy it."

I haven't been to a library since I finished my studies, although I do buy novels sometimes; maybe it's time for me to renew my library card and branch out a bit on my reading material. "I'll go tomorrow," I tell her as I put my socks and shoes back on.

"Now, drink some water because it will help with the clearing process of the treatment. I hope your appetite will be better too. The trouble is, what works for one might not work for another. That's why there is no one cure for everybody as we are all so different – it would be a lot easier if there were but also a lot more boring." I laugh as she has such an expressive face, showing exactly how she feels about everything. She would be a hopeless poker player.

I reach for my wallet to pay her but she stops me.

"No need for that, James, Jenny has already paid me. Just in case you hated it and threw me out, she didn't want me to be out of pocket. And those are her words, not mine."

"Yes, I am a terrifying boss," I agree as I open the door and usher

her out in front of me. "Where is your car parked?"

"Oh, it's just around the corner. I was lucky with a parking space, although I did ask my parking angel for one and she didn't let me down."

"Your what?"

"My parking angel," she smiles, looking at my bemused expression. "If you need a space, all you have to do is ask your parking angel for one and you'll get one. You'd be amazed how often it works."

"Right," I reply dryly.

Katrina is still thinking about James as she pulls into the car park of the Tranquillity Healing Centre where she rents a room, and on entering the building the first person she encounters is Tara. She smiles and just knows that she has to mention him to her although she rarely speaks about her clients with anyone.

"Oh, I'm glad I've bumped into you. I've just been telling a new client all about you and how you might be able to help him understand his karma."

Tara's bright blue eyes widen and she looks at Katrina with interest as she runs her hand though her shoulder length blonde hair. She is surprised. Karma is not a subject many people are interested in.

"Really?" she asks.

"Yes, so if a James Wylie 'phones you, you'll know who he is," she says and leaves it at that.

As Tara watches her go, her heart begins beating a faster at hearing his name and she shivers, wondering if this could be the 'J' that Harper had mentioned and if he would bring good or bad news.

"Are you alright, Tara?" Karen at Reception asks, and she realises that she's standing frozen to the spot, which must look very odd.

"I'm fine, Karen" she smiles, making her way to her treatment room in a bit of a daze.

Eight

I awake the next morning feeling better than I have in ages, with no headache. My appetite is back and for breakfast I tuck into several pieces of toast washed down with two large glasses of ice-cold milk, my favourite tipple, straight from the fridge. It feels good to be full again and I am not nauseous at all. This improvement lasts for five days. I also then renew my relationship with the local library and manage to pick up several of the books on Katrina's list. I start reading one about chakras, another thing I had never heard of, but it's interesting even if I'm not completely sure I believe it all.

But on Tuesday morning I feel bad again and it seems the reflexology treatment has worn off. It takes a superhuman effort for me to make it to the bathroom where the mirror only confirms how I feel, my skin a nice tone of grey and my eyes dull and puffy. Not a good look and I can't face any breakfast today. I get down to my office before Jenny arrives so that I don't have to pretend that I am fine as I pass her desk. I don't think I could pull it off. If she had been there and seen just how much effort it takes for me to get from my flat, downstairs and across Reception into my office she would probably have called for an ambulance. On the way past her desk, I pick up a pile of papers she has left out for me.

"God, I feel terrible," I say to myself. I'm so weak and shaky, I can barely hold up the card Katrina had given me to read the `phone number.

"Hello," she answers.

"Hi Katrina, James Wylie here."

"Oh, hello James. I wasn't really expecting to hear from you again."

"I know, I wasn't exactly your most enthusiastic patient, was I? But I really felt so much better after the treatment that I'd like another one, please."

She laughs again and says triumphantly, "Another convert!" I smile at that but make no comment as one good treatment does not a convert make. "I'd be delighted to treat you again, James. When were you thinking of?"

"Can you fit me in today?" I ask with my fingers crossed.

"Um, no, I don't think, so but I can do tomorrow at 5.30. I'm seeing another client not far from your office so how's that for you?"

"Okay, that will be great." I'll have to hang in there until tomorrow, then, and somehow get through the next two working days.

Now I have to ring Jeremy, who will be back from his holiday, as we have to get the business sorted out; until we do, I can't set a date for my retirement. The more I think about my life, the more I am realising how dealing in stocks and shares is a soulless way to make a living. Why haven't I seen this before? Does it take something like being told we have a terminal illness to wake us up? I am feeling angry too, not just about the brain tumour but also with myself. Why haven't I done more with my life? I've wasted so much time doing… what? Just making money. But it hasn't kept me happy or fulfilled.

No, I don't believe in organised religion having suffered in my youth the Hell-fire-and-brimstone teachings of our local Catholic priest, but right now I'm thinking that I do need something spiritual in my life. As if to answer me, just as I start going through the pile of papers a book drops out onto my lap: it's 'Saved by the Light' by Dannion Brinkley. I have no idea where it came from; perhaps it's Jenny's or she put it in there for me… The book seems to be about someone who had technically died but then come back to tell us what happened. I shiver and put it away as it is a bit too close to home for me, but all day it sits there on my desk looking at me accusingly until I give in and begin reading it.

Next day I pick up the `phone and ring Jeremy but it rings and rings until finally the answer machine picks up with the usual banal message.

"Hi Jeremy, James here. Look, I really need to talk to you about the business. Aaah, something's come up and, well, we need to talk … Call me. Thanks." I put the `phone down quickly and sigh, wishing he had been there so we could get something sorted. I feel restless and conscious of time ticking away, every day one less. Then I watch the clock slowly crawl around its face until it finally reaches 5.30 and Jenny pops her head around my door.

"James, Katrina's here. Are you ready for her?"

"Yes, Jenny, please send her in. And put all incoming calls to voice-mail now as I am officially off duty."

"Aye aye, sir," she replies with a mock salute. Seconds later my office door opens and Katrina struggles in with her chair and bag. I get up quickly to help her.

"Thanks," she says. "I should have muscles on my muscles carry-ing that thing." Even though she is wearing a tee-shirt I can't see any bulging muscles as she sets up the chair and tests it. "Okay, it's safe for you. I wouldn't want you to collapse in an undignified heap – though you'd never be undignified in that suit."

I guess she has a point as I am wearing my favourite, a midnight blue Giorgio Armani, which fits me perfectly; but under her scrutiny I suddenly feel a little self-conscious so to cover this up I sit in the waiting chair and bend over to take off my shoes while she busies herself with her creams and towels. I let her get on with the treatment for a while, enjoying the sensations, but more questions keep coming into my mind.

"I got a couple of those books on your list from the library the other day," I tell her. "I've been reading about chakras but I'm not sure if I believe in them."

"Yes, it is hard when you can't actually see things. It's like the aura."

"The what?" I have to ask.

"The aura." She pauses, then says, "We are all surrounded by seven layers of energy which each have a colour and represent a facet of our being – like the emotional layer and so on. When we are healthy and emotionally balanced, the aura is complete and strong. But it can be damaged and have areas that are weakened or even missing, which allows in illness or dis-ease…" – she pronounces the word deliberately – "… and some psychics can actually see people's auras."

"Seven layers and seven chakras?"

"Yes, and their colours are important to our state of health. The seven chakra colours and the seven auric colours are the same."

"All right, but what I don't really understand is how these chakras work." I've read that the word chakra is Sanskrit for wheel, and now Katrina asks me to imagine seven wheels or portals about four inches across sitting along the centre of my body. She says they are normally open but can also be shut, plus they spin and when they do they draw in what she calls 'life force' which gives us our energy and vitality. But if they stop spinning or are not working in harmony with each other, we are energy deprived and can get problems all over, not just in the body but the mind, emotions and spirit too.

"Does it hurt when I do this?" she asks as she massages my big toe a bit harder than last time. I consider the sensation I am experiencing and try to describe it.

"No, it doesn't hurt exactly, just tingles and burns a bit, like having hot pins and needles."

"I wish I could see auras," she comments. "It would make my work a lot easier because I would be able to see the state of someone's health without having to rely on their answers to my questions. A lot of people can't or won't tell me what is really going on or what they are really worried about. Anyway, I'm working on it."

"How do you work on something like that?"

"Spiritual development is like anything else, the more you do the better you get. So I go to classes."

"They do classes in all this stuff?"

"Of course. But like anything else it's essential to find the right teacher. The spiritual path isn't an easy one to follow. It takes courage and a lot of commitment and it also brings about many changes in your life, which can be very disruptive especially to relationships. Sometimes your friends and family just don't understand why you have changed and they can't cope." This sounds heartfelt.

"Who is your teacher?"

"Tara. I told you about her last time. I gave you her card. She's very gifted and apart from owning Tranquillity and giving healing she also runs a fortnightly development circle with another medium, Harper, which I'm lucky enough to be in." I have no idea what a development circle is and let this go as Katrina continues to work in silence for several minutes until, inevitably, she shocks me again. "Sometimes when I'm healing, I connect with the client's spirit protector guides. I know you don't have a clue what I am on about, James, but if you keep going through my reading list you will." This is beginning to sound just like my doctor's prescription list: 'Keep taking the tablets and it will be alright.' I sigh because I'm beginning to feel stupid. Why have I never heard of any of this stuff before? I guess I've never needed to nor come across a person like Katrina and this new world, though it's starting to seem important to me.

"Do I have one of these protector guides then?" I ask.

"Of course, everyone does, they are with you even before you incarnate and they stay with you until you return safely to the spirit world. They are usually someone you have been close to in another lifetime." She speaks about reincarnation and other lives as if it is as natural as talking about what you watched on TV last night. "It would help you to get to know them."

"True," I reply. If the doctor is right, I will soon need mine to help me across to that spirit world. She looks at me quizzically and then gets my full attention.

"Would you like me to try and connect with yours for you?" No-one ever asked me something like that, so I nod weakly. "Well, I've nearly finished here so then we'll sit in silence so I can tune in to you. We'll see what happens. No guarantees." When she's done, she ask me to lie back and close my eyes and we stay silent for what seems an age before she speaks again.

"Right, James, you can open your eyes now."

I look up and she is grinning at me. "Did you see anyone?"

"Oh yes, I certainly did."

I am suddenly a little afraid of who I might have watching my back, but it is too late to back out now. "Alright, who is it?"

"Well, at first I seemed to be in a very dark place and I couldn't make out anything. Then I saw a full moon, only I was looking down, not up, which was strange and it took me a few seconds to realise I was seeing its reflection in a circular pool. Then I saw that this pool was in a clearing in a forest and standing around it were about twenty women." She pauses and blushes – why is she embarrassed? "They were all naked," she says and giggles.

"Are you saying I have naked women following me around all day?" I have to ask. She throws back her head and laughs and it takes several minutes for her to regain control of herself.

"No, James, although that image is very amusing."

Well, it isn't to me. I'd much prefer a warrior or an Indian chieftain myself, although when I leave this world it might be more fun to follow naked women into the afterlife. I'll have to think about this.

"There is more," says Katrina. "There was obviously a ritual going on and a priestess stepped forward and started chanting in a language I have never heard before. It might have been Norse as the women were all blonde with fair skin and blue eyes." She grins at me and then continues. "Then the scene changed and I saw the same priestess in a large log structure with a fire pit in the centre of it. I got the feeling it was a long house and she was sitting on the ground casting runes to foretell the future." She glances at my puzzled expression and says, "I'll tell you what runes are in a minute, James, but let me finish while I still remember the details. I know this woman is a shaman and a powerful healer and she also has second sight. Anyway, she is your protector guide and I think you were with her in that lifetime though I didn't see who you might have been. Her name is Freizal, or that's what it sounded like. She was then about five feet eight inches tall, with long blonde hair and strikingly ice-blue eyes, very strong and athletic. She is quite formidable."

As Katrina talks I get a flash in my mind, like a vision, and for a moment I think I see her. She is beautiful. I close my eyes and try to see her again but she has gone. I open my eyes to find Katrina hovering anxiously over me. I smile up at her and say, "I think I saw her." Katrina looks surprised.

"You did? That's great. So now you know she's there you can start to get to know her again."

"How do I do that? She's not in the `phone book, is she?"

"No," she laughs, "but when you are quiet you can speak to her and she will be listening. Do you meditate?"

"It's not something that stockbrokers do very often."

"Well, it's easy and everyone can and should do it. Really it is, James. Look, I have some guided meditation tapes at home that really helped me when I started to meditate. I'll lend them to you. It's easier for most of us to follow directions and go on an imaginary journey than just sit still and try to clear the mind. These tapes are designed to lead you into an altered state without you really trying. Anyway, if you'd like to give it a go I can drop them in tomorrow when I'm passing."

"Okay, thanks." I know I should try anything now.

I get my socks and shoes on then open my desk drawer to take out my cheque book to pay her. I have already written it out after finding out from Jenny what her fee is. She smiles and takes it, then looks thoughtful.

"James, the effects of the treatment wore off after five days?"

"Yes, so I'd like to book another one for then."

"Really, that's interesting," she says as she gets out her diary. "I have to write everything down straight away as I have a head like a sieve," she explains, opening the blue book and flicking through the pages. "Can we do it Monday, then?"

"Sure, not a problem," I reply, hoping that it won't be. When she is out of sight, I remember that she didn't tell me what runes are. Maybe the library can help.

Nine

Next morning I feel better again and enjoy a hearty breakfast before facing another day at the grindstone. Last evening I had read 'Saved by the Light' and finished it, leaving it on Jenny's desk this morning. It is fascinating and a bit scary. The author says he had a 'near death experience' of Heaven. I had never heard of this NDE before and I'm not sure I believe it or not, but it's a compelling read.

Before ten I get a `phone call from the Estate manager to say the owner is more than happy to sell Mam's house and accept the price I offered. I'm not surprised as I had looked up the market value and then offered more. With a sitting tenant they can't evict, the best possible way out for them is to sell it to me on behalf of my mother. I ring Craig and give him all the information he needs to get the legal side sorted then I ring my mother who is delighted.

"Trish says I must make a Will now as I'll have property," she says. I bet she did, I think.

"It's a good idea and it does make it easier on those left behind when the time comes."

"Do you have one, James?"

"Yes, I do," I sort of lie as it is still being typed up after I found a few errors in the draft Craig sent me.

"Does it cost a lot to have one made Jimmy?"

"No, you can even do it yourself as long as it is dated and two witnesses sign it – someone like your doctor or solicitor though, not family."

"Would that young man Craig you have do it for me?" So inevitably it turns out that I'm going to have to organise it for her with Craig, though I can feel my stomach knotting up and my blood pressure rising because I don't need this right now as I have a list a mile long that I would like to get though before I die. But at this rate I'll not make it to the fourth item on it. I tell her to write things down and send it to me before Friday when I have an appointment with him. She pauses again. Mam does a lot of this especially on the telephone and it's something you have to live with even though it is so frustrating.

"I'll try Jimmy," she says slowly, then adds, "Why are you going to see him?"

"I am selling a house," I tell her. Obviously I'm not going to tell her that it's several.

"Your house?"

"Yes and no. It's a house I bought some years ago and I've been renting it out but now I want to sell it." I have explained this to her before but I'm sure she never listens to a word I say.

"Oh, you have two houses?"

"Yes, but I'm selling one, need the money," I add jokingly, one lie after another. There is another pause.

"Is your business going wrong, dear?" with a note of concern in her voice.

"No, Mam, its fine. I've just decided I want to… travel." It's the first thing to come into my head and from her reply she obviously swallows it.

"Oh, that's nice dear. Maybe you'll find a nice young lady and settle down." And produce more babies…? I don't think so but if that's the fantasy she wants to create then who am I to disillusion her.

"You never know," I say.

It's around 4.30 and it seems to be about this time most days that I suffer a major energy dip. However much I try to stop them, my eyes keep closing until I give up the struggle completely and slip into a strange place.

I find myself floating over rolling green hills where sheep are peacefully grazing. It is a beautiful sunny day with a blue sky and small puffy white clouds skipping across it. Somehow I know this is Dorset and that the lovely old farmhouse I can now see nestling between the hills in a river valley is the one Jeremy's wife Carol grew up in. I move towards it as if I am a bird and pass straight though the walls into the large, traditionally furnished country kitchen. It has an Aga and a huge oak table in the centre, around which Jeremy and Carol sit drinking coffee and talking. Jeremy looks tanned and healthier than he did when he left nearly a year ago, his skin golden brown, his blond hair shiny as are his green eyes. He has also put on a bit of weight, which suits him. I can't help listening to their conservation and as Carol talks her dark brown hair falls across her broad forehead covering upturned eyes that always remind me of a cat's. She has never liked me and the feeling is mutual: something about her disturbs me although I don't know why.

"You know you hate London and your old life, Jeremy. We've discussed this before," she says.

"I know. I don't want to go back, I love it here and so do the kids. But I can't let James down."

"Why not? He's a real bastard to you. You don't owe him a thing, especially after the way he spoke to you last year."

I shudder, remembering the abuse I hurled at him when he told me about his plan and how I've behaved towards him since. I am not much of a friend and I feel ashamed, but I didn't want him leaving me. His leaving would make me look at myself and question what I'm doing with my life, which scared me.

"Oh my God!" I mutter.

And suddenly I am struck with the reason I hate Carol so much – it is jealousy. I see her as a threat, taking Jeremy away from me and getting between us, ruining both our friendship and our partnership. I resent her for marrying him and having children, trapping him. I've wanted him all to myself as my friend, my oldest friend. He is like a brother to me.

In the beginning, starting up on our own had been exciting and fun; we worked long hours and even shared a flat to save on rent so we could spend more on the business. Then he was introduced to Carol and it all changed overnight as I found myself side-lined. I'm afraid my ego couldn't cope with that, so I tried to throw as many spanners in the works of their relationship as possible. It's amazing that they didn't break up, but somehow his love and capacity for forgiveness was great enough to overcome the obstacles I put in their way. He even made me his best man, though Carol tried to make him change his mind. I've been a thorn in her side ever since, so maybe she is right and I am a complete bastard. Maybe if I had been nicer to her she would not have the need to make Jeremy choose between us.

"You'll have to tell him you're not coming back and you have to do it now… or I will," she says in exasperation.

I know Jeremy, he hates confrontations or hurting anyone's feelings. If we have to sack an employee or terminate a business agreement, it would be me who did it. So I know he will find it next to impossible to tell me the truth. Now I want so much to tell him it's fine because I'm quitting too – but he can't see me. Next Carol gets up, walks to the old sideboard, picks up the `phone and hands it to Jeremy.

"Call him now."

I know that look of hers and it isn't pretty. She'd give Attila the Hun a run for his money and Jeremy doesn't have a chance against her. So he begins to dial. I jump back into my body at the sound of my `phone ringing.

"Hello?" I croak, half-awake.

"James, is that you?" Yes, it is Jeremy! For a few seconds I think I must still be dreaming but I quickly pull myself together.

"Jeremy, it's great to hear your voice. It's strange you have called just now as I was about to ring you with my news." I don't want him to feel guilty about breaking up our partnership as I know he will, so I will do it for him. I owe him that and much more.

"Your news?" He sounds surprised.

"Yes, I've… well, I've decided to give up the business. So I hope you aren't ringing to say you want to carry on."

"Er, no, in fact I was going to tell you the same. I just can't face going back to the old grind again."

"I know. I'm the same. Life's too short to be stuck behind a desk seven days a week and there's so much more to do," I lie.

"Yes, I agree," he says weakly. "That's how I feel with the children growing up so fast. I want to enjoy them while I can."

"Sure, you don't want to miss out on that. That's what life should truly be about, family." I pause, wondering if I have gone too far with the family bit. There is dead silence on the other end of the line and I think my news has completely thrown him. Why I am not telling him the truth about the tumour, I don't know. Maybe, deep down, I don't want his sympathy or for him to feel guilty about leaving me in the lurch last year. So for now I'll keep it quiet. Still, he knows me too well...

"Are you sure you want to pack it in?" he continues. "I mean, you've always been so focused on the business profits."

"Yes, and look what I have to show for it. No, I want more and maybe I'll meet a nice young lady and make my Mam's dreams come true." I'm surprised that he thinks money is my driving motivation as really it never has been; the devil on my back is the fear of failure and becoming like my drunk of a father. That is my inspiration to be successful and I can't say I cared much in which profession I made it, as long as I could go back to Lambourn with my head held high.

"We need to meet up to discuss the details," he says quietly at last, "and there is also Harry to think about."

"He's your problem, not mine," I snort. "He'll have to find another office." Jeremy knows how much I dislike Harry so surely he can't expect me to let him stay here now that he's not coming back.

"How about Tuesday, then? Carol has a friend coming in from the US to stay with us for a while so we'll be near London anyway."

I glance at my appointment book and see that it is empty for Tuesday. And I decide to drop the second bombshell now.

"Yes, that's fine. Maybe we could all catch up over lunch? My treat. I'd like to see Carol again and apologise for my appalling behaviour to her over the years. I realise what a bastard I've been and I'd really like the opportunity to say 'Sorry'." There is a deathly silence at the other end as Jeremy has gone into shock. "Yes," I continue, "I can see now that I was jealous of her for taking you away from me. You were my friend and there she was coming between us. Pathetic or what?"

"No, not pathetic," he says weakly at last. "Maybe just human."

"I bet Carol doesn't think I am human," I laugh.

"Well, you know, she…" He ran out of words and I can visualise her glaring at him right now.

After the conversation, I sit back and smile as I had almost forgotten how well we go together; even when we haven't seen each other for months, we slip back into the same easy friendship. Neither of us has to pretend to be anything other than we are and that is rare these days. I miss him and can't wait to see him again in a few days' time.

Tara sits on the floor opposite her client and sends out a request to her healing guide, Ala Oki, to help her unravel some of the karmic knots that are causing so much heartache. A beautiful perfume of tropical flowers announces her presence and she floats into Tara's subconscious to join her.

"Greetings, dear one," she says. "I am here to help but this task is heavy – so much karma. It is going to be a long process and I fear the soul is not going to complete it."

Tara sighs as she has felt that too. Although Gillian says she is ready to start this task, she has no idea how much time and effort it is going to take to do it. She is impatient and somewhat pig-headed, so Tara can only see difficulties ahead.

"I know, but we have to try to help her," she says and Ala Oki smiles.

"Yes, of course we do. Don't be downhearted. Soon we will be helping someone who will see it through."

Tara is surprised, as never before has she said anything like that.

"And I can't wait for you to meet him," Ala Oki adds with a smile.

Tara shivers as somehow she knows that she means this 'J' man. But she just nods and together they return to Gillian.

Ten

I have had a pretty good week. The reflexology has really helped with my symptoms and life is so much easier if you don't feel sick and dizzy all the time. When I can get a good night's sleep I feel quite upbeat and positive, more than I did before I was diagnosed. It is strange, but I feel I have a real purpose now which, if I am honest, I haven't felt for several years. Now it is Friday morning and I have another appointment with Craig. It is only a short distance to his office and the sun has made an appearance today, so I'm looking forward to the walk.

I open my office door and there is Harry, leaning over Jenny's desk and spouting his opinions in that upper crust, condescending way of his that instantly makes my blood boil. Jenny looks over at me and he stops talking, having lost his audience. He looks up with his round face, red and burnt like he's been boiled, his pale piggy eyes almost lost between his oversized cheeks and bulbous eyebrows. He is becoming piggier every time I see him, which is thankfully rarely; he pays the rent Jeremy used to pay for his office and half of Jenny's wages, and that is all the ties we have. He smiles – or is it a sneer? I am never too sure which.

"Aaah, James, how goes it with you?" he says, as if he cares.

"Absolutely brilliant, old chap," I reply with an unpleasant smile and in the most exaggerated upper crust accent I can muster. His smile falters for a second as he is not sure whether I am sending him up; he is not the sharpest pencil in the box. Jenny is looking down, trying hard not to laugh, her shoulders gently shaking. "Well, sorry old bean, can't stop as I have an important appointment to keep, don't you know," I continue as I walk past and open the front door. As I leave, I hear him ask Jenny where I'm going, but he won't get anything out of her. She'll tell him to mind his own business as she knows where her loyalties lie.

My biggest regret at giving up the office is that Jenny will lose her job and I must tell her soon so she can start looking for another; and when I meet Jeremy we must discuss a settlement for her. She has been with us from the start and it will be a wrench not seeing her cheerful face every morning. I am sure we can come up with a glowing reference about how efficient and capable she is and with her personality and professionalism she will be snapped up in no time. Even so, I still feel bad about it. I must be developing a conscience.

"How are you, James?" Craig greets me.

This is why I haven't told anyone that I am dying yet as all I will get is questions about how I'm feeling. They'll expect me to look worse all the time, becoming decrepit right before their eyes, but from what I have gleaned from the leaflets this is unlikely to be the case. I will have pain to look forward to (a lot of it) and nausea (yep, got that already), increased dizziness and disorientation and maybe even fits. But on the plus side I will probably look fine and then I could drop dead if I'm lucky. It is only at the very end, if it drags on, that I'll look like I'm dying. So for now there is no outward sign of my impending doom.

"I'm good, thanks," I tell him.

"Great," he says and smiles a little nervously. He opens a file in front of him and hands me some papers.

"I've corrected the errors you pointed out so if you'd like to check it… and if it's all right my assistant and partner will witness your signature." I look down at my Will. It isn't very long and takes me only a few minutes to see that everything is in order.

"This looks fine. Shall I write the reasons for leaving my money to charity here at the end?"

"Yes, but I'd like Andrea and Scott to watch you write it so they can witness that too, just to prevent any arguments." Craig is obviously covering all the bases. A few moments later, under the gaze of three people, I write my reasons for not leaving money to my family:

"I, James Wylie, leave all my hard earned lolly to the above
charities because they will use it for the good of the under-
privileged and disadvantaged and to make this planet a
better place to live, whereas I fear my family would squan-
der it all on plasma tellies and other material crap, thereby
helping to accelerate the destruction of this planet instead."

I sign it underneath and on the other line Craig has marked for me and
hand it over to him. Craig reads it and a small smile plays on his lips. The
tall, very slim man who must be Scott, bends forward to sign and date it,
adding his address and occupation before handing it to Andrea Hawks,
Craig's partner (in both business and in private). From the way she looks at
me, I am sure she knows about the tumour and I feel she wants to give me
a hug or maybe a pat on the head. I cringe inside and smile weakly at her.

"Thanks for that," I say dryly as they both leave the room.

"Right," Craig moves on, "and now the houses. I've had two estate
agents look at each of them for a valuation and I should get their
reports next week. And I've written to all the tenants and informed
them of the sale and of your offer." He pauses for several seconds. "Are
you sure it's what you want to do?"

"Yes, I am very sure. Look, you can't take it with you, can you?"

"I suppose not. Anyway as soon as I get the valuations they will
then have a few weeks to decide what they want to do before the dead-
line." I wince at his choice of words but keep quiet and he doesn't
notice. "Hopefully I'll be able to get any properties not sold to tenants
on the market six weeks from now."

I'm impressed, as time is short, but I am sure his bill at the end of
all this will reflect the effort he is putting in. And now there is another
item I have to add to the account.

"I've talked to Jeremy and we have decided to end our partnership,
so do you have a copy of the partnership agreement?" I don't tell him
I couldn't find the damn thing last evening because a blinding headache stopped me in my tracks. He rummages in my personal file and
finds it easily. "Will there be any legal complications dissolving this?"
I continue. He shakes his head.

"No, this is the least complicated business partnership I've ever done. All you need to do is give your clients one month's notice so they can make other arrangements to find a new broker. And as you own the office building and Jeremy pays you rent, it is up to you when you stop this arrangement. The only complication is Harry."

"He's Jeremy's problem," I tell him. As I prepare to leave and pick up my briefcase, I suddenly remember I was going to ask him about Mam's will. "Oh, I nearly forgot." I place my briefcase back on the desk and open it, taking out a white envelope Mam has sent me; I haven't looked at it, although I have been sorely tempted to. "My Mam asked me to give this to you. I think it could be her Will."

"Really?" he sounds surprised.

"Yes, she was muttering about making one now that she is to become a woman of property and you're the only solicitor she's heard of so you've got the job." His face registers a mixture of confusion and horror all at the same time and I have to hide a smile. But he can deal with her and hopefully I'll keep right out of it.

"Aaah, fine… I'll see to it."

"Just add it to my bill," I tell him.

Next day I make a return visit to the library, armed with Katrina's list, and I now know where to look. I'd had to hunt out an assistant last time after spending ages walking around unable to find any of the books I was looking for. I lean over and begin to read the titles on their spines.

"Nope… nope…" I mutter to myself as I run my finger along the line. Then I find one, grasp it and pull it out to check it is indeed on my list. 'Only Love is Real' by Doctor Brian Weiss. Yes, this is definitely one I am looking for as it is about past lives and this is a subject I have never considered. Well, let's face it, it isn't really something that comes up at a dinner party. This book is about love and how you can meet your lovers in different lifetimes; I am already anxious to start reading it, not having a lover.

I move along looking for more until I think I see one on the top shelf and start to pull it out. Suddenly another book comes flying towards my head. I don't have time to more than duck and it whistles past my ear to land with a thump at my feet. It is a slim volume to have made such a crash and I turn it over to read the title: 'Runes – the ancient divination tool of the gods'. I feel my fingers tingle and I smile as it would appear that this book wants my attention. Someone wants me to learn about them.

"I get the message," I mutter under my breath. "You don't have to throw the book at me." I decide to get out of here before anything else is thrown at me and reach my apartment to settle down with a nice cup of coffee to begin reading.

Eleven

My coffee has been forgotten and sits cold and congealing on the table in front of me as once I started to read I became so involved with the stories that nothing else came into my head. I feel emotionally drained but also awed and fascinated by the stories in the book as they are both sad and heart-rending but also inspirational. I've always been a cynic when it comes to love, maybe because I've never really found it. I have had girlfriends and lovers but there was still something lacking in all of those relationships – although that could be me. I have certainly been accused of being 'cold and unemotional' and that's one of the kinder comments I have had thrown at me over the years. Showing my feelings makes me feel vulnerable and scares the heck out of me.

Perhaps I don't have feelings, yet I do get emotional over sad stories as long as they are someone else's. I feel protective and caring towards animals and the Earth; it's just people I have a problem with. Well, all this introspection isn't getting me anywhere. But at least this book has opened me up to the possibility that I might find answers to questions about my lack of feelings: maybe past life traumas with members of my family? I'm going to investigate this idea further, another thing to add to my list of things to do.

Sunday arrives and I feel sluggish, my head muddled like it is full of cotton wool and the effects of the reflexology have definitely worn off. I really don't think I can do anything physical today so I sink back into my soft bed and start to read the book on runes. I hadn't realised that runes were used for divination, but as I look at the pictures of them something clicks in my head, as if I knew them once, a long time ago. They are familiar to me and yet I have forgotten so much… Then a sharp pain fills my head and I gasp and drop the book. It's no good, I reach for my painkillers and swallow two of them, waiting for the pain to recede as I close my eyes.

There is a light up there. It is hidden by something then slowly it becomes stronger and I realise what it is.

"The moon," I say softly as I watch the clouds disperse, leaving the full moon shining brightly above me. My breath is visible as smoke and I shiver with the cold. I look around and there is snow on the ground and on the branches of the tall pine trees that ring the clearing I am standing in. To my right is a log building.

"A long house." I am surprised that I know what this place is – I have been here before – but why am I here now? I shiver again because this cold is intense and I know I can't survive outside for much longer; I have to get into the long house so I move cautiously to the door and push it open. A rush of warm air hits my frozen face and I can see a fire burning brightly in the middle of the room. A female voice speaks from the depths, making me jump.

"Come. Welcome. Close the door and join me." I see a young blonde woman in a red dress sitting near the fire and instantly I know who she is. Freizal! My spirit guide and protector. This place is somewhere in Norway.

There is tension in the air. She is frowning as she casts the runes onto a skin laid out on the floor, her face drawn and exhausted. I move closer to look and I seem to know instinctively that the runes are not predicting good news; she is casting them for our tribe and I am one of them. Our leaders want to attack another tribe who have been poaching on our land, but the runes are saying that this would be disastrous for us. Then suddenly I find myself outside lying in the snow; I am hurt, there are bodies around me and the long house is burning. I start to float upwards and look down onto the scene as a deep sadness fills me.

This fades and I find myself as a child hiding in the woods near my family home to avoid the school bullies. I had forgotten this incident but now I remember it clearly as I had been chased from school and knew that if they caught me they would give me a beating as bad as any my father had given me. But I have a plan. If I can get to the woods, my domain, I know where I can hide and they will never find me. I've spent a lot of time in these woods and know them intimately. I spend an hour listening to the boys getting more and more frustrated until in the end they give up and leave. They will never bother with me again.

Now this fades too and I am older and living at the youth hostel in London. I see Isabella who is teaching me to cook; it was only with her help that I learned how to take care of myself in the big city. She was a lonely Italian widow, a voluntary helper at the hostel, and for some reason she took a shine to me and took me under her wing. With her help I learned how to cook, mostly Italian classics like lasagne, how to iron my clothes, to polish my shoes so that they shone and how to sew too. She was like a second mother to me and I kept in touch with her after I finally had enough money to leave the hostel. But she died some years ago now and I still miss our talks and her wise advice.

The next face I see is a real surprise. Rodney Green had been a new trainee at the brokerage firm I used to work for, a real East End boy with an accent to match and a cocky attitude. My boss told me to mentor him as, and I quote, "You should have a lot in common, being working class." That had hurt because I had worked hard to educate myself, lose my Berkshire accent and look like I belonged in the City; I doubt anyone meeting me for the first time would guess my humble origins. To class me with this cockney boy, who positively reeked of the slums and was so proud of it, was insulting.

Rodney, or Rodders as he insisted he wanted to be called, put my back up and for the next six months I did my very best to get rid of him. Reliving it now, I am ashamed at my behaviour and the ugly emotions he brought up to the surface in me. I never knew what became of Rodders as Jeremy and I had been planning our escape for over a year by then, and we left in the May to set up on our own. I guess Rodney was one of many people pleased to see the back of me. I see his face clearly now and know that I have some karma to 'repay' to him…

I jerk awake. It is a struggle to push my unwilling body through the motions of getting out of bed, dressing and going downstairs to my desk. I have a lot to do today and thankfully Katrina is coming over later to give me another treatment.

I need to start selling off my own share portfolio. I should get good prices as the markets are buoyant at the moment; but as this can all change overnight, today is a good day to get the ball rolling. There isn't a large amount as over the years I have gradually cashed them in to buy property, usually at auctions where you can still pick up a bargain. But to make life easier for Craig it will be best to get rid of my remaining investments now and put the money in the bank for when I am gone.

Why am I so calm about my approaching death? For some unknown reason, I am. Maybe it's because I have so little going for me in my life that it really doesn't seem so bad to leave it – all I want is to go quickly and not suffer too much pain in the process. The death bit doesn't worry me, it's the pain I could have to endure that does. I seem to have somehow accepted it and in fact it's a relief because I no longer have any worries about the future. I am surprised by how much weight has been lifted from me by realising this. I don't have anyone in my life relying upon me or will even remember me a year after I am gone; sad but true, I am just a ripple in the world, not a wave.

I struggle on until finally I can sit back in Katrina's comfortable chair, relax and let go of some of the pain I have had today. I have spent the day bringing to a close my life as a stockbroker and now I realise that I never set out to be one in the first place. It just sort of happened. I just went where the first job I was offered took me and ended up here; in all that time I have never questioned it, never asked myself why I was a stockbroker or even if I liked doing it. For the very first time, I realise that I don't. That's quite a shock!

It's making me ask what I should have been doing instead. Do I have a gift that I have overlooked? I know it's a bit late now to change but I also know I have to find the answer before I die – this is important, even though I don't know why. I must have sighed heavily because Katrina laughs as I open my eyes.

"That was deep," she says.

"Yes, I was wondering why I became a stockbroker," I tell her, smiling.

"I gather from the sigh that you didn't get an answer?"

"No," I shake my head, "but that's only one of many questions I seem to have."

"What are some of the others?" she asks.

"Well, I've been back to the library and I read a book about past lives, so it's made me think about who I might have been before." She nods wisely, not at all surprised by what I am saying. It is good to be able to talk about this stuff with someone who is both knowledgeable and unfazed by my questions. She is the only person I know who wouldn't think that my tumour is causing me to become a little odd.

"I have always been interested in that too," she tells me.

"So what have you done to find out about who you might have been?"

She grins as if she knows I won't like the answer. "If you remember, I told you that I joined a development circle and that's where I met Tara and learned how to meditate. It helped me to centre myself, get rid of the mental clutter so I could focus on things a bit more clearly. Then I did some one-to-one regression work with Tara and began to relive my past lives. It also helped me understand my karmic issues better."

"Aaah, karma, yes. That is a thorny issue." I hesitate before taking the plunge and telling her about my strange visions of Carol and Rodders. She raises her eyebrows.

"Oh, that really is interesting. What are you going to do about it?"

"I don't know. I'm not even sure if that's what the dream was telling me."

"You know, don't you, that you want to sort some of this out – and if you don't it will drive you crazy?" As much as I don't want to admit it, I know she is right, so I nod reluctantly. "Then I really think you should meet Tara. I know you are resisting the idea but she is great and not scary at all."

"I'm just not sure," I tell her, though I don't know why. Is it what I might find out, or am I just worried about meeting her?

"Look, Tara is going to be at the 'Mind, Body and Spirit' festival for the next few days here in London and I'll be helping out on the stand. Why don't you drop in there and meet her? There's no pressure – if you don't like her I promise I'll never mention her name again, cross my heart." She makes the appropriate gesture and smiles sweetly. I can see that she won't give up mentioning this Tara women until I give in, so perhaps it will be best to get it over with without committing myself.

"Okay, you win, I'll come to your shindig."

"It's hardly that," she laughs. "If it's anything like last year it will be bloody hard work. I'll be doing some healing and handing out leaflets and talking to people about our therapies. It depends on how much space we're given, hopefully enough for at least two couches and my chair as well."

"So how many people will be manning your stand?"

"It's not my stand, it's the Centre's. Tara opened a healing and spiritual development business called Tranquillity a few years ago. Therapists hire rooms there and use the Reception for bookings and advertising. It is very hard doing this work alone but there you get support from the other therapists. We all have the same problems, like finding enough work to keep us going. And it means you can work part-time with a base to work from. I rent a room there two days a week and then the rest of the time I go to clients' houses, like with you."

"So tell me when and where it is and I promise I'll be there."

"Good, that's one person at least. And there will be a lot there that you will find interesting."

I nod and close my eyes again as I feel the tight band that has been squeezing my head like a vice all day releasing its grip on me. The pain has got worse lately – the painkillers still help a bit but not like they used to. Hopefully the reflexology will keep the pain at bay for a little while longer. It is six weeks since I got my diagnosis, six weeks less to live. Yet I have learned so much about myself in that time and know there is still so much to find out; but the clock is ticking, making me conscious of just how precious each day is.

"There you go, all done." Katrina's voice brings me back to the present and I have to get on with what is left of my life as I open my eyes. As she gathers up her bag and folds her chair preparing to leave, she suddenly stops and says, "Oh, I nearly forgot. I have a book on runes for you. I forgot to tell you about them last week, didn't I?" She fishes in her cavernous bag until she finally produces a very familiar looking book. It is the same one I got from the library, so I grin, open my desk drawer and pull out my own copy.

"Snap!" I say. "It almost brained me by leaping off the top shelf."

"Aaah, synchronicity," she says with a wise nod.

"Synchro-what?"

"Synchronicity is when everything falls into place, like runes coming up with your guide and then a book about them literally falling at your feet."

"Some would call that a coincidence," I counter.

"Don't believe in them," she replies with a shake of her head. Somehow I knew she was going to say that.

There is still a huge list of things to get done for the festival stand in a few days' time, but even though Tara has `phone calls to make she can't keep her eyes open. Her head nods and she drifts off into an altered state, suddenly finding herself seeing the 'Tranquillity' stand which looks amazing. The new banners she has had made advertising the Centre fit perfectly and the colours she had thought might be too garish look just right.

Then the area fills with people and among them is a tall, dark-haired man – she knows he is coming to see her. There is an intense red light around his head and she senses his pain and fear; he is hoping that she can save him… Although she has never seen him before, she instantly knows that this is 'J' and he is an important person for her to meet on her life's journey. But why? Before she can go any deeper the `phone rings.

Twelve

Next morning finds me feeling well, with a clear head and an appetite. Jeremy is coming today and I am really looking forward to seeing him again. It is good to enjoy breakfast again and then head downstairs to my office. I am early as I have something I want to look up on the professional register of brokers: Rodney Green has been haunting me and I awoke this morning with his name in my head, so I sign on to the website to find out where he is now as this is getting on my nerves. It only takes a few moments to find him.

"Ah, there you are, Rodders," I say to myself as I highlight his name.

In seconds, there is Rodney on screen in all his glory and I begin to read his biography: I am surprised that he has left our old firm and set up on his own. That takes guts, believe me, and I didn't think he had that in him so maybe I misjudged him. It looks like he left them suddenly last November. No reason is given, but I guess he got tired of being the token working class whipping boy, just as I did. I know what they can be like as it's a kind of club and if you didn't go to a top school like Eton you're just never accepted. You would always be an outsider, excluded from their rarefied world by accident of birth, nothing to do with your ability or intellect. To survive, I'd put on my mask of protection and became known as a hard man not to be messed with; with this reputation, I began to turn the tables on my detractors and establish myself enough to break away from the confines of the firm. I cultivated 'the look', a withering glance that could put them back in their cages. I did not respond well to their patronising manners and kind of enjoyed my bit of power over the privileged classes.

But Rodders was not like me, he was actually naive enough to think they liked him and his cockney accent and all; in reality they were laughing at him and I heard many derogatory comments about 'the barrow boy' behind his back. At least I was up front with him, I told him I didn't like him and I made it tough for him with no favours from me. I figured that if he were to survive he'd have to grow a hard skin or get eaten alive. Well, I feel bad about my attitude now. Maybe I should have helped him more but I just didn't want him around, reminding me where I had come from. Selfish, yes, but there is something I can do to make amends now so I make a note of his business address and `phone number before closing down the site.

I open my office door and look into the Reception area to see Jeremy with his back to me, listening intently to Jenny. She looks past him to see me standing by the door and nods to Jeremy, who turns and comes towards me. I am surprised to find his blue eyes are blazing with anger.

"Why didn't you tell me?" he demands. So Jenny has told him and I give her a resigned look. She mouths "Sorry" back to me, obviously thinking that I had already told him about my tumour.

"And it's lovely to see you too, Jeremy," I say and he stops in his tracks, his anger dying quickly as it usually does with him.

"I'm sorry," he says and shakes my hand warmly. I usher him into the privacy of my office so we can talk and he sinks into my client chair as I retreat behind my desk. I take a deep breath and begin.

"I take it Jenny has blabbed about the tumour?" He nods and leans forward. "Well, this whole thing has been a bit of a revelation to me too." A look of surprise crosses his face.

"How so?"

I remain silent for a moment. How do I put into words all I have learned about myself since the diagnosis? Eventually, I tell him that it's made me think a lot about myself, almost as an outside observer, and I can see what has motivated my behaviour much more clearly than before – like my jealously towards Carol and the reason for driving myself so hard.

"I've realised that the reason I wanted success was to show my father how much better I am than him." I smile. "Stupid isn't it?" He shakes his head.

"No, not at all. I think we are all influenced by our parents and the need to get approval from them, whether they're good loving parents or not."

"Another thing I have found out," I continue after a long pause, "is that I don't like being a stockbroker." I wait expectantly for him to be shocked, but I am the one in for a surprise.

"Yes, well I've always thought you'd be a lot happier doing something else."

"What?" I exclaim.

"James," he smiles, "you only really come alive when you buy a new house and start planning its refurbishment. You love the planning and the visits during development. You never look that excited about buying stocks and shares."

"Why didn't I see this?" I ask him. I'd never realised that; it's odd looking at yourself from someone else's eyes. He shrugs.

"Don't take it too hard, you are far from alone. I've done exactly the same thing. I hate being a broker too but I did as my father expected me to and followed him into the City. I never questioned this until Carol persuaded me to take a year off. She knew I wasn't cut out for this life and without her I would still be living a kind of half-life, sleepwalking through the years."

We sit quietly together thinking of all the time we have wasted doing a job we loathe. In the end I break the silence. "So what are you going to do instead?" He looks a little embarrassed.

"Well… I've always loved working with wood so I've been on a few woodworking and furniture restoring courses – and I'm pretty good at it. There's still a fair bit to learn but I think I can make a modest living, with Simon, a chap who already has a workshop in the village. Anyway, we've decided to sell the house here and we've found a perfect farmhouse in the village, near to where Carol's parents live."

I can only congratulate him. Jenny brings us coffee and we sit in silence for a while as we drink it.

"So tell me," Jeremy ventures, "when you found out about the tumour… is it operable?"

"No, terminal."

His face drains of colour and naturally he has to ask the question I dread, about the prognosis. I tell him that the doctors don't know but so far at least the reflexology is helping. His eyebrows shoot up almost to his hairline, knowing me so well, and I blame it all on Jenny. He understands now, having heard her views on complementary therapies over the years.

"Yes, one of her friends, Katrina. I wasn't keen at first but she booked it without telling me and suddenly this nice young lady is there to do my feet. So what could I do but give in gracefully?"

"That's our Jenny. It's going to be awful telling her that we're quitting."

"I think she's already guessed. After all, she knows about my tumour and I think she sussed that you weren't coming back the day you left. She must be psychic."

"She's certainly more clued up on us than we are."

A few minutes later, we get down to business, or rather deciding when to end the business. Our client contracts give them one month's notice and today is September the 25th, so allowing time for the letters we shall officially dissolve the partnership on the 1st of November. I can't wait to finish now.

"I suppose we should get Jenny in and break the bad news," I sigh, "and then you have to tell Harry. Once upon a time it would have been a pleasure for me to tell him but I'm trying to turn over a new leaf – I don't need any more karma."

"Karma! Good God, don't tell me you are going New Age on us, James?"

"Maybe. I'm learning a lot of new things at the moment, so who knows what I'll find out before the curtain falls? Anyway, look, all I want is to be treated normally. I don't want sympathy so please don't tell anyone else about the illness."

"Not even Carol?"

"Heavens, no. I'd hate her to know and the same goes for Harry. If he came in being nice I think I'd throw up."

He laughs at this but knows I am deadly serious, so reluctantly he nods agreement as he gets up to leave my office and talk to Harry. I am alone to ponder my own future for a few minutes. Then I open my top right-hand drawer and pull out two pieces of paper. One is a draft letter to our clients and on the other a reference for Jenny; I want to get Jeremy's approval for them both before we talk to Jenny and there is also the question of a financial settlement to show her how much we appreciate her dedication and loyalty. We struck gold when we employed her and I regret losing her from my life as she does brighten up the day.

Jeremy returns grim-faced and flops down into my client chair.

"Grief, he's an insufferable bastard," he growls.

"Have you only just worked that out?" I ask him. "So what did he say?" I have to ask if only to find out why Jeremy has changed his own opinion of Harry.

"Oh, just that he can take over both my clients and yours and make a much better job of them than we do."

For a moment I am stunned by the sheer arrogance of the man but then I see the funny side of it all and throw back my head and laugh. This reaction is clearly not what Jeremy was expecting, but quite frankly I can't be bothered anymore.

"What's so funny?" he asks.

"Harry's funny," I manage to say at last, controlling myself enough to inform Jeremy how the blubbering mound of lard has managed to deal with his clients between the boozy lunches and the frequent weekend breaks that usually include Friday and Monday. "The reason, my dear friend, that he hasn't lost all your clients is the redoubtable Jenny and the fact that I have made sure he didn't screw up. Harry has no idea how much effort it takes. He believes the computer does all the work for him." I hadn't done all this out of the kindness of my heart – remember, I don't have one when it comes to business. No, I did it so that the idiot wouldn't damage the company's reputation.

"Well," mutters Jeremy, "if he wants to retain my clients he'll have to win them over. And if they are foolish enough to stay with him, then they deserve what's coming." He pauses, then asks, "What about you, James, who you are going to recommend to your clients if they ask you?"

I hesitate to tell him what I've been thinking as I am still not sure if I'm going through with it or not... but what the hell. "I've been thinking about Rodney Green a lot lately." The look of total surprise on his face gives me a certain satisfaction.

"Good grief, there's a blast from the past. But didn't you hate him?"

I don't answer that, but tell Jeremy what I've found out about Rodders. Still, I want to check him out and ask Jeremy if his old school friend, Peter Gorman, who still works in the firm, can tell us more. There had been talk of Peter leaving with us but his wife is the daughter of one of the firm's founders and she objected to that. I must say I was relieved at the time. Peter is fine but he is Jeremy's friend, not mine, and I would once again have ended up being treated as less than an equal partner.

"No problem, we're having dinner with him and Sarah tomorrow night. I'll ask him why Rodney left and whether he's a good broker." He sighs. "But I still don't understand why you are considering this."

I can't really tell him about my 'karma issues' so I come up with another reason that he will understand. "I just feel that if he is any good I should help him a bit – especially as I was less then helpful before."

"That's an understatement. You were absolutely bloody to him."

I look down, embarrassed by his comments as I know how true they are.

"Yes, well maybe I want to make up for that now."

We smile at each other and sit for a moment, savouring our mental pictures of Rodders and of Harry's likely downfall. After a few minutes I pick up the two papers I had extracted earlier and hand them to Jeremy.

"What do you think of these?" I ask, sitting back and waiting while he reads Jenny's reference and settlement first. He looks up and nods.

"Yes, I agree with everything here," he says as he hands it back to me. Then he begins to read the other letter for our clients. Two minutes later he is done, looks up and smiles his agreement. "Right then, we had better have our chat to Jenny now."

Thirteen

Jenny comes in and sits down on the spare client chair while Jeremy nods to me that I should start. It seems that I have been elected to give out the bad news; some things never change.

"Aaah, Jenny… Jeremy has decided he wants to try something new and as I am not going to be around much longer we have no choice but to end the partnership and close the office." I watch her face and it remains pretty much expressionless. "So I'm afraid we have to give you a month's notice. We'll be closing on the 1st of November." She sighs and nods.

"Yes, I've been expecting this," she says sadly. "I have really enjoyed working for you two and I'll miss you both." Her eyes are glistening a bit with unshed tears.

"We'll miss you too, keeping us in order," I tell her.

"Oh, you're not so bad," she smiles. "When I first came here I was a little scared of you, James, but I soon realised your bark is worse than your bite. And you," she turns to Jeremy, "are a pushover."

"I know," he nods in agreement without a trace of embarrassment.

I hand her the reference and letter of settlement I had prepared and that Jeremy approved, and ask if it's all right for her. She starts to read and I study her face as she does so, noting her eyebrows going up and down a few times and a smile playing around her lips. Then suddenly she stops and looks up at us, her big blue eyes wide open in surprise.

"Oh guys, this is far too much," she says and I guess she has got to the sum we want to give her for her dedication, often above and beyond the call of duty. "Not at all," says Jeremy. "We could never have built up this business without you. You're the glue that has kept it together and this is just a token of our appreciation and esteem."

"It's one hell of a token," she grins. "Well, who am I to argue with my bosses… Still, I'm amazed, flattered… and…" She runs dry so I finish it for her.

"And happy, we hope?"

"Both happy and sad. It's the end of an era." We are all silent for a few moments, reflecting on the past, until Jenny asks, "So what happens now?"

"Well, firstly we need to inform all of our clients so if you could get a copy of this letter out to them as soon as possible, please -" I hand her the other paper "- that's a start."

"No problem. Er, what's going to happen to Harry?"

"Hopefully he'll disappear back to whichever hole he came from," I reply with a shrug.

"Spoken like the James I have come to know and love," she giggles. "Okay, maybe that was a little harsh. But he's Jeremy's relative, not mine."

"Yes, and aren't you glad of that!" he retorts.

"Quite so," I tell him. "But then mine are no great shakes either. Still, I'm sure he'll be fine. Harry is a bit like a cat, always lands on his little flat feet. But he can't trade under our name as it will cease to exist soon, so he's on his own." Jenny gives me one of her looks. "What? You know as well as I do he's a pain in the backside and a lazy sod."

"Oh, that's a little unfair, James," she counters. "He's not so bad when you get to know him."

"Really? Then why were you complaining to me recently about his cavalier attitude to work?"

"All right," she concedes, "sometimes he is very annoying – but he's not callous or mean."

"Not like me then?" I reply and she smiles sweetly.

"No, nothing like you, James. You're a one-off." I'm not sure whether that's a compliment or an insult but Jenny quickly changes the subject as she gets up from the chair and heads for the door. "Oh, I nearly forgot… I managed to get you a table at George's for 12.45 and the flowers will be delivered to the table about 1.30."

"Great. Thanks, Jenny."

She leaves us alone and Jeremy raises his eyebrows. "Flowers?" he asks.

"To soften Carol up," I tell him.

"Really, well it's never worked for me. I wish you better luck."

We are sipping our first drink by the time Carol and her friend Beth joined us. I see her coming across the room, a look of grim determination on her rather horsey face. I take a deep breath to steady myself as I am determined not to rise to any bait she may throw out at me; all snide comments are going to be ignored and returned with a smile. Well, that is my intention. We stand as she and the other, smaller woman arrive at our table.

"Carol, lovely to see you again – and looking so great," I say. Maybe I am gilding the lily a little bit and I notice that Jeremy's eyebrows have almost vanished under his fringe and Carol's mouth is hanging open. Thankfully my greeting has rendered her speechless so I turn to the rather mousy, plump woman behind her and hold out my hand. "Hello, you must be Beth. I'm James. It's a pleasure to meet you." She smiles shyly and offers a rather weak handshake.

"Hi, James, thank you for inviting me." Her accent is New York.

"Not at all, my pleasure. Any friend of Carol's is a friend of mine." I hear a spluttering coming from Jeremy but I ignore it and pull out the empty chair next to me for her. She seems impressed by my British manners and smiles as she sits down. So far so good. She looks across at a startled Carol.

"It's so nice to meet a real gentleman in this day and age," she says. Jeremy pulls out the remaining chair for Carol but at first she doesn't make a move, still stunned by what she has just witnessed. Suddenly she snaps out of it and sits down heavily. I hide a smile, realising that this could turn out to be much more fun than I had anticipated; so far

I have confused the hell out of her and out-gunned her though I'm in no doubt that she'll come back at me soon. Still, I appear to have won round one.

Jeremy sighs, obviously fearing that the worst is yet to come. I know he loves us both and has tried his best to keep the peace, mainly by keeping us as far away from each other as possible. To quote him on this, "It's so I don't have to stand by and watch my two best friends tear each other apart." I look across the table at him in the hope he might start up a conversation, but he still looks like a rabbit caught in the headlights of an oncoming car, so I turn to Beth.

"Is that a New York accent?"

"It sure is. I'm from the Bronx originally, although I don't live there anymore. It seems like I've known Carol forever. We met at summer camp when I was a high school senior and Carol was on her gap year. We were looking after ten year-old spoilt brats in Pennsylvania for two very long months. Boy, it was hard work but you made some great friends too." Like a wind-up toy she kept going, mainly about quaint old England as if it were a medieval theme park, and about having gotten tickets to the Palace.

"Perhaps you'll meet Her Majesty," I tease. Seeing her frown, I add, "The Queen."

"Oh really? That would be neat." I keep smiling but it is beginning to hurt. After a few moments of silence, Carol decides to attack cautiously.

"So, now that Jeremy is moving on, what are you going to do, James?"

"Well, I've also come to the conclusion that it's time to live a little so we are dissolving the partnership and getting on with our lives. If Jeremy is ready to try something else then maybe it's time I do the same. We've already set it in motion and we will cease to be on November 1st – in a manner of speaking." I get a jolt of pleasure from seeing Carol's shocked face – no doubt that's another bit of karma I need to pay back, but I enjoyed it – as she looks to Jeremy for confirmation of what I have said.

"You're not going to fight us on this?"

"Of course not," I reply in a shocked tone, smiling sweetly.

The waiter arrives with our wine and the menus, which gives Carol time to digest what I have said. I can almost hear the wheels going round in her head. From her face I know she can't work out why I am being so co-operative and it's driving her mad. I glance at the menu though I don't feel particularly hungry, deciding on a chicken dish as it is the only thing I can digest easily at the moment. Jeremy, as usual, is reading his from top to bottom and I know from past experience that it will take him an age to decide what to order. This usually drives me mad but that is Jeremy and he'll never change. Carol is more decisive and now looks across the table at me so I smile back.

"Jeremy tells me you've found the perfect house in Dorset?"

"Oh, did he?" she replies, glancing at her husband who wisely keeps his head stuck firmly in the menu.

"Yes, it sounds idyllic. I'm sure you and the children will prefer the country to London. And you'll be near your parents too." She really has no idea why I am being so nice or if I am just faking it, but I must say this is almost as much fun as fighting with her. "I can just see Jeremy as a carpenter, too."

The waiter then comes back to take our orders, which gives Carol time to think as Jeremy keeps him waiting while he finally makes up his mind. Once the waiter has departed, she comes back at me on the attack.

"So, James, what do you really think?" she says, leaning forward in a rather threatening manner. I smile again.

"I think, Carol, that you should wear that colour more often. It suits you."

Jeremy splutters, sending drops of wine across the table, and Carol's reaction is of total surprise. Her eyes are wide open, as is her mouth, which I have to say is not a pleasant sight, and for the second time today I have rendered her speechless. I fear this happy state won't last for long and I am right.

"Oh, very funny, James. What game are you playing?" she asks angrily.

"Game?" I raise an eyebrow. Beth is looking from one to the other of us as if at a tennis match.

"Yes, you heard me. You love money too much to give up the partnership without a fight. So what is your devious mind really planning?" I try to look shocked that she could think such things of me but I am not sure how successful I am.

"Carol, I am hurt. I never realised you thought I was that kind of person. And I have never meant to give you any cause to dislike me. I do realise that at times I have been jealous of the time you have with Jeremy. But in my defence, remember that he and I used to spend a lot of our time working and socialising together. And when your best friend gets a girlfriend, all that goes out the window." She stares at me as if trying to look right through me, then across to Jeremy who smiles at her and nods.

"James is telling the truth, Carol. He told me all this only this morning." She frowns and purses her lips and I can see from her expression that she isn't sure what to believe. I press my advantage and give her the story about having enough money and wanting to travel, hoping that Jeremy will keep his word and his mouth shut. I know he hates to keep secrets from Carol but he also knows that a promise is a promise.

"Well… that's good," she finally concedes. She doesn't seem as pleased as she might be, but perhaps she misses sparring with me as much as I do. Still, I have enjoyed being nice to her today. It's been a pleasure.

Our food arrives and the conversation moves on to other less thorny topics as the rest of the meal passes in relative harmony. Right on time, the waiter brings the flowers I had asked Jenny to order to the table. He's not sure which of the two ladies at the table they're for, so I gesture towards Carol who, for a record third time today, sits there like a stunned mullet.

"Carol, these are for you to say sorry for my less than gallant behaviour in the past. I do sincerely apologise."

She blinks a couple of times and looks down at the bouquet, trying desperately to come up with something to say and possibly worried that it might explode in her arms. No, I am only really trying to be a better, kinder person and reduce some of my karmic load, not add to it. It seems that my being nice is going to be hard for some to accept, but finally the power of speech returns to her.

"Um, thank you, James. What a nice gesture."

I glance across at Jeremy who is suspiciously wiping his mouth on a napkin to hide a grin. "I hoped you would like them. Jenny said they're your favourites." Yes, I had even taken advice on what to order – I only know the difference between roses, carnations and chrysanthemums – and Jenny had told me to leave it to her as she already knew what Carol likes best. Now Carol smiles, perhaps the first genuine smile I have received from her since we met four years ago.

"They are lovely, thank you, and please thank Jenny for me too."

"I will," I tell her, just as the waiter comes back with the bill. I give him my credit card and as he departs with it Carol is again staring at me as if I have suddenly grown two heads. "My treat," I say.

All right, maybe in the past generosity might sometimes have been an issue with me, but I am trying to turn over a new leaf and all. I just have to pay as a final act of defiance, a breaking of the old James mould and the emergence of the new. I had already told Jeremy I wanted to pay for lunch and he was more than happy to let me. God knows he has paid for me enough times in the past, especially when I first knew him and had no money at all. Well, so much has changed for both of us since those days.

We all get to our feet and walk out onto the pavement. It is a strange moment for me as this will probably be the last time I see Carol; I am not expecting any invitations down to Dorset in the very near future.

"Beth, nice to have met you," I say and she giggles as if she has thoroughly enjoyed the play she has witnessed. Then I turn to Carol. "I hope Dorset lives up to your expectations and that everything goes well for you all."

She looks me in the eye, an unnerving experience, and then suddenly relaxes into a smile, taking my hand. "Thank you, James. And I hope you find whatever it is you're looking for too."

I wonder what that is as I watch them go and suddenly I feel a bit sad. But I still have work to do so I turn and walk back to the office alone.

Fourteen

Saturday morning arrives and I don't feel great but, unfortunately, not bad enough to pull out of going to the Mind, Body and Spirit festival that Katrina had invited me to. It doesn't take me long to get there on the Tube, which is surprisingly neither crowded nor smelly, and after a few stops I find my way to the festival. The doors have just opened and a large crowd is waiting to go in, so I join the back of the queue and file inside. I am surprised at how big the hall is. I'm not sure what I was expecting, maybe a dozen stalls, but this is a huge place crammed with over sixty individual booths. To one side there is also a large stage area where there will be demonstrations, music and dance going on during the weekend. On top of that, according to the programme, there will be lectures going on in smaller rooms given by people who have come from all over the world to speak here. It's a much bigger deal than I ever envisaged.

I set off up the first passageway and find myself in a very new and strange world. There are people being massaged and given healing in various ways and stalls selling crystals, clothes, books and all manner of health products, even a roped-off section reserved for Tarot card readers and fortune tellers. I steer clear of them as I don't believe anyone can tell you what is going to happen in the future: what would they say about mine? I find myself in amongst some very peculiar folk, stopping in surprise at the sight of a woman lying on a couch in front of me with what appears to be a candle sticking out of her ear; another woman dressed in a rainbow-coloured kaftan, with wild black hair and a headband, comes towards me at full sail.

"Would you like to try it?" she asks. "It's very therapeutic." That's as may be, but there is no way I am lying down in front of all these people and having a candle shoved into my ear, however good for me it is. I dodge around her and make my escape.

This place is like nothing I have ever seen before, like I have been dropped onto another planet, and I must stick out like a conservative sore thumb amongst the brightly clothed exhibitors even though I have dressed down in my corduroy trousers, blue shirt and black leather jacket. I have never seen so many exotically dressed people before in England. And the noise is ever-increasing. I can feel the beginnings of a headache so I must find Katrina before I have to leave.

"James, over here," a familiar voice cries. I look around over the heads of the multitude and see a hand frantically waving at me from a stall on the other side of the passageway, so I push my way through the stream of people who are flowing past. She has a huge grin on her face as she watches me approach.

"Hi there, you came!" she exclaims.

"As if I had a choice," I roll my eyes. "Anyway, I said I would and I am a man of my word. I must say I didn't think it was going to be such a big event."

"Oh yes, and it goes on for days. I'll be here on and off but don't worry, I haven't forgotten our appointment on Monday."

"Good. I think I'll need another treatment by then."

"You and me both! Anyway, come and meet the others."

Their exhibition space is bigger than many of the others and once inside there is some peace. The space has been divided up into four, with screens of beautifully patterned textile banners in swirling purples, blues and pinks, making it into a sort of sanctuary from the hustle and bustle outside. The first area is the information hub with its leaflets and cards and the other areas are being used for what they call taster sessions. They all appear to be occupied already. A short, red-haired lady with bright blue eyes gets up from a chair to meet me as Katrina makes the introductions.

"James this is Rosie, our acupuncturist."

"Hi there, I'm afraid I'm not great with needles," I blurt out and she throws back her head and laughs. I bet she hears that a lot.

"Okay, I promise I won't attack you with any," she says.

"Rosie, be nice or you'll scare him away," Katrina chides her.

"It's all right," I offer. "I am also trying to mend my wicked ways."

"Well, they do say that God loves a trier," says Rosie.

"I do hope so," I reply, as I might be meeting Him quite soon.

"James is really here to meet Tara," offers Katrina. "Karma issues."

"Oh right, well you've come to the right person to get a handle on them," says Rosie, clearly not one to mind her own business. "She's great."

"You've had karma problems too?" I ask, though I don't know why.

"James darling, the whole world has karma problems, it's just that most people don't know it. You'll learn so much about yourself – why you think like you do, who has been in past lives with you … It's a little spooky but it will explain a lot."

I open my mouth to reply when a pain like a bullet entering my brain hits me and "Aaah!" is all that comes out. All my senses are scrambled, my eyes won't focus, the world is slipping sideways and I can't do anything about it. I try to hold my head on but the pain is burning inside my brain so intensely that I can't stand it anymore; from somewhere I hear myself cry out but I'm somehow disconnected to it and my legs are going from under me… Someone grabs me as I fall and I hear my name, but all my synapses are firing at once and my body is on fire.

"Oh God, take me now," is the only thought I can muster.

Nearby, someone is calling for help – I hear the voice but the name is slowing down somehow… T…a…r…a…

She hears a crash then Rosie shouting for her, making her heart sink with dread. Rushing to the commotion she sees a man lying on the floor with both Rosie and Katrina frantically trying to communicate with him but to no avail. Rosie gets out of the way saying, "I'll ring for an ambulance" and she gets her first good look at the man.

Her hear misses a beat as, for a moment, his face is that of the brother she lost on Skye three hundred years ago, but then it changes before her eyes to that of a handsome, living man who is obviously in great pain.

Immediately, Ala Oki is with her and tells her to put her hands on each side of his head so that she can send cooling energy to him. Tara does as she is told and feels the healing pouring through her hands like an icy river.

There is someone different kneeling next to me; I don't know who this is but suddenly cool hands are touching my temples with the effect of pouring cold water onto a fire. The cool energy enters my head and almost immediately the pain decreases to a more bearable level.

"Aaah, better," I mumble as my muscles begin to relax and I can breathe again. A flow of energy is now enveloping me and I am conscious of a pink light around me, calming and peaceful; I just want to fall into it as more of the pain is receding. It is like being held in a warm blanket that is now beginning to deepen to a lovely magenta and as it does so I feel myself shutting down. "If this is dying," I think, "it's not so bad at all."

How long I stay in that warm world I can't say, but for me it isn't long enough; the real world is slowly making a comeback and with it the remnants of that terrible pain. I hear the rumbling of gurney wheels over polished floors and feel that I am being moved along horizontally. "Why is that?" I wonder and then realise that I must be in hospital, which is not where I want to die. I have got to get out of here. I groan and try to open my eyes, then a hand touches my shoulder and I hear soft words.

"James, you're going to be fine, just lie still."

I'm not at all sure about that as it feels like I have done ten rounds with Mike Tyson; that wonderful feeling of warmth and comfort is going now and in its place I have a thumping headache. I have another go at opening my eyes and this time I make it, turning my head away from the glare of bright overhead lights to find a blonde beauty looking down at me with the bluest eyes I have ever seen. She smiles.

"Hi, James, I'm Tara."

"Oh!" is all I can come up with, not at my wittiest at the moment, but my senses are returning and I know from the smells around me that I have indeed ended up in hospital. I hate them, so I try to sit up and manage to struggle onto my elbows. "Let me off this thing," I demand weakly but the male nurse pushing me along looks at me with a grin.

"No can do, mate," he says with an Australian accent. "You're on your way for an MRI." I groan at this, having had one of those before and I didn't enjoy the experience one bit. It was like being squashed inside a metal tube and the panic of not being able to move had been terrible, so I really don't want to go through that again. I struggle to get my legs under me when Tara places her hand on my arm.

"Calm down, James, you will be all right." A wave of peace flows over me as I look into her eyes and I believe her, although I have no idea why. "Trust me, you're going to be fine, I promise." She seems to look deep inside me so I know I will be if she is with me.

"Okay."

"Good," she smiles. "Now lie back and behave yourself."

I do as I am told. The nurse chuckles and we trundle on past many doors until the right one is pushed open and I am wheeled into the MRI suite. Tara has to stay in the anteroom but before I am wheeled away she pats my hand and smiles, which is reassuring somehow. I lie back and sigh as I am pushed through the double doors to the dreaded machine.

"Right, mate, up you get," says the nurse I am calling Bruce so I struggle upright and gingerly move across onto the slide that will retract and pass me into the bowels of technology. Before I lie down I have one more glance at the glass window and Tara is there, smiling encouragingly and raising her hand, so I return her smile and take great comfort that she is still there. "Okay, time to go," Bruce says.

This is what I hate the most: losing control and being held down. It dredges up a deep fear from somewhere and I can already feel the panic rising up in my stomach. I close my eyes and try to shut out these feelings by thinking of something else. But I am parcelled up like a chicken ready for the oven so moving is not an option and it's hard to think. Then a beautiful face pops into my head … so, that is Tara. There is such warmth and compassion in her amazing eyes and even though we've only spoken a few words I feel I've known her forever. I wonder if she feels the same or… I guess I didn't do much for her reputation, having to be stretchered out of the hall, and I groan inwardly with embarrassment. Still, no point in worrying about that now.

I'd rather try to remember every detail about Tara and commit her to memory. I'd say her face is oval in shape, with skin like porcelain, a wide mouth and a smile to die for. Ah, wrong choice of words. Now, her nose… um, I'm not sure how to describe it, it just fits perfectly with the rest of her face, one I hope to see a lot more of in the future. Um, the future is not my favourite topic anymore. If the pain I have just experienced, which was beyond agony, is what I have to look forward to then I'd rather kill myself first. Maybe we'll find out when they get the results of this scan. A buzzer goes off somewhere and I start to move forwards out of the machine.

In the anteroom, a tall man in his thirties and wearing a white coat is looking at the images of whatever is inside my skull on a computer screen and sitting in one of the chairs is the women whose face I have been rebuilding. I sit down next to her and we wait patiently until the doctor looks up at us as if he has only just noticed that we're there.

"Let me introduce myself," he says. "I'm Doctor Tillman and when you came in someone informed us of your ongoing condition. I have managed to have a quick word with your GP too." I wonder who could have given them that information and then it comes to me.

"Katrina," I say.

"I don't know," Doctor Tillman shrugs, "but anyway I've had a good look at the images. The tumour appears to be larger than the last time you had a scan. I believe you were told this would happen?" I gulp and nod. "Well, I can't estimate how fast it might grow and therefore the time scale of your illness."

"You mean my death," I reply as I dislike ambiguous language: let's call a spade a spade. He looks a little taken aback by my words.

"Er, yes," he concedes. "Still, there is -"

"I know it's inoperable," I interrupt, "and I don't want pointless treatment."

"I don't think chemotherapy is pointless," he says, a little tetchily.

"You don't, but I do," I reply. He refrains from arguing further and I suspect he already knows it would be useless. I have already made my wishes very clear to my GP. "So as there's nothing more you can do for me, I'd like to go home now. I'm not in any pain now,"

I lie. I still have a headache but it is very mild compared to what I experienced earlier.

"That's interesting," says Tillman, leaning forward towards me. "Did you receive any pain medication when you arrived?" I look at Tara who places her hand on my arm so that I know she doesn't want me to say anything about the healing she has given me. I nod to her and then turn back to Doctor Tillman.

"No, I wasn't given anything. It just went away."

"I don't understand…" he frowns.

"Well, I don't either," I shrug and smile back at him. "Anyway, as I see it there is a lot about the brain that even you lot don't yet understand so let's add my disappearing pain to the list." A small smile hovers on his lips as he accepts defeat.

I sign the 'Cover your arse' form to say that I'm leaving the hospital against medical advice and soon we are out of the building and into the street. I look around and realise that I don't have a clue where we are or even which hospital this is.

"Where the hell are we?"

"I know," Tara giggles. "The Tube is this way." She takes my hand and that warmth flows into me again. Her head only comes up to my chin so she has to look up to my eyes. "Are you really free of pain, James?" she asks as we walk towards a distant Underground sign.

"No, of course not. But it's all right, for now anyway."

"Then let's get you home and if it's still there maybe I can help to get rid of it."

"I'd like that." We walk on in silence but it is not an uncomfortable one; I feel safe with her by my side.

Fifteen

It is a strange journey home as there is no need for words, we seem to be in harmony as if we have been together for many years, yet we have only just met. I have never felt this comfortable with anyone before. It is as if we already know everything about one another and are happy just to be together. I can't explain it any better but I think she feels the same. We reach my front door and go inside where she looks around the Reception area with interest.

"I live upstairs, come and see."

"No, James," she shakes her head, "I can't come up now. I think you need to rest for a bit and I need to go back to the festival and see if they are coping without me." I had completely forgotten that she has responsibilities other than me. I look at my watch and am amazed to see it is already past two o'clock.

"I'm sorry, I've taken up so much of your time."

"Well, I'm not sorry. We have finally got to meet – even if you did have to collapse in my arms to do it." There is a gentle smile on her lips for all her teasing. "But for now you need to rest and I need to get back to my stand. I'll come back later if you like." Do I like?

"Yes please – and I'll take you to dinner to thank you for rescuing me."

After she leaves, I can't get the smile off my face and nor can I wait for her to return. But she's right, I am exhausted and climbing the steps to my apartment is a struggle. I sink into my soft bed and close my eyes thinking about Tara: something deep inside me has moved… is that the right description? Maybe 'opened' is a better word, yet even that doesn't describe how I feel inside. There is now a warmth where there had only been emptiness and cold, so is this what love feels like? I have never felt like this before. I might have deluded myself that I was 'in love' but it was a pale imitation. Somewhere in all this musing I fall asleep.

It is almost dark when I awake and for a moment I am disorientated. Then I remember and smile. It has just gone seven and she could be arriving at any moment, so I must get up and give my apartment a once over. I straighten the chocolate brown satin bedspread and rearrange the cushions on my iron-framed double bed, as they do in all the Good Homes magazines. I have always enjoyed the interior design of my properties, getting them ready to rent or sell, and I'm surprisingly good at it for a mere male. I check the bathroom and it's fine as I hate mess; I can be a bit obsessive if truth be told and it has got on some of my former girlfriends' nerves. They haven't appreciated me telling them how to tidy their apartments, for some reason.

Stepping into the lounge, I pace around the coffee and cream carpet and see that everything is in fact tidy. Has my life been altogether too tidy until now? Yet I love the feeling of this room, the ivory walls and the black contemporary furniture, comfortable chairs around the large plasma TV in one corner. Above the modern fireplace hangs a large oil painting of racehorses straining every muscle and fibre to be first past the post, full of energy and style but also reminding me of Lambourn. On another wall is a magnificent David Shepard painting of a male lion relaxing on the plains of Africa, which I bought at a charity auction; I often sit and observe this, imagining I am on safari – another thing I have never got around to. No point dwelling on that now.

And no time for the hoover because the buzzer rings and she's here.

"Come in, I'm up the staircase on the left of Reception." I take a deep breath, smooth down my rather wayward hair, open the door and am very pleased to see her. "Hello again, come on in. I live above the shop," I explain, rather unnecessarily as the name emblazoned on the outer door says it all.

"Yes, Katrina told me." I'm wondering what else she may have passed on. "She thought you might contact me for some sessions on karma." She smiles at my obvious discomfort and continues, "I understand why you didn't, so let's forget it, shall we?"

I nod in relief and show her to the lounge where she takes a seat on one of the sofas. Suddenly I feel awkward and embarrassed, yet earlier today I had been so comfortable in her company. Is it because here, at home, I am exposed and more vulnerable? I don't quite know what I should do or say. Then I look around and see the bottle of wine I had got out earlier and sigh with relief.

"Would you like a glass of wine? I have a nice bottle of red here... or I could get white from the `fridge... or maybe you don't...?" I'm rambling like a schoolboy.

"I love red wine, James, thank you." She smiles up at me and I feel my heart beat a little faster. Such an idiot, I can't even string a simple sentence together while she, on the other hand, seems completely at ease. I manage to open the bottle without spilling anything and take two glasses from the cabinet before, with an almost steady hand, pouring the wine.

"I hope you like it," I say as I hand her the glass then retreat to my favourite chair. I watch her face carefully as she takes a sip because for some reason it is important to me that she likes it.

"Oh yes, that hits the spot after the day I've had. Do you mind if I take my shoes off? My feet are killing me."

"Please, go ahead. Me casa su casa." Did I really just say that? She laughs.

"Your pronunciation is a bit off but thank you for the sentiment." She leans over and pulls her shoes off, curling her shapely legs under her and settling back with a serene smile on her face.

"I'm sorry your day was a bit of a disaster. And I had more than a bit to do with that."

"Actually," she shakes her head, "rescuing you was the highlight of my day."

"Heavens, if that's true then the rest of your day must have been really crap."

"It was."

"Do you want to talk about it? I'd love to hear what topped me being carried out of your stand on a stretcher. Tell me, what was so bad?"

She gives a deep sigh. "I suppose it's the energies that a show like this attracts," she says.

"Energies?" This is a new kind of language for me.

"Yes, there are a lot of wonderful people there, don't get me wrong, people who genuinely work with love and integrity. But where there is light, naturally there is darkness too – you can't have one without the other. So therefore there are also people who are only there to make money. Some of them, I think, believe that they are helping others but in reality they are just helping themselves. Their energy is very dense and I can't bear to be near them. I get psychically sick and have to be protecting myself all the time from it. That's exhausting."

"So how do you do that?" I ask. I have never had this kind of conversation before and have no idea how one protects oneself from the dark side.

"Well, everyone has their own pet method, James, and as you work in this field you find the one that suits you best. I use what I call 'the golden ring' – I visualise a ring of golden light around me like a kind of shield."

"And that protects you?"

"Yes, if you believe in it then it will. All healers must protect themselves or they will pick up illnesses from their clients. Protection is the most important skill anyone should learn and perfect when doing any spiritual work." She sighs again and yawns. "Anyway, I feel better now I'm out of there with a glass of wine in my hand. I just hope I can survive the rest of the festival, though I won't have to be there every day – I have ten therapists working at Tranquillity and they all want some time to promote their skills, which means I can escape for a day or two."

I'm now feeling guilty for dragging her here when I suspect that all she wants to do is go home and get something to eat. But that's something I can do for her, to repay the kindness she has shown me.

"Food, then!" I say. "You must be starving. Do you like Italian?"

She looks interested at least. "Yes I do, why?"

"Because it's the speciality of the house," I tell her. "I can rustle up a very edible pasta dish in twenty-five minutes if you'll risk it?"

"Bring it on," she says. And she sits back, closing her eyes while I head to the kitchen and get down to work.

Sixteen

"This looks good," she says. She doesn't need me to encourage her and for several minutes we eat in comparative silence until she has satisfied her immediate hunger and slows down. "This is very nice, James, thank you."

"It's the least I could do for my saviour," I reply. She laughs and waves a fork at me.

"I must say you did liven up the day somewhat with your dramatic collapse. Don't worry about it, James. I'm sure the girls on the stand have seen worse and it gave everyone something to gossip about – although I'm not sure if the extra people who visited us were there for treatments or to find out what happened."

"Oh well, at least I was good for business."

"You were," she grins. "It was the busiest day we've had at any exhibition."

I look at her for a moment and then have to ask what's been in my mind. "Didn't you give me healing?"

"Well, strictly speaking I can't give healing, James, only the Creator can do that. No, all I did was focus His power to where I was told it was needed – in your case, obviously, it was your head. Think of me as an electric cable between you and the Creator," she says.

"The Creator?" I ask, not sure if it's the same one that the Catholic priests used to talk about.

"God – or whatever you think created everything."

"I see… and you're a cable?" I raise a teasing eyebrow.

"Metaphorically speaking," she says, grinning. "The healing current flows through me but I don't produce it. This power is then directed to where it can do the most good, provided it's appropriate for you to receive healing – sometimes permission is denied."

"Denied? Why?"

"Sometimes I'm not given a reason," she shrugs, "but maybe because it's not the right time for the person to be healed, or they need to learn something from their illness first…" She pauses. "Or they are not going to be healed. In these cases I am usually allowed to give pain relief, but that's not quite the same sort of energy."

"And you can tell the difference?" I am desperate to know which category I fall into, but perhaps it would be indelicate to ask.

"Oh yes," she answers. "When you work with energies you begin to feel the difference between them. My guides feel very different too and the energy also changes subtly when it's used for other purposes. It's a learning process. But you are not given more than you can handle at any one time. I've been doing this work since I was a child and I'm still learning new things every day."

As we go back to our food, I have a hundred questions going round in my head. This is a new world for me and it feels very important. I want to know whether anyone can learn to heal, or use this energy. Tara nods several times and becomes really passionate about this, and angry at the medical profession's rejection of complementary therapists, as if they were a threat.

"Sometimes, using allopathic medicine is the right course to take and I respect their work," she says. "I just wish they would respect mine. I dream of a time when we can all work together to heal people in the best way possible."

"So how do you do it, I mean, healing?"

"I don't, remember, but I know what you mean. Everyone's a bit different. Some have a structured way of attuning themselves to the energy while I just do it intuitively. Like I said, I ask for permission and I don't need to know where the healing is needed – I just get guided to different parts of the body and somehow I know when they have had enough. I don't need to understand how it works."

She looks closely at me to see if I understand and, strangely, I think I do. What she has said somehow makes perfect sense to me; it is as if I already know it but had forgotten it and somewhere in my mind things are falling into place. And then the evening takes a whole new turn as I lean across the table and touch her hand.

"To your own self be true," I say, as surprised by my own words as she appears to be.

"What?"

"Um, I don't know why I said that," I confess.

"I think I do," she smiles. She takes my hand and looks deeply into my eyes. There's an electric silence between us for a minute before she continues. "I hope this isn't going to freak you out, but here goes…" She leans back and breathes deeply. "My spirit guide told me recently that a man with the initial 'J' was about to enter my life. He said I'd feel as if I've known this person a long time. There's a past life connection between us and he would teach me a lot." She is studying my surprised face and is clearly relieved that I haven't got up and run out of the room screaming. "He also said that I would be sure it's the right one when he says what you just did."

"What?" I exclaim. "That's amazing."

"Yes. And it's true, there is a familiarity about you. Do you believe in past lives, James?" I tell her about my conversations with Katrina and the book I read recently, which suggested that we have all lived before, maybe even hundreds of times. "Right," she nods, "and the life we have now is always connected to those from the past. That's where we need to look to find the answers we need in this life – why certain people are causing us problems and why we have phobias, prejudices and what pushes our buttons."

"So if I had a difficult relationship," I ask the obvious question, "with, let's say, my father – could this be something carried over from a past life?"

"Yes, it could. And resolving it in this life may well prevent a repeat performance in a future one. All our lives are changed by the decisions and choices we make and they play out in our futures too. This is bound up with karma. It's complicated but fascinating as well."

"Hmm, karma … Katrina has told me about this. In fact, that's why I was coming to see you!"

"So it's not all bad," she laughs. "And there's positive as well as negative karma, you know. The thing is to try and diminish our load and not add to it."

"To become karma neutral?" I reply.

"I like that. Yes, karma neutral. We should all be looking to reduce our karma footprint – it would make the world a happier and safer place." She leans back, sighs and yawns. "Oops, sorry."

"No, don't be. I've kept you here talking when what you really need is a good night's sleep." I get up and reach for the `phone. "I'll get you a taxi."

Ten minutes later I am waving her off in the cab of a company I have an account with and I miss her already even though the cab has only just turned the corner. I have never felt like this about anyone before. Still, I'll be seeing her again very soon as we have arranged a consultation for me to start finding out about my karmic legacy. I touch the spot on my cheek where she kissed me goodnight and smile like an idiot again. I don't think I'll stop smiling for quite a while.

I open my eyes next morning fully expecting to feel rather delicate but to my surprise I don't, in fact I have no headache or side-effects at all except one – recurring thoughts of Tara. I smile as feel a fluttering in my heart. I don't think I have ever truly been in love before. There was Angie, my only long-term relationship and in fact my ex-fiancée. She loved me, I know, and I would say that I loved her but it wasn't real. I was good at saying terms of endearment, especially if they got me what I wanted, but they came from my head and not my heart. As Tara's face floats through my mind again, I lie back in my bed and wonder: is this it? Has love finally found me? If it has, then it has left things a bit late … It seems that God's got a very warped sense of humour.

A few hours later, after spending some time working on the computer, I give up due to lack of enthusiasm. Very soon our clients will have been informed of our retirement and in a few weeks I shall never have to spend another Sunday working. I'll not miss it. It has taken a brain tumour to knock some sense into me and get me to look outside the box I built for myself. A sound by my elbow startles me out of my daydreams back to the present and I pick up the `phone. It's Jeremy.

"I'm just letting you know that I'll be coming into the office tomorrow to start tying up loose ends."

"Great. How is Harry taking it?" I ask. "I haven't seen hide nor hair of him since you told him our decision."

"I don't know, I haven't seen him. He's probably lying low for a while. Or perhaps he's planning something." I have a feeling Carol's sister may be sticking her oar in the mix, to help the lump of lard she was foolish enough to marry. "Anyway, I talked to Richard last night about Rodney Green. It seems our Rodders got fed up with being the butt of office jokes. And with other brokers claiming the credit for his work."

"Aaah, why am I not surprised?" I say. I'd had a very similar experience when I started, but my approach to the problem had been a little different. For one thing, I made very sure to claim the credit for my efforts with back-up proof. Secondly, I did some work on myself and began a programme of self-education: reading books on etiquette, art, history and anything else I could think of that would come in handy when talking to toffs. That's how I discovered my love of architecture, for example. "So, he's gone out on his own has he?" I ask. "That's gutsy." We both knew from experience that the first couple of years of going solo is either foolhardy or courageous.

"Yes. And Peter is quite surprised by how well he is doing."

"Is he any good, though?"

"Oh yes, I get the impression that Peter is regretting him leaving. They are only now realising that he might sound like a barrow boy but he's got a good business brain and knows how to use it."

It is good to have my intuition confirmed, but I decide to go and see Rodney before recommending him to my clients – and dealing with that particular piece of karma. There is a sharp intake of breath from the other end of the line when I tell Jeremy this.

"You're going to visit him?" Jeremy's voice rises an octave. "That could be downright dangerous. Didn't you almost come to blows in the conference room last time you met?" He's right. I had deliberately goaded Rodney into a reaction and then ridiculed his lack of polish and self-control. Now I shift uneasily in my chair; once upon a time I had enjoyed doing things like that but now I am appalled by my past behaviour. If Jeremy could see my face he might notice it going a delicate shade of red, with embarrassment and a hint of shame. "Well, if you want to risk it," he continues, "it's your funeral… oh God, sorry I didn't mean…"

"It's all right, don't stress Jeremy. We all have to go sometime. Anyway, if Rodders feels the need to punch me I guess he has every right to. I'll make the appointment to see him in another name, then at least I should get though the front door. What happens after that is anybody's guess."

Seventeen

Monday dawns grey and gloomy which corresponds beautifully with my mood as I awake with a tingling in my left arm and hand plus a brain that feels sluggish and unco-operative. I take some painkillers but there isn't much improvement and I fear it is going to be a long and difficult day.

The only bright spot on the horizon is my appointment later with Katrina. Perhaps I can elicit some more information about the delightful Tara since I know so little about her. Is she in a relationship? She didn't mention anyone and she was free to have dinner with me... Still, I can't be sure though I expect Katrina will know. Not that I am looking for a long-term relationship, for obvious reasons; but to love someone, really love someone before I kick the bucket, well yes, I do want that. Am I being selfish? I mean, if she falls in love with me too and then I die – she'll be hurt and I don't want that.

I am pretty much resigned to the fact that I haven't got long; I am not happy about it but I am a fatalist at heart. So I must get a grip and get down to some of those things I have on my 'To do' list. Rodney Green is on the top so I pick up the `phone and dial his number.

"Rodney Green's office," a chirpy female voice answers, "this is Miranda. How can I help you?" She is as cockney as her boss and I have an instant mental picture of her looking like a young Barbara Windsor in one of the old Carry On films, all bust and bleached blonde hair.

"Good morning, Miranda," I reply. "I would like to make an appointment with Mr Green, please."

"Okay, let's take a look-see…" I hear the rustle of pages as if she is searching for a slot to fit me in, yet I have a feeling she is just moving one page backwards and forwards close to the 'phone for effect. I smile, remembering a time when I did the same thing before we could afford Jenny; but at least he has a secretary. Finally Miranda returns.

"He has a slot on Thursday at 10.30. How does that suit yer?"

It suits me fine as I am no longer interviewing potential new clients and am not tied to the office. "Yes, that is good for me."

"Right, and yer name?"

I have already decided on a suitable nom-de-plume. "Mr Ano Nymous."

"Oh, heavens, that's an unusual name. Foreign is it?"

"Yes, I believe so." I try my hardest not to laugh at her delightful accent as I lean back in my chair later and smile; like Jeremy said, Rodders has a lot of guts as our profession runs on the Old Boy network, yet here he is shoving his working class roots in their faces.

I get another stab of pain. The headaches are becoming more frequent and harder to shift, an indication that the tumour is growing. How much time do I have left? I doubt it's another year, maybe six months if I'm lucky.

"God, it's so bloody unfair," I mutter. "I am just beginning to see life's possibilities and You're going to take it all away from me." Then it hits me that it's only because of the tumour that I am even aware of these new possibilities at all. If I hadn't been diagnosed, I would probably be raging about Jeremy giving up the business and I'd be impossible to be around, throwing myself into my work to take my mind off the anger I'd feel. That old James, I am embarrassed to admit, was a perfect bastard. I just hope that I have enough time to make amends to some of the people I've hurt and reduce a bit of my karma. And enough strength to keep up this account of it all.

Tara's face swims into my consciousness again and I cling on to the thought of seeing her tomorrow when I have my first karma appointment. For now, I must try and drag myself into work mode and concentrate on selling some of my own share portfolio without starting any rumours or runs.

Katrina's healing hands slowly release the pain I have been unable to shift all day. I take a deep breath and feel my tense shoulders relax and let go. "Oh that's better."

"Good," she laughs, then after a pause she adds, "You gave me a terrible fright on Saturday, James. Are you all right now?"

"Well, I am as all right as a dying man can be," I reply dryly. I open one eye to look at her and am surprised to see a tear on her cheek. "Come on, don't go all mushy on me. I'm okay, really I am, and I'm sorry I scared you. Truth is, I scared myself too."

"Lucky Tara was there, then," she says.

I want to cheer out loud as she has just brought up the one subject I want to talk about; but if I had mentioned Tara first, I wouldn't have been able to hide that my interest in her goes beyond her healing skills. "Yes, it was," I reply. But then there's another silence as I'm desperately trying to find a way of asking all the questions I have about Tara.

"James," Katrina says eventually, "can I ask you what you felt when she touched you?" She says this without looking me in the eye, as if she is embarrassed about asking.

"Well, the pain in my head was like there was a fire inside it... it's not an easy thing to describe though, pain I mean. I could hardly tell what was happening. Then it was as if a jet of cold water was poured into each side of my head, putting the fire out. That must have been when Tara touched my head, I suppose." I sigh. "But then I don't remember anything until I was being wheeled to the MRI scanner at the hospital."

"And when you woke up then, how did you feel?"

"Apart from acutely embarrassed, you mean?" That makes her smile. "I was tired and had a faint headache, but apart from that I felt quite good."

"Tara didn't get back to the hall until after three o'clock," she says, looking up at me with a glint in her eye.

"Yes, well, she insisted on taking me home in case I had a relapse on the way."

"And I suppose she had to check on you later too, just in case," she adds with a grin.

"Of course, she's very conscientious," I reply. It's an effort to keep my face straight but Katrina's grin is growing wider so in the end I can't help joining her. "Yes, so I like her, sue me," I say. "And I think she likes me too, so you can stop fishing and answer some questions I have."

"All right, that's only fair I suppose," she replies. "What do you want to know?"

"Everything."

She laughs and I have the feeling she is a born romantic at heart.

"Let's see. She's single and unattached though she was engaged once – something happened but before you ask, no, I don't know what that was except that it was when she was living in Malvern, where she comes from originally, before her move to London.

"I met her five years ago when she set up Tranquillity. She was advertising for therapists and we've been friends and colleagues ever since. Whatever happened before she came here, she doesn't talk about. She's very private. I call her a friend but we're not bosom buddies, she doesn't encourage that sort of friendship. Not stand-offish, just… I don't know, self-reliant? She doesn't need to be surrounded by lots of people. I do know she hates clubs and loud parties – she told me once that she'd rather go to the theatre or out for dinner."

"That's useful to know. What sort of shows does she like – musicals or drama?"

"I think you should ask her, James." She rolls her eyes at me.

"Does she have any family? Where was she born? When's her birthday?"

"Whoa, boy," she says, putting one hand up to stop me, with a look of mock horror on her face. "Slow down, James. Let me think. Well, I do know her birthday. It's March the 28th – she is Aries."

"And how old is she?"

"A gentleman," she snorts, "would never ask a lady's age."

"Maybe not, but I don't have time to be a gentleman, so spill the beans."

"Alright," she sighs, "but you must never tell her I told you. She'll be thirty-four next year and she's not looking forward to it. I think she'd like to have children and mid-thirties is considered to be getting on in the fertility stakes."

This gives me pause for thought as I can't say that children have ever really featured in my plans; but that is more because I haven't found the right woman yet. Or have I, when it's too late? After a long silence, Katrina sits back having completed my treatment.

"There you go, James, all done. I do hope your intentions are honourable?" She raises one eyebrow and grins at me while I struggle to keep a straight face.

"Absolutely not."

"Good, she laughs, "Tara needs a little excitement in her life. And I think you could do with some fun right now, too." She is nearer to the truth than she might imagine.

I replace the `phone at five o'clock two days later and switch it to voicemail. I rub my eyes, which feel gritty and dry, and stretch my tired muscles; my neck and back ache from hunching over my desk all day. Since we sent out our retirement letters the `phone has been red hot, so much so that Jeremy has had to move into my spare room so he can be on call at the office to answer his clients' enquires. He has also moved back into his old office, much to Harry's annoyance because he now has to work at the small desk in Reception. He is not a happy little piggy at the moment but I am enjoying his discomfiture, except that he is driving Jenny mad with questions about why I am retiring. Still, she is a formidable woman and I know my secret is safe with her.

As for my clients, I have been surprised that quite a few of them, mostly my oldest ones, have decided to sell their portfolios rather than move to a new broker. I have been a very touched by the high regard they have expressed for me and I have even shed a few tears. I must be going soft. I make my way upstairs and meet Jeremy on his way down.

"I'm just out to meet Peter at the club for a drink. Do you want to join us?"

"No, I've got a better offer, thanks," I say, shaking my head. From the look on his face he doesn't believe me but it is true, though I haven't told him about Tara yet. In front of my open wardrobe I sigh at the rail of expensive suits and crisp white shirts but not a lot else. I haven't a clue what one should wear to go to Tranquillity and discuss karma, but I'm guessing Armani is not it. My collection of casual clothes is also woeful as I just don't do casual very well; I suddenly realise that my life is a lot like my wardrobe: work-orientated, conservative and frankly boring.

What have I got that isn't? I scour the room and spy an old chest of drawers sitting half-forgotten in a corner. Rummaging inside, I find a dark blue polo shirt and a cream vee-neck; they look clean and are not too wrinkled though I can't remember where they came from or how long they have languished here. They still fit me anyway and it seems I am thinner now than when they were given to me. Then I find a pair of black jeans, brand new with the label still on them, and I do remember that Angie had talked me into buying them over six years ago. Once bought they had never seen the light of day again until now.

After a shower and a shave I pull on my new wardrobe and stand in front of the full length mirror to survey the results. I look ... different. I'm so used to the uptight, restricted version of me that it is a little unnerving to see this less constrained person staring back at me. I'm not sure I know this person at all but perhaps I will get used to him eventually. Will Tara like this different James? That flutter is back in my chest and I can't stop a smile spreading across my face.

She closes her eyes and tried to take herself to her sacred place to centre herself before James arrives. He has stirred up her life already and she wonders if she'll be able to sep-arate her growing feelings for him from her responsibility as his therapist.

So far, this hasn't been a problem but now he is all she can think about. Even her meditations have been invaded by images of their past life together in Skye and how, as his brother, she had failed to save him from being killed. She has the feeling that this time she has to do more to help him; but she also knows that this isn't going to be easier. Tara sends out a request for help to her guardian angel and feels his presence around her, like being embraced in angels' wings. All the tension and anxiety leave her and she smiles.

"Thank you," she says, knowing that he will help. She opens her eyes to look at the wall clock, realising that James is due very soon. There is a mixture of happy anticipation and sadness within her now, knowing that she has some karma of her own to work off with him and that there is no way to avoid it. What happens now, she isn't sure; she only knows that she is already falling in love with him.

A quick trip on the Underground and I return to the surface, walking the five minutes to Tranquillity. I turn the last corner and there it is, tucked in off the main street. There's a small Japanese garden in front of it while the building itself is quite modern, with steel columns and plate glass at the front and a huge, wooden double door with a red lintel over it. It has a very Eastern feel about it, chic and minimalist, and while it is impressive it is somewhat of a surprise to me. I don't know why but I had imagined her working in an old building of faded elegance.

"Well, I guess I'm wrong again," I tell myself. But if I got this so wrong, have I made other false assumptions as well? I have thought Tara might like me – more than like me – but perhaps she sees me only as a client and nothing more. It would be the finally indignity if, just as God decides to lower the curtain on my life, I fall for someone who doesn't love me. There is only one way to find out.

Eighteen

I look at my watch and find that I'm early for my appointment but as it is getting cold I decide to venture inside anyway in search of warmth. So I walk with more confidence than I feel towards those imposing front doors and push them open, finding myself in a semi-circular entrance hall with a semi-circular Reception desk behind which sits a beautiful oriental woman. She looks up at me and smiles, one of those smiles you see from receptionists everywhere, a professional meet-and-greet smile that never quite reaches the eyes.

"Good evening, sir. Do you have an appointment?" she asks me in a pleasant sing-song voice.

"Yes I do, with Tara."

She looks down at the large appointment book in front of her and finds my name. "James Wiley? You are a little early so please take seat." She waves me towards some very uncomfortable looking chairs to the left but my attention is drawn to an enormous tank of tropical fish that stretches from the window to the end of the Reception area along the back wall. It must be over twenty feet long and full of brightly coloured fish. I have always loved tropical fish and even did some diving in the Caribbean and the Red Sea some years ago, a truly magical experience. I've always dreamed of diving off the Great Barrier Reef; but that's another ambition I'll have to shelve now. So I walk along the tank watching the fish dart in and out amongst the coral-like outcrops and the waving grasses. They look very content. I recognise several of them, like the Clown fish, but there are many others that I don't. There is so much going on in there that I am mesmerised by all the action, so much so that suddenly Tara is standing next to me.

"Hello, James," she says in her soft voice. I turn round and I swear that my heart does a complete skip and I am speechless. "James? Are you alright?" she asks as I stand there like a stunned mackerel. With enormous effort I pull myself together.

"I love tropical fish."

She smiles, takes my arm and steers me away from the tank and down a corridor to a door with her name on it where she ushers me inside and invites me to take a seat. I look around to find myself in what looks at first glance like an ordinary sitting room. There is a small couch by one wall and an armchair to match under the windows; a beautiful wooden coffee table sits in front of them on a gold and cream rug, over an oak wood floor. It is all very tasteful but the stock ornaments on the shelves giving it an impersonal feel, reminding me of the many show houses I have been around – and some I have helped to create. I sit on the sofa while she takes the chair and opens the folder in her hand.

"Right, James, I need to take a few details for my records, if that's okay."

I sigh inwardly as this is not going quite as I had hoped. But then I am a paying client so I suppose I should expect to be treated just like any other new one. "Fine, what do you need to know?"

"Well, I have your name, address and `phone number so I need your GP's name and number, please." I tell her even though I have no idea why it is necessary.

"Now, as you are here for a karma reading I don't need the rest of what's on here and I already know you have reflexology with Katrina. Are you having any other treatments, either complementary or allopathic?"

"Nope, the doc says they can't do anything so….oh, except I do take a fair amount of painkillers."

"Prescribed ones?" I nod. "Do you take anything else, like any supplements or multivitamins?"

"No, I don't. Do you think I should?" She tells me about a particular natural supplement that can help to prevent strokes, which I'm at risk of, and writes a few notes before putting the folder aside. I'm feeling uncomfortable, with so many thoughts in my head, but she stays professional. We talk for a few minutes about the concepts of karma and past lives.

"Don't be so anxious, James," she says, picking up on my feelings. "It is a lot easier to understand than you imagine. Let's begin. All I need you to do is relax for a few minutes while I tune into you. Are you alright about me doing that?"

"Sure," I say, "though why do you need to?"

"Well, I am a medium so I have to tune into another person to be able to help them, both for healing and to see their 'karma knots', as I call them. It's the nearest description that I have come up with to describe what I see when I do this work. These knots represent karmic events both in this life and from the past and they're the ones that need clearing. You may have more that can't be cleared at this time but we'll leave them for now."

I can't say I understand but I keep my mouth shut and listen, hoping it will become clearer eventually. She describes seeing areas like ropes all knotted up. Sometimes if one is already working on a karmic issue they appear loose but there are others that look tightly knotted and unyielding. They are also coloured, which helps Tara identify which area of one's life they relate to.

"Once I see them," she continues, "I ask my guide to tell me which ones we should start with and how they came into being. I might only get a vague idea what caused them but you will know what it's all about, if you stay open to the process. I should tell you that it's not comfortable, James, and it can get very emotional too. You have to face up to your own flaws – but if you are serious about doing something positive to undo some of these karmic knots, then that's essential."

I swallow hard as I have a feeling this isn't going to be pretty and I might not like what I hear. But I do know that I have to go through with this if I am to save myself a lot of future pain. She now asks me to relax and start thinking through my life, to see where I may have created karma, not dwelling on anything but moving on. I'm not sure how good I'll be at this but I'll give it a go, though feel very self-conscious sitting here in silence while she scans me for karma. It feels like one of those dreams where you end up naked in public. I shudder at the thought and decide I had better focus on my life as she asked me to and let her do her job. I can't say I know what I am looking for exactly, but I start with my childhood in Lambourn and then my move to London. It all begins to feel shallow and meaningless though at last her voice rescues me from becoming depressed.

"All right, James, that's enough. You can open your eyes now. You've done great." I do as I am told and find her reading notes that she must have made while tuning into me.

"Is it bad?" I ask hesitantly.

"No worse than anyone else's," she smiles. "Why, are you really a serial killer?"

"Some people might think so."

"Well, I don't," she says and that flutter in my chest is back. "Anyway, from what I did see you have already been working on some of this."

"Yes, I am trying. I guess if I'm honest I already know where some of my karma might come from and I have been trying to undo some of the damage."

"That tallies with what I felt as one knot is almost undone. I got a name with it too – does Carol mean anything to you?"

I laugh and tell her about Jeremy's wife. "I have apologised to her for my behaviour," I say. "Is there something else I still need to do?" She sucks the end of her pen and looks past me into the distance, then after a few minutes she nods and says I have to keep it up. Now that I understand why I didn't like Carol, it will be a lot easier to be nice. Tara goes on to tell me about another knot loosening, something to do with work, green in colour and again she got the name: Rodney! This is embarrassing, like washing my underwear in front of her.

"I'm not proud of how I treated Rodney," I admit. "He was everything I had tried so hard not to be. So to my everlasting shame I took my discomfort out on him and made his life hell."

"We've all felt these things, James." She nods and I feel her empathy. "But it was wrong to use it against another and it did create karma for you."

"Yes, I see that now." I sigh, feeling ashamed. "But I am going to see Rodney tomorrow, to explain to him why I was so rotten and ask him to forgive me… though I have no idea how he'll react. My partner Jeremy thinks it could get violent but, well, I hope it doesn't."

"Does he know you're coming?"

"Aaah… no. I made the appointment under another name so at least he'll let me in. After that, who knows what will happen. But I hope to get to say what I want to." She smiles encouragingly.

"I wish you luck," she adds. I think I'm going to need it.

She glances down at her notes again and is silent for quite a while. When she looks up, our eyes meet and my heart flutters again as I feel the connection between us. I'm almost sure she does too because she blinks twice and then blushes and averts her gaze; a warm feeling fills me as I watch her studying her notes, regaining her composure. When she continues she is still looking down so I can't see her eyes.

"Ummm, where was I? Yes, this strange knot. It's like two knots tied together so I think it's to do with your relationships."

"Well, it must be from a long time ago then. My love life hasn't been exactly scintillating lately."

"No, this is from about…" she glances up quickly then looks down again, "five or six years ago. I don't understand. An angel?"

"Angela," I tell her. "We were engaged."

"Oh, what happened?" She raises her head to stare directly at me, making me feel uncomfortable. I think she's trying to sound politely interested but it doesn't come over like that. I pause, trying to think of a way to explain the break-up so I don't look like a total jerk – but there isn't one. There is no nice way to do it so I get it over with.

"Well, it was all my fault. I got cold feet and pulled out. We met through work and started dating, then after a year or so she asked that question…"

"Where is this relationship going?"

"Yes. I was quite happy with it just the way it was but unfortunately she wasn't, so if I was going to keep dating her she demanded we get engaged. I guess I hoped that in time I'd feel, oh, I don't know, ready. But I just felt panicky and trapped. Then I took a long, hard look at our relationship and realised that I didn't love her – well, not enough to marry her and have kids, which is what she wanted."

"So you broke it off?"

"Eventually. But I should have done it months before. I suppose I'm a coward – or maybe I hoped it would all work itself out in the end. It just got more and more complicated and messy instead. As soon as we announced the engagement her family went into hyperdrive and within weeks they had the wedding all arranged." I pause before adding, "That's when reality kicked in and I began to realise that I couldn't go through with it."

"It happens, James," she says quietly. "And it was for the best in the long run. To enter into a marriage without wholehearted love and commitment is foolish and almost certainly doomed to failure." She sighs and it sounds to me as if she is speaking from experience; but now is not a good time to ask that. I shudder as I remember the terrible weeks of recriminations, arguments and explanations. It was horrendous so I'm not surprised there's a lot of karma associated with it.

"Where's Angela now?" she asks.

"I haven't a clue," I shrug. "She quit her job and vanished. I'm sure I could have found her if I'd wanted to… but I didn't even try, which must tell you a lot about me. To tell the truth I was just relieved that she'd gone. Does that sound awful?" I am surprising myself with my own honesty. It feels important to open up to Tara.

"No, not awful, just human." Then she surprises me. "Have you ever been in love?" I bow my head and stay quiet for a while. This is difficult. I never had any role models for love and, no, I've probably never felt real love, before now. Thankfully, Tara remains professional and asks me what I'm going to do about Angela… But I haven't a clue. I sit there trying desperately to come up with something but my poor brain has seized up.

"Er, I don't know. Can I do anything?"

"Of course you can. Did you tell her the real reason you broke off the engagement or did you lie?"

"I tried at first. But she was so angry and just kept shouting at me until in the end I just agreed with her that I was a stupid idiot who didn't deserve her and got as far away from her as possible."

"Very mature," she says with a wisp of a smile on her lips. I blush. "Well, perhaps you need to tell her the truth now. It may be the resolution she needs as much as you do. You may think you have put it in the past but there is unfinished business between you which created karma and you need to close it once and for all. Karma is like bubble gum, it sticks to you."

I sigh heavily to myself as I really don't want to get in touch with Angela again, even if I knew how to. It feels tantamount to opening Pandora's Box and letting all the demons out. Then again, she has always been on my conscience, so much so that I have deliberately stayed away from any relationship that might become more than just a bit of fun. It's made me ruthless and shallow and I don't like myself for it, but I kept doing it anyway. Like most men I need sex, but I don't need love. Or so I've told myself. Tara smiles at me encouragingly and leaves these thoughts with me. She wants to move on to another four knots, to do with my family. I am alarmed that there seems to be so much karma… She asks about my parents first.

"My Mam's alive but Dad drank himself to death." My answer is a bit waspish but talking about him always makes me angry.

"Oh? What drove him to drink, do you think?"

"Lack of backbone, probably," I reply.

"James!" she says reproachfully.

"Okay, I'll tell you about him. He wanted to be a jockey and came over from Ireland to fulfil his ambition. But he grew too big to be a Flat jockey so he rode National Hunt instead. He had a few wins but he didn't have natural talent – or the gumption to work hard at it. So he was dropped from riding and ended up as a stable lad, which he resented. He got fired from several yards until no-one would employ him at all." I shrug. "He wasn't great at being a husband or a parent either. A bit of an all-round failure really and I can't remember a time when he wasn't drunk and violent."

"Did he hit you?"

"You haven't lived with a drunk, then? Yes, he hit whoever he could grab hold of. It didn't matter to him. If you didn't move fast enough you'd get it."

"So that means your brother and sister as well?" I'm surprised by her question as I haven't mentioned them. "I can see two red knots which mean males to me and two blue ones meaning females. It's not just your karma I'm seeing here, it's all entangled with the family. However," she glances at her watch, "I think we'll have to look deeper into this another time."

I agree as I am a little shell-shocked by the whole experience and need time to process it all and understand the implications. We agree to book another session and she leads me back to the Reception desk, now unmanned. The lights are dim and I realise that my appointment has overrun and we are the last ones here. She opens the appointment diary and flicks though the pages.

"Can you make November the 4th?"

"After the 1st, I can make any day. I'm retiring."

"Oh, really?" she seems surprised and smiles at me.

"Yes, I'm looking forward to it. Up until now my whole life has revolved around work and I haven't done much else. But this tumour has given me a wake-up call and shown me just how much I'm missing out on by being so tunnel-visioned."

"So what are you going to do with yourself?"

"Try new things." I shrug. "It depends how my health holds up. Unfortunately I can't travel far so some of the places I always promised myself I'd visit are out. But I'm sure I'll come up with something." I need to lighten the mood and I also know that I have to walk out of here now, so I blurt out, "Will you come for a drink with me, Tara?"

"I'd love to, James," she smiles, "but not tonight. Tell you what, ring me after Saturday and I'll say yes. That's the last day of the festival so I'll have more time and energy once it's over."

I feel pleased that I'm only being turned down because of work. I can relate to that.

"Keep Sunday free then," I say.

Nineteen

I sit nervously in Rodney Green's Reception the next morning, waiting for my appointment. I am a little disappointed that Miranda, the rather plain and petite brunette, is not at all as I had imagined her from talking to her on the `phone. The door that must be to Rodders' office opens and a tall lady walks out, tucking an elegant briefcase under her arm as she heads for the outer door. Miranda observes her departure, consults her appointment book and looks up at me. As I am the only person waiting in this small, though surprisingly stylish Reception, it doesn't take a genius to work out that I am probably next. Miranda smiles.

"Mr Green will see you now."

I cringe inwardly at her flattened vowels and head for the door. This is it. I have no idea how he is going to react when he sees me, so I take a deep breath and take a firm hold of the handle before pushing the door open. Rodney is sitting behind a large desk on which is a computer and paperwork. It looks a lot like mine. He has a smile on his long face which slowly vanishes as he recognises me.

"You!" he exclaims with a mixture of horror and disbelief in his voice.

"Hello Rodney," I smile, "long time no see. You're looking well." I stride towards him with my right hand extended but his mouth has dropped open and his brown eyes are wide like a stunned rabbit, so I sit down in the chair opposite him and wait. Finally his mouth snaps shut and he rises from behind his desk.

"What the hell do you want?" he splutters.

I grin. That's more like it. "If you calm down, I'll tell you," I reply. He grunts and sinks back down into his chair, but he still does not look like a happy bunny. Nor is he very calm but at least he has stopped shouting. "That's better," I say. "Now, I have come to apologise." He frowns and looks confused.

"Why?" he asks. I take a deep breath and launch into it.

"Because I was a real bastard towards you, so I'm apologising and I hope you'll be big enough to forgive my shameful behaviour." Slowly his frown disappears and is replaced by a small smile.

"Good God, James, I'd forgot you talks like a bloody dictionary. Shit, I've missed that."

"Well, I apologise for that too," I add and he laughs.

"You, James, are a piece of work. But yeah, I see now you told it to me straight up – in me face an' not be'ind me back like all the rest of 'em. Oh, I know you didn't like being classed with me – that I under- stand, but you was right."

"I was?" Now it's my turn to be shocked.

"Yeah, it took me a while to get it … an' even longer to do summat about it. But you was right. To be me, I `ad to go it alone. An' I'm doing okay – not like you, mind, in yer fancy upmarket office, but yeah, I'm me own man, so no complaints."

"Good, well I'm glad about that."

"Yeah, well if you've salved yer conscience you can go now. But before you do, I wanna say this…" He pauses and I brace myself for something unpleasant. "You was a total shit and I hated you back then, with yer phoney manners and voice. We used to call you 'Mac the Knife' behind yer back, us juniors. We was all scared of you, more'n the bosses."

"Really? I am surprised," I say, as I had no idea about that.

"Yeah, you can be scary. Part of yer act, I s'pose, just like that shark – that's where the nickname comes from." I have no idea what he is talking about and he sees my confusion. "The advert. Don't you remember? There was this advert on the telly where a shark sings Mac the Knife – can't remember why, doesn't matter – and it reminded us of you … that smile just before the knife goes in."

"Bloody charming," I say with a grimace.

"It's true, though, innit? Yer don't suffer fools." I nod and have to agree. "So why're you really `ere, then?"

"Because you are not a fool," I tell him. Now it's his turn to look confused and I guess he's wondering if I'm being funny so I decide to put him out of his misery. "I've checked you out, professionally speaking, for two reasons – first to apologise and second to see if I should recommend you to some of my clients. I am retiring." His mouth drops open again in surprise and I find it a trifle unprofessional; he really should work on a poker face.

"You're retiring?"

"Yes, and although some of my clients have decided to cash in their portfolios I have others who need a good broker to take care of them. Are you up for the job, Rodney?" I can't bring myself to call him Rodders. He swallows hard.

"Yeah, thanks, I am."

"Good. Then I'll forward your details to them – though it will be up to them if they contact you or not." I think this news has stunned him more than my apology. I smile again while he regains his composure but have a feeling he has something else to say. I am not wrong.

"Aaah, don't get me wrong, I'm grateful for a `elping hand, but why me? I mean, you must know loads o' brokers?"

"You're right, I do, and most of them are plonkers."

"You're priceless." He laughs at my use of one of his favourite words.

"I'm honest," I remind him. "But the other reason is that I admire your guts, going it alone, so if I can help you I will since I didn't before."

"I'm gobsmacked."

It's time for me to go before he asks any awkward questions about why I'm retiring as I don't like lying; but there is no way I am going to tell him about my tumour so I get up and hold out my hand again. This time he takes it firmly.

"It's bin… interesting," he says. As I turn to leave, the world suddenly tilts to the left and I have to hold onto the desk to stop from falling over. But I take a deep breath, the dizziness disappears as suddenly as it came, and I just about get away with it.

The fresh air helps a bit but I still feel nauseous and there is a thumping starting up in my right temple, which I know from experience will only get worse. I had come by Tube but I don't think I can face that as I need to get home fast. I look around for a taxi but there isn't any sign of one so I pull out my mobile and call the taxi firm I often use. To my relief it pulls up in front of me in five minutes; by now the pain in my head has intensified, even with the painkillers I've taken, and it's well on the way to becoming the worst one yet. I stagger towards the cab and find Roger behind the wheel.

"Are you all right, Mr Wylie?" he asks as he comes to help me.

"No, Roger, I'm not feeling great, that's why I called you."

He takes my arm and with his support I manage to make it to the cab and sink gratefully into the back seat and close my eyes. Another wave of dizziness hits me and it takes a real effort not to throw up; I don't think Roger will be too happy if I do. He asks if we should go to hospital instead of home but I tell him I'm fine, it's 'just a virus'. He probably doesn't believe me but stays quiet and a few minutes later the dizziness begins to recede and the pain killers have started to work. I think now I can make it up the stairs to my apartment with my dignity intact. Roger watches me climb out of the cab and walk slowly and as straight as I can up the five steps and inside the building. Jenny is at her desk, takes one look at me and comes running to my side.

"James, are you alright?" I am so fed up with being asked that.

"I will be once I've had a rest. Can you just take messages if anyone wants me and I'll look at them later?"

"Of course, you go and lie down and I'll take care of things." There is fear and concern in her eyes, which I find touching.

I turn and walk to the door that leads to my apartment upstairs. Once through that and away from prying eyes, I lean against the cool walls and take some deep breaths. I feel weak and my head is thumping, but the worst thing is my vision getting fuzzy and making me feel sick. Looking up at the stairs rising in front of me I groan; there seem a lot more of them than there used to be yet somehow I have to get up there. Grasping the handrail firmly, I push myself off the wall and up the steps, each one a great mental and physical effort, and by step six I feel exhausted and my breathing sounds like a train. I have to lean against the wall again and it takes several minutes before I am able to carry on to the top, but somehow I make it and arrive at my front door, a sweating wreck. I fish in my pocket for the key but even doing that makes me feel dizzy again so I put my hot forehead on the cool door and wait for it to pass. I have never felt this bad before and the pain in the front of my head is now in my nose and I feel it running. I touch it and feel warm liquid and look at my hand, to my horror finding it covered with blood.

"Oh, my God, no!" I am shocked, watching the blood drips through my fingers onto the floor, so I pull out a handkerchief to cover my nose before finally turning the key in the lock and stumbling gratefully into my home, making my way as fast as I can to the bathroom. I can't remember the last time I had a nosebleed, probably when I was a kid, and I hate the sight of blood especially my own. Now I need to lie down before I fall down so I make my way slowly to the bedroom. If this is a sign of things to come, I am not impressed.

Twenty

I cannot say the next couple of days are very good, with more blinding headaches and having to rush to the bathroom twice to throw up before making it downstairs to my office. Gradually through the morning I start to feel a little more human, maybe because I now have something other than myself to think about, and I manage to work through until the afternoon when I finally have to admit defeat and retreat upstairs to my flat. On Friday, I finally sink down into my armchair and notice the pile of unopened mail sitting on the coffee table in front of me. I groan, knowing that if I keep looking at it I will become depressed, feeling like I am losing control over my life. Unopened mail symbolises this as I usually deal with it as soon as it arrives; but I have felt too sick to bother.

"The first steps on the slippery slope," I tell myself as I lean forward and scoop it up.

I leaf through the envelopes. Most are the usual bills and as I pay things by direct debit I only have to check them. A white envelope stands out among the brown ones and I recognise Craig's company name on it. It is good news. Two houses are to be bought by the tenants as well as two of the six apartments, which means that only four apartments need to be sold and that should be pretty straightforward. What surprises me though is my complete lack of feeling for this one way or the other. I remember how excited I had been when I bought my first house and all the fun I had planning its refurbishment; but now I am just happy to get rid of them. I wonder if I am more ready than I thought to check out of this life.

I glance at my watch and see that it's only 5.30 yet I am exhausted and all I want to do is sleep. Jeremy has gone back to Dorset for the weekend so I can relax and do my own thing without his furtive glances of concern dragging me down; I find his presence hard to bear when I'm feeling so awful. I am heading for the bedroom when the `phone begins to ring. I look at it from across the room and wonder if it is worth the walk over there to answer it. I decide that it is.

"Hello?"

"James? It's Tara."

"Hi, it's lovely to hear your voice." I am smiling, despite the pain.

"Thanks… um, I'm ringing to invite you to dinner tomorrow. Only…" She stops there, leaving me wondering.

"Only?" I prompt her.

"Only my kitchen isn't very good."

"So you'd like to cook here?"

"Yes," she laughs. "But isn't that a bit…"

"…cheeky?" I finish for her and she giggles wonderfully. "That would be nice although I've been off my food the last few days so I hope you'll not be offended if I don't eat much." I don't add that I might throw it back up too as that is hardly romantic. There is a pause while she thinks.

"Are you in pain?"

"On and off, but I guess I can't expect otherwise, can I?"

"No," she says softly.

"But don't let that put you off coming over. I'd love to see you." I put the `phone down with a big smile on my face, so glad I made the effort to answer it.

I check my watch again and I've lost count of how many times I've done that since six-thirty. Tara is only five minutes late but when you have been counting the minutes since waking up in the morning this is a big deal. I couldn't help wondering if she had changed her mind; it can't be much fun going out with a dying man since there's no future in it… Or maybe that's the attraction? I'm certainly not going to be looking for commitment from her, am I?

I stand at my front window looking out onto the street below, but even with the streetlamps it is pretty dark out there. Then around the corner comes a cab and it slows down as it reaches my door; I watch the back door open and my heart skips again at the sight of her. I hurry to the door, quickly checking in the hall mirror that I don't look too sickly before going downstairs to reach the front door just as she rings the bell. I feel as awkward as a teenager on his first date. Why does she have this effect on me? Luckily she doesn't seem to notice awkwardness and smiles at me in a most beguiling way. I'm sure I'm blushing.

"Sorry I'm a little late but the traffic was awful."

"I hadn't noticed," I lie. "Here, let me take that bag for you." I relieve her of a large carrier bag leaving her with a wicker hand basket and show the way upstairs to my apartment where we make for the kitchen. She nods approval of my cooker.

"Now, I know I said I'd cook here but I managed to cook a chilli at home. All I have to do is reheat it and cook the rice. It's one of my stand-by dishes. I never seem to have enough time for cooking usually but I had some unexpected free time yesterday."

"How did that happen?"

"Oh, a new therapist is joining Tranquillity and wanted to promote her work so I let her have my place for a while. I was grateful actually. As I told you, after several days of running backwards and forwards from the clinic to the festival I'm really thankful it's over for another year." I smile at that because although I was only there for about an hour before I collapsed I still found it noisy and stressful.

"So it's over now, then? " I ask.

"Yes, thank God. And I had plenty of helpers to take down the displays so now I can get back to my real job. There's a bit of a backlog to get through but I'm taking tomorrow off just to relax." I'm wishing she would relax with me but I guess that isn't going to happen. "Now," she pauses and looks at me, "why don't you open a bottle of wine and I'll put the rice on. It only takes ten minutes then dinner will be served."

I do as I'm told. Soon we are sitting opposite each other, the aroma has stimulated my jaded taste buds and I dig in. It is good, not too hot but with a bit of a bite, just how I like it. We leave conversation for later while she relaxes until finally I push my empty plate away and sigh with satisfaction. She laughs at me.

"Was it all right?"

"Brilliant," I tell her.

I refill her glass and we move to the more comfortable chairs in the lounge where she flops down on my sofa. I hesitate before opting to sit in my armchair. I'd love to be closer but I'm not sure how that would be received – she is not easy to read. I think she likes me but is that just as one of her clients? Perhaps she just feels sorry for me – that would be terrible. I can't risk overstepping the mark and maybe losing her, even if all she wants to be is my friend, so I decide to play it cool.

"Tell me something about yourself, Tara."

"What do you already know?" she counters, taking a sip of wine.

"Sod all," I reply dryly.

"You are funny, James," she says.

"Me, funny?" I reply sardonically. "Sure, just ask the people I work with."

"Ah, but which James do they know? Your professional persona or your real self?"

"Oh, I see. Well, I guess most people only get to meet the professional me as I don't have many friends. I'm a bit of a loner by nature, but then I've also buried myself in my work with no time to socialise."

"Yes, I see that a lot with people who are passionate about their work. It becomes all-consuming."

"But there's the rub. I realise now that I never really have been passionate about it. It's been about making a success of my life, not being a nobody."

"Like your father?" That makes me squirm; she has me sussed all right. Then I'm telling her about how I escaped home at sixteen and headed for London and fell into broking because I'm good at making deals.

"So what would you have chosen to do, given the chance?"

"I don't know." It's true, I've never really thought about it for years. "I love animals and once thought about becoming a vet. But I hate needles."

"Yes," she laughs, "I can see that could be a handicap."

We are silent for a moment before I realise that she has neatly evaded my question about her and managed to extract more of my life story instead. She is very good at this. She says that she hates talking about herself because it's 'boring'.

"I don't believe that. I think you're exciting," I say before my brain gets into gear to stop me. She blushes.

"Not really."

"Why don't you let me be the judge of that?" I reply, grateful that my faux pas seems to have been unnoticed. So she tells me about being born in Worcester and growing up in Malvern with an idyllic childhood, living in the countryside with loving parents and a younger brother who was great most of the time and annoying occasionally.

"Darren, my brother, is the clever one and went to university and then on to Law School, so at least one offspring made it. He's in New York at the moment, working for some large corporation. I have no idea what he does and I haven't seen him or his wife Penny for years. I wasn't academic and I didn't want to go to university, much to my parents' displeasure. Dad is a GP and Mum works as his practice manager. They're a great team." She pauses and smiles wistfully at that as though she envies them. "It took me eight years and many different jobs before I stumbled on my vocation."

"How did that happen?" I prompt her as she stalls again, not as self-confident as I have thought after all.

"I met someone, Marcus, a trance medium. I've always been fascinated about past lives and he specialises in discovering them. So of course I had to have a reading and this led to me joining a development circle and that led me into the complementary medicine world and karma and hundreds of other subjects…" She has a dreamy expression on her face. "It's funny how one meeting can change your whole life." I'm beginning to believe that myself now.

"Destiny?" I suggest.

"Yes. I believe strongly in that. Destiny is something that is going to happen – like my meeting with Marcus – but then there's free will too. I could have ignored Marcus, or not had that reading, and then never have found my true vocation. But instead that meeting changed my life."

"So you began to study complementary medicine?"

"Yes, and I love it but it's not my greatest passion. It was a means to an end. I learned a couple of therapies that I could earn money doing, which in this world is essential if you want to eat, but I also met some amazing people who taught me so much more, like spiritual healers who opened my eyes to spirit and the energies that are invisible to our eyes. I met Kalke, who's Australian, half aborigine, and she showed me how her people see and feel the Earth's energies and how they interact with plants and animals. I also met Ray Trees, a Native American shaman whom I'd love to study with if only I had the resources to hire a manager for Tranquillity for six months while I swan off to South Dakota."

She smiles a little sadly when she says this and I can almost feel her longing to do this. Suddenly I have an idea of how I could help her with this… but that will have to go on the back burner for now. Instead, I ask her how she learned about karma as that seems to be the most important thing between us.

"Learning new spiritual skills often happens very naturally. You don't go out to learn it in the conventional sense – there are no courses on what I do, it just happens. It's my gift, I suppose. I don't know how else to describe it. One day in the development circle I began telling everyone about their karma, just like that, and I've been doing it ever since."

"But where does this knowledge come from?"

"My spirit guides. After I had freaked out a bit, they explained it to me. I never set out to do this, it just happened, a bit like you and your career."

"Not quite, though I see your point. But my career was never my soul's purpose."

The evening is passing pleasantly and we seem comfortable with one another, though I can't help wishing it were more than this. I keep forgetting that this is early days yet. But it turns out that we have more in common when she tells me about her love of animals and her healing work with them. We also agree that we both probably like animals more than people. After all, they give you less grief and they don't lie or stab you in the back. If they like you they show it and if they don't you'll soon find that out too.

"Do you work with a vet?" I ask.

"Good grief, no. Most vets wouldn't be happy if they knew that one of their patients was receiving spiritual healing. I am usually called in when the vet isn't doing very well and the animal isn't getting any better. This all started out of the blue when my friend's dog got sick and the vet said he had cancer and would have to be put down. She rang me in floods of tears and begged me to try and help him. I wasn't at all sure if I could do anything – I'd never treated an animal – but as soon as I started he settled down and slept for the first time in a week." She smiles at the memory, leaving me hanging.

"So what happened?" I ask eventually.

"Oh, sorry. Well, it was wonderful. I laid my hands on him and immediately they became really hot and tingling. It was like I could almost see the tumour so I sent love and light into it and that's all I did for about half an hour. It felt so beautiful and peaceful and the colours I saw around him were amazing. He accepted the healing with a grace that humans often lack. I had never felt such bliss before. It was a magical experience."

"And what about the dog?"

"Cured. The tumour vanished and he's still alive today. Of course, the vet said he must have misdiagnosed his condition but with all their equipment that's not possible. And I know there was a tumour there because I saw it." She shrugs. "Well, after that I started to get a lot more calls about animals needing healing so now about half my time is spent working with animals and the rest on karmic issues and running Tranquillity."

I'm amazed by all she does. Did she say her life is boring? Her story has also triggered something deep in my mind and I ask if I can come and watch her when she's next healing animals. She just smiles, nods, and says that maybe I should have a go myself.

"Me? I wouldn't know what to do."

"Neither did I, James, when I started. But it's not hard. All you have to do is sent love into them and the Creator will do the rest."

"Love? Is that all? Remember, I don't know what that is."

"I'm sure you have a lot of love in you," she says, and grins at me. I feel uncomfortable now so I get up and head for the kitchen.

"I'll get the coffee," I say.

> She watches him walk to the kitchen and a feeling of contentment grows inside her, catching her unawares with its intensity. She knows that she is setting herself up for heartbreak – his tumour is aggressive and advanced – but even if they only have a few weeks together she'll take that rather than pull away from him now.
>
> She feels Juliette close by and hears her say, "Love never dies, Tara, you know that." But unfortunately human bodies do and his body's time may be almost up. She feels tears beginning to well up but pushes them back, not wanting to cry in front of him and vowing to be strong for them both.

Twenty-One

I wake several days later hot and sweaty after a very disturbing dream and struggle to get upright, pushing away the covers that envelop me and shudder as I remember the dream. I had seen Angela. She was screaming at me to help her but I was being held back by some sort of demon that was too strong for me, dragging me back. I woke up still feeling the cold emptiness of it; somehow I know that I can't pretend any longer that I don't need to see her again and put things right. I have a feeling that if I don't this won't be the last time I have that dream. The problem is how to find her as I have no idea where she is. After six years she could be anywhere, married with kids and a new surname. I suppose I could hire a private detective to find her for me, but I'll keep that option until I run out of other ideas. I'm sure I can come up with something.

I'm still mulling over my options while I work through the correspondence that Jenny has placed in my in-tray. She has sent out letters to all my clients who asked me to recommend a new broker, giving them Rodders' name and address, and as a consequence my mail pile has decreased dramatically in the last week. With only seven more working days to go, I am hoping it'll shrink even further. I occasionally get a twinge of sadness about retiring but it doesn't last long. A knock brings me back to the present and Jenny pops her head around the door.

"Do you have a minute?" she asks me. She smiles but looks a little nervous. "Ah, I have a favour to ask you, James." This is new, she has never asked for one from me before.

"Okay, go ahead," I tell her.

"It's Harry." She takes a deep breath before continuing. "He's asked me to work for him." My face must have shown my surprise because she hurries on. "I know you don't like him, but really he's always been generous to me."

"Really?" I reply dryly.

"Yes, and I know how to handle him." I grin as I bet she does, although it's not a skill I've ever wanted to learn. "Anyway, I have agreed on one condition."

"Oh, and is that where I come in?" I ask.

"Yes…" Another hesitation and I think I know what's coming next. "I love this house and my office and I don't want to move anywhere else. And I know Harry loves it too."

"So he wants to rent the office and Reception, does he?" She nods and looks at me with pleading eyes. I try to look sternly back at her but I'm afraid I can't keep it up any more; my heart is just not in it and anyway she's always been able to see through my hard-faced act. She smiles.

"Thank you, James."

"Hey, I haven't said yes yet." I object.

"I know. But you will," she replies and she's right.

"I would have preferred Harry to have the guts to come down here and ask me himself," I observe.

"And he will. I'm just testing the waters. They seem to be warm," she says with a grin as she makes for the door. Then she turns and says, "He has an appointment with you at two o'clock."

I open my mouth to complain but she has already slipped out of the room before I get the chance. I have been Jennied. It's not entirely Harry's fault that I can't stand him as he has never done anything to upset me personally. It's just the way he makes me feel about myself when I'm in his presence, defensive and prickly; he only has to open his mouth and I feel my hackles rise. But I know that I must try to be more forgiving, however hard.

That afternoon, he pushes open my door and strides in as if he owns the place and lowers his widening rear end into my client chair without being invited. Then he swallows hard and it hits me that actually he's nervous; this is a revelation as I've always thought him as confident, even arrogant, though maybe all that is just an act. He clears his throat and asks me about renting the place, but I decide to play the game.

"Well, I'm not sure I want the disturbance," I reply with a deep frown.

"Oh, we wouldn't disturb you. I mean you have your apartment entrance and of course that's sacrosanct. You won't know we're here. And it'll be income for you."

Trust Harry to think I'd be persuaded by money, which is the least of my concerns now; but as he has mentioned the subject I begin to wonder how much he thinks the space is worth.

"Hmm, there is that," I say. "So what's it worth to you, Harry?"

"Ah, well, I don't have a figure for you yet but, um, I'll get my accountant onto it. I'm not here to dot the i's and cross the t's, James, no, no, I'm just, er… you know, seeing if it's a goer, so to speak."

I hide my smile and decide to keep him on the hook just a bit longer. In truth, I am not at all sure I want him around the place but on the other hand it would be lovely to see Jenny every morning and to know that someone is in the building in case of, well, an emergency.

"Well, Harry, it may well be as you say a goer but even if we do come to an arrangement it will only be short, until I decide what I am doing in the future." He nods vigorously and his chins bounce up and down.

"Oh yes, of course, but I assure you it will be of great benefit. And dear Jenny will be so pleased to be working for me."

"You mean she hates working for me, do you?"

"What?" he exclaims, startled. "No, I didn't mean it like that. No, um, it's just that… ah, she likes it here…" he finishes lamely, swallowing hard again and shifting uncomfortably in the chair. He looks like he would really like to escape now but doesn't know how to without causing offence. Just as he's about to launch into probably another ill-advised comment there's a knock at the door and Jenny's head pops around it.

"Sorry to interrupt, James, but Harry has an important call from the US."

I raise an eyebrow at her and she blushes. I have a feeling she is telling me a white lie to get her potential new boss out of the hole he is digging for himself. Harry breathes a huge sigh of relief and gets quickly to his feet.

"Thank you, James, I'll get those figures for you. Thank you."

"It's been a pleasure," I reply with a sweet smile, and for once it has been. But sparring with Harry has worn me out – I don't have the appetite for these games like I used to. So I tell Jenny to hold my calls for an hour and lean back in my chair.

Within seconds of closing my eyes, I'm asleep and dreaming again, finding myself in a lovely rural landscape which somehow I know is Kent. I am walking up a track carrying a heavy wooden basket over my arm; it is very hot and humid and I am sweating and uncomfortable. I seem to be wearing a lot of heavy clothes for such a hot day and when I look down at my legs I realise that I'm a women, wearing a heavy, patched and shabby skirt made out of a coarse and scratchy material.

Up ahead at the top of the rise is a windmill and that's where I am heading, as I live there with my husband the miller. I feel apprehensive, hoping that Walter will be in a good mood and not drunk. He has never been a patient man but lately his temper has been much worse and he is always finding fault with me and shouting. He scares me and I know he is going to hit me and I won't know what to do. I have nowhere else to go. Most of the women in the village envy me as millers' families never go hungry. And Walter always has money to spend on ale. There are whispers that he is short-changing the villagers and I wouldn't put it past him; he is certainly becoming unpopular and making enemies.

I slow down, not wanting to reach home even though the sky is getting darker and the wind is picking up with a storm on the way. The sails of the mill are turning again and perhaps this will make Walter happy; for the last four days there has been hardly a breath of wind and he has been unable to work, making him frustrated and angry. Now at last the storm we need to break this heaviness is on the way.

I stand at the bottom of the stairs and look up at the doorway of our small dwelling. I used to love our little place up in the sky and when we first married I dreamed of bringing up our children here. But that was eight years ago and no children came. Walters blames me for that and maybe he's right, but lately everything else is my fault too including the weather.

When I push open the door I find him pacing the floor and feel his anger hit me like a wave. I know he is going to hurt me. He turns to face me and I can't believe it – it's Harry! I know it's him, even though this man is thin with black hair and a beard, I know it is him.

"Where've you been?" he screams. "You're a lazy, useless woman. You can't even give me a child. You're nothing but a burden to me."

I am stung by his venom and the hatred I see in his eyes. He is drunk and crazed, his face red and patchy as he mutters to himself and paces up and down the floor. I don't know what to do or say so I stay as still as I can and watch him warily. Suddenly he swings around to face me.

"What are you doing to me, woman?" he screams, moving quickly towards me with a deranged look on his face. I'm so terrified that I can't move to get away. "You bitch. I'll bet you've been with all of them behind my back. Who are they?" he screams, raising his hand and closing in on me. I know he is going to hit me and somehow I manage to unfreeze my legs and run for the door, making it just before him and running out. There's a thud as I'm hit by the windmill's sail and I feel the pain as my head explodes and then there's nothing at all.

I awake with a start, knowing that I had been killed outright and, in those moments between living and dying, I had blamed Walter and vowed to get even with him one day. So is that why I dislike Harry so much? I must ask Tara next time I see her. This past life stuff is interesting, but I have a job to complete while I'm still here. I stretch and rub the sleep from my eyes before turning on the computer to check the markets just as the `phone rings.

"James, Katrina's here," Jenny informs me. I'm surprised to realise that it's already four o'clock and I've been asleep far longer than I intended. Seconds later Katrina enters with Jenny carrying in her chair, a concerned look on her face. "Are you alright, James?" she asks.

"Yes, I'm fine. I just dozed off but I feel better for it."

"Don't worry," says Katrina with a smile, "I'll sort him out." I'm sure she will and once she has set up the chair and has me in her clutches she pounces. "Right, James, what's up?"

She has got to know me well over the last couple of months but then, with the exception of Tara, she is the only other person I have felt comfortable enough with to open up to. Even Jenny and Jeremy really don't know me as well as they think they do; they know the professional mask I wear but not the real me at all. That one is a lot more contradictory and complex – I'm still trying to puzzle him out myself. With Tara's help, I hope to know me better by the time the grim reaper comes to claim me. I just hope that's enough time to make a difference as I have only just scratched the surface of karma. Now that I've started, I want to get as close as possible to being karma neutral. A tall order.

"Have you ever dreamed about one of your past lives?" I ask her. She purses her lips and has to think about it.

"Well, it wasn't a dream, more of a flashback," she says with a smile. "While I was working on a new client I suddenly had a vision of us as children a long time ago. I think we lived in Africa, in a small village. We were toddlers and I saw us playing together outside a roundhouse."

"Really? But you knew it was a past life, even though you saw so little?"

"Oh yes, I'm sure of it. In those few seconds I knew he had been a friend in the past."

"So did you tell him?"

"Good God, no," she laughs. "He wasn't into alternative stuff. It was his wife who made him come to see me and she was sitting in on the treatment." She pauses and then adds, "And from the way he talked, I don't think he'd have appreciated being told he was once black. He's quite well known for his racist views, so I found it quite ironic."

"Yes, I can see that," I observed. "But it might have been interesting if he had been told…"

"Why'd you ask? Have you had a dream?"

For some reason I'm a bit embarrassed by what I saw but I want her opinion so I bite the bullet. She listens intently, a small frown between her eyebrows, and when I have finished she stays silent for a few minutes before responding.

"I can see why you don't like Harry. His presence is a reminder of that lifetime on a subconscious level, even if your roles this time around are different." She then adds cheekily, "I'd love to have seen you as a woman." I raise an eyebrow.

"I'll have you know I was a very attractive woman," I assert, although I could be lying as I never saw enough of myself.

"I'm sure you were, James," she says as she continues to work on my feet. "So you know what you have to do with this new information, don't you?"

I suppose I do. "Yes Katrina, but I don't know if I can forgive and forget."

"We don't forget these things from the past, that's impossible, but we can make an effort to forgive. After all, James, this was a tragic accident. I know you were scared but it was a very different time with different rules. You need to try and see it from a higher perspective now, see the bigger picture."

"And what is the bigger picture?" I ask.

"Well, we all have lives that intertwine and in some we are friends and in others we are enemies. But in the big picture of all our lives over the centuries, isn't taking revenge for some mistake in the past a bit pointless and ultimately self-harming as it's our own karma we're increasing? If we realise how brief these trips to the Earth school are, then we can see that the only way to get off the merry-go-round is to learn to forgive."

I know in my heart that she's right, but forgive Harry? Well, maybe I can try.

"Am I right or am I right?" she smiles.

"I guess you're right," I tell her.

Twenty-Two

The first day of November finally arrives and I awake to my last day as a stockbroker, not entirely sure how I feel about it but now I have no choice. I've been getting so tired lately and I've noticed that my left hand is often numb in the morning, although this does wear off in a few hours. Of course, I've read the depressing list of symptoms that I can look forward to and a loss of feeling like this is one of them with a lot more of the same.

For a few minutes, I lie back thinking over the last few weeks and how they have changed me. I have been on five wonderful dates with Tara, unfortunately as friends although I'd like our relationship to be more than this; I don't know if she wants to take it further. We have been to the theatre and an art gallery, which I wasn't expecting to enjoy but I did very much, and we've been out to dinner a couple of times as well as a lovely walk in the park followed by a cosy afternoon in front of the fire. I smile at this memory, my favourite one. I have never felt about anyone the way I do with Tara and my heart does its now familiar skip as I think about her. I just wish I knew how she really feels about me. So far we haven't got further than a goodnight kiss. Maybe I'm fantasising about something that will never happen.

Jeremy and Carol have arranged a party for later and I've asked Tara and Katrina to come, hoping that with Katrina there Tara will feel less uncomfortable around a lot of people she doesn't know. Tara is quite shy really, not a natural party-goer. I am quite looking forward to it and just hope I don't get one of my headaches or have a dizzy spell and disgrace myself.

It's no good, I will have to get up and finish tying the final loose ends of my professional life. Most of my old clients who wanted a new broker have taken my advice and moved to Rodders, so apart from the last few stocks of my own to sell there's little to do today. A couple of hours later and I have sold the last of my own portfolio and I am staggered by how much they are now worth. I log off the computer and turn my attention to the contracts I need to sign for two of the properties I am selling as Craig needs them back today. The numbers are extraordinary, especially when I remember how much I paid for them seven years ago. I sign on the dotted line and then it really is the end of an era. There is just one other thing I have to do today and that is to have a talk with Jenny so I pick up the 'phone and ask her to come into my office. She settle herself in the chair as I clear my throat.

"I just want to ask you if you really are happy about staying on here and working with Harry."

"Yes, it's great," she smiles, "and it's sweet of you to ask."

"Sweet?" I exclaim and she grins.

"Yes, under that impenetrable exterior you're a pussycat."

"And there was I hoping that people were scared of me," I say, with my tongue firmly in my cheek.

"Oh, some people are but not me. I saw that pussycat a long time ago." Then she leans forward and whispers, "Harry is terrified of you, though." This makes my day although I'm sure I've added some karma points for enjoying the revelation.

Then I gather up the contracts I have signed and hand them over to her. It's the last act.

"I'd be grateful if you could get these back to Craig, please."

"Sure, no problem. And if you need anything typed up or sent in the future just ask me, James. I'll be happy to do it for you."

Later that evening I look around the room and smile as the party is going well. Carol has done us proud, arranging the food and drink which is all in very good taste. If it had been left to me and Jeremy it would probably have been a few bottles of wine and some nibbles. If we'd remembered.

I am also conducting a bit of an experiment. In talks about karma with both Katrina and Tara, we have discussed people we do not get on with, such as Harry, and Katrina told me of a technique she's heard of for dealing with these people.

"I've tried it and it works. But when I tell you what it is you'll think I'm nuts," she warned me. "Now I use it whenever a problem person pops up and it's never failed yet."

"Right then," I'd agreed, "whatever it is I promise to give it a go… as long as I can keep my clothes on to do it."

"Okay," she giggled, "you don't have to remove a single item." She went on to say that all one has to do is to imagine the person covered in a cloud of pink light, pink being the colour of unconditional love. So you're sending this person love in a pink cloud.

"And this works how?" I asked.

"I don't know," she shrugged, "but it has an amazing effect. Within hours they seem friendlier, less antagonistic, nicer. And the longer you keep it up the more they change. I even become friends with one girl I used to hate on sight when I had to work closely with her on a project that I couldn't get out of."

And so despite my scepticism my experiment is now on and my test subject is just coming into view. I started imagining Harry inside his pink cloud earlier today and although it isn't as easy to do as it sounds I have kept it up. Tara has also suggested that I try to forgive him for hurting me in the past. As she has pointed out, none of us is blameless; we have probably all done terrible things to each other in the past. So if we cast any stones they'll only rebound and hit us. Now I look over at Harry, who is busy pontificating to a bemused client, and quietly say, "I forgive you." This is getting easier; the first time I said those words they got stuck in my throat.

A hand on my arm brings me back to myself and I find Tara smiling at me. A warm feeling flows over me.

"Are you having a good time?" I ask, worried that she might be bored or uncomfortable as I know these are not her kind of people, but her smile is encouraging.

"You know what, James, I am," she says and sounds surprised. "You were very good at describing these people the other day and I think I could have recognised most of them just from what you said."

"Really? And what do you think of them? I'd really like to know."

"Well, Harry is a seething mass of contradictions. I think he envies you because of your talents and because you got where you are with hard work and dedication. He feels insecure. He hasn't got the same talent." Her insight makes a lot of sense.

"Well, I've been trying my affirmations and putting the pink cloud on him," I tell her. As we both look over towards him he must have felt us because he stops talking mid-flow and turns to look at us. I raise my glass and he blinks, a look of amazement on his chubby face, and then slowly he raises his glass in return, a hesitant smile flickering across his features. Tara and I exchange grins.

"You never know, miracles do happen," she says, just as my next subject, Carol, arrives with a bottle and refills our glasses. I smile, hoping she'll move on, but she has no intention of doing so. Of course, it isn't me she's interested in, it's Tara.

"Hello, Tara isn't it?" she asks. "We haven't had a chance to meet properly. I'm Carol, Jeremy's wife." Tara smiles sweetly and holds out a hand.

"Yes, it's a pleasure to meet you, Carol. I hear that you are responsible for this wonderful party." I swear I can hear the ice crack under that well-timed compliment and Carol smiles happily. Tara has a great talent for saying the right thing. "It's amazing, especially the food, and you achieved it all in such a short time."

"Oh," Carol simpers, loving adulation, "it's nothing. Tell me, have you know James long?" She doesn't waste time. It becomes clear that this is the real reason for seeking us out, an intelligence-gathering mission since today is the first time either she or Jeremy have met Tara. She will soon go on to how we met and what Tara does and once she gets her teeth into you she never lets up, like a pit-bull. I wouldn't be surprised if she'd worked for the Spanish Inquisition in a former life. But I already have a strategy planned to change the subject fast.

"Carol," I interrupt, "I wonder if you can help me. Your sister – sorry, I can't remember her name?"

"Sarah," she says sharply, taken off guard.

"Oh yes, Sarah. She was very friendly with Angela Morton wasn't she?"

"Angela!" she exclaims, her mouth dropping open in surprise.

"Yes, I wonder if Sarah might know her address now."

Carol looks at me suspiciously and then glances meaningfully towards Tara, who smiles back.

"I know," is all she says. Carol hasn't expected that and her mouth snaps shut. For a few seconds we all stand there in silence until she regains her composure.

"I expect Sarah has her address. I believe she's living somewhere in Wales."

"Oh, is she? Do you think Sarah would give it to me?" I ask pleasantly.

"She might," came the clipped reply. This is like pulling teeth and I can see that Carol does not approve of this at all. I can only hope she will do as I ask. With a cool look back at us, she stalks off.

"What was all that about?" Tara asks me.

"I haven't a clue. I mean, it is nearly six years since we broke up so why all the secrecy? Carol definitely seems to have a problem. I just hope I do hear back from Sarah."

"I hope so too," she agrees. "Well, you're certainly trying, James." She raises her glass and says, "To you, James, and your quest for karma neutrality."

Twenty-Three

I am a bit nervous today as I am about to attempt an exercise called 'Breaking the ties that bind', supposed to cut energetic bonds that are no longer appropriate. In this case, it's Harry. Now that I know why I have a problem with him, I can get on with releasing us both from the restriction; I am a bit sceptical about all this but if it will make me feel more free then I am willing to give it a go.

Over the last six weeks I have been meditating daily, alone and with Tara, and my focus and clarity have improved greatly. I never thought I'd be any good at this but, to my surprise, I am. It makes me feel different, somehow more centred and a lot calmer; I also use it when my headaches start and it has helped to control the pain. I have also met my 'doorkeeper' Freizal several times now and can recognise her presence by a smell of fresh pine needles, finding it very comforting to know she is nearby. She has told me that she will be with me when I die and not to be afraid – she will make sure my soul will get safely to the other side.

"Take a deep breath," Tara says, "and now visualise Harry sitting opposite you in another circle." I am sitting on the floor in her therapy room at Tranquillity, in a circle I've drawn in chalk on the wooden floor. Tara is behind me talking me through the process and providing spiritual protection. "Now visualise the circle you are sitting in joined to Harry's. They meet at one point only. Now there is a blue line going around your circle, James, and I want you to focus on it. Make it as real as you can…" I see a neon tube with pulsing blue light "… and extend this light around Harry's circle too, so it forms a figure of eight."

I do as I am told and very soon it is really there in my mind, a blue current moving around and between us – I can even feel it, which is weird. Tara now tells me to move my circle slowly away from Harry's, with a gentle force between the points where the circles touch until they are only holding on by a thread. The blue line is becoming thinner and thinner until I visualise a pair of golden scissors and cut the last thread.

"With love and light, forgive Harry and release him from your life," she says softly, and as I do so he and his circle move away into the distance until they are gone completely. I have a smile on my face as I open my eyes, and Tara talks me through grounding myself.

"How was that?" she asks.

"I don't know yet, but I do feel… lighter? I'm no good at describing how I feel. Anyway, I'm tired too."

"Well, you've been sitting for nearly an hour," she tells me. "I'll get you a glass of water."

But I barely make it to the chair when something explodes inside my head, closely followed by a blaze of fireworks and a wave of excruciating pain as I begin to shake all over. Oh my God… this pain… it's as if my whole head is on fire and someone is stabbing me in the eyes for good measure. I can't stop myself from crying out. The shaking is getting worse and the throbbing is like giant waves thundering through my head, crushing me and scrambling my senses. Somewhere very far away I hear a cry of alarm and my name and then a cool hand is placed on my burning head as I am hit with another wave. I feel cold fingers penetrate my skull and send a cool river inside to stem the raging fires. The pain spikes again but it doesn't last quite as long and then the coldness soothes it to a bearable level.

"Oh," I groan, "that's much better," I manage to say as at least the flashes and bangs have stopped.

"Just relax and try to breathe normally." Her calm voice is reassuring. I try to let the pain flow 'out of my feet' – it's an exercise Tara has taught me that I've found helpful before – and then I move on to stand under a waterfall, allowing the cold water to put out the fires in my head. It doesn't take long before I actually feel cold and the pain has all but gone.

My vision is a bit blurred and at first I can only make out the outline of her face but soon it clears and I smile. She looks very concerned but I feel all right now, which is amazing considering that I thought I was going to die a few minutes ago. "Are you in pain now?" she asks.

"Not really, but that was bad. I feel a bit weak and shaky," I tell her.

"Let me help you stand up in case you go woozy."

I nod and start to push myself up as she slips her shoulder under my armpit. But I am over six feet tall and she is quite a bit smaller so we must look a queer sight. As I straighten up I lose my balance and she can't hold me, so she has no choice but to come with me as I end up on the sofa.

"Well, I've been hoping to get you in a clinch for weeks but this isn't quite how I planned it," I say before my brain is in gear. She laughs as I try to roll off her. "Sorry, I'm squashing you." I manage to move sideways enough for her to extract herself from underneath me and I watch her push back her hair and smooth down her clothes. There is a smile on her face so maybe my faux-pas hasn't damaged our relationship.

"It's okay, James, I'm fine. I'm stronger than I look. And I was going to suggest you should go to hospital but with chat up lines like that I don't think there's too much wrong with you … not now anyway."

"No, there's nothing they could do anyway except poke and prod me then send me home. I just feel a little tired but most of the pain has gone now."

"You're probably right, but I'm going to take you home. We can pick up a take-away en route. I'll go and telephone your taxi firm now, so stay there."

I can't stop a big smile from appearing on my face at this news as it would appear that getting sick has some perks after all, although the pain part is a bit of a downer. I lean back and close my eyes, wondering if maybe tonight I'll ask the question that I have wanted to ask for weeks now and find out once and for all what her feelings are for me. I know I love her but … ? My symptoms are getting worse every day. My left hand is numb and I have a tingling in the arm that is fast becoming a regular occurrence, as are the headaches. So if I don't ask her soon I might be too incapacitated to do anything about it. It's now the second week of November. Will I be here at Christmas?

She opens her eyes and sighs contentedly, finding herself beside James in his lovely apartment. It feels just right being with him, this gentle lover with so much to live for and to discover about himself. He is like a flower bud about to explode into bloom, but will he have time to complete his transformation? She shivers at that thought. Although she gives him healing daily and he has Katrina treating him too, he is still going downhill. She has talked endlessly to Harper about what she should do; he took her hands in his and looked her in the eye.

"You, my dear, are here this time to love and support him. So let go of the outcome and just enjoy your time together. The Creator will see to the rest."

She knows he is right but it is hard to do. Then she feels him stirring and knows he is awake, so it is time to put her fears to one side and concentrate on helping him.

As I awake next morning, I feel her body next to mine and turn to find a tuft of blonde hair sticking out above the duvet. My heart beats a little faster and I feel on top of the world; for a man who's dying of a brain tumour, I'm very content. Last night turned out so much better than I could ever have imagined in my wildest dreams. Once we had arrived back here and eaten our Indian take-away, I grasped the nettle.

"Tara, there's something I have to tell you." I then hesitated a moment but somehow managed to carry on. "I'm in love with you."

Her eyebrows rose and she looked surprised but not horrified by my words. But the seconds lengthened and she didn't reply so I began to worry that she was trying to think how to let me down gently. She then smiled, which I took to be a good sign.

"I…" she started, and then stopped.

"Yes?" I prompted. "I mean, I can understand why you might not… you know… my condition… I mean, it's not great timing, is it?"

"No, it's not. And that's the problem."

"Ah."

"Yes, because, James, I've fallen in love with you too. It's hard, you know, I want to be with you…" She stopped again and her eyes were welling up. "Oh shit," she said. "James, I want to grow old with you but…"

"That's not going to happen. Yes, I get it."

She took my hand and looked me in the eye. "I do love you. I've tried very hard not to because I've been hurt before. It was a long time ago, but… stupid, really."

"No, it's not. And I know I'm not a good catch with my built-in expiry date – but at least you know that already. I wish I could change that, but I can't."

"And do you think if you could… would you still love me?" she asked. I didn't need to think.

"With all my heart! Every time I see you my heart does a skip and it's never done that before."

"A skip?" she grinned. "I like that. I've never made anyone's heart skip before." She got up and moved to sit beside me and put her head on my chest. "Oh, James, why is this happening?"

"I don't know. Aren't you the one with the access codes to them upstairs?"

"Believe me," she laughed humourlessly, "I've talked to them already only they haven't been very helpful."

"What, no tips on where we go from here?"

"Nope, not one."

"So I guess we'll have to wing it," I said.

"Wing it?" she said, pulling back to look me in the eye, smiling. "Okay, let's do that." We cuddled up close again and I have never felt so comfortable and loved before. We stayed like that for a while before she said, "It's no good, James, I can't stop loving you, even if we don't have much longer together. Let's go to bed."

So I have my answer and I'm the happiest man on the planet this morning. Where we go from here, I have no idea, and for once I don't give a damn since it has taken a terminal illness to teach me what is truly worth a fortune. Just take it from someone who knows that having a million pounds in the bank doesn't make you happy. Nothing you can buy will ever fill you up like love can, however much the advertising industry tells you otherwise.

I also learned that as I no longer hunted for love, it somehow found me when I least expected it to. If I hadn't got sick I would never have meet Tara at all. Coincidence? I don't think so, not anymore; there are no coincidences but there is destiny. The timing seems a little off but you can't have everything. Is that another lesson? Still, I am thankful for the time we have together, however short that may be. I used always to want to know what was going to happen in the future – I was a broker – but all that is irrelevant now. This present moment is the only time that I know for sure I have. So I am going to make the best of it.

Twenty-Four

Tara stirs next to me, her head emerges from under the duvet and her eyes blink a couple of times in the bright winter sunshine flooding my bedroom.

"Good morning, Skip," I say and am rewarded with a beaming smile.

"Hi there, handsome," she replies.

"How did you sleep?"

"Wonderful, but who wouldn't after all that exercise?"

"Yes, well, I didn't want to disappoint."

"You didn't, honey," she says as she kisses my cheek. I can't keep the grin off my face as I slip out of bed to start breakfast. She wolf whistles.

"Nice butt," she giggles. I grab my bathrobe and throw a smaller robe at her and in no time at all I have eggs scrambled on toast, mushrooms and tomatoes cooking and the coffee percolating.

"Wow, this smells wonderful," she says from behind me, looking amazing in the fluffy white robe with her blonde hair all curly and damp from the shower. I have already laid the table so we take our seats and I smile, happy that she's enjoying my food. It's been a while since I've had such a good appetite at breakfast too. Nothing else is said until our plates our empty and Tara leans backing her chair.

"Oh, I enjoyed that, but I'm stuffed now." I'm finding it hard not to stare at her. "So, James, what are we going to do today? It's Saturday and I have no appointments." She has been working seven days a week to catch up on the appointments that had backed up when the festival was on, but finally she has a whole weekend off which I hope she'll spend with me. "Let's go out and enjoy this sunshine," she says.

We go back to the bedroom to get dressed and I open my wardrobe; in front of me are the neat rows of suits, shirts and shoes.

"Good God," she says behind me and I frown as I turn to look at her.

"What's wrong?" I ask her. She just points at my wardrobe.

"James, you're so… Don't you have any casual clothes?"

"No, not really, just these." I show her the few things I'd found before, on the day we met, and she wrinkles her nose up at them.

"Pitiful," is all she has to say. "I'll have to take you shopping."

"Is that really necessary?" I ask, as clothes shopping is not my idea of having fun. She looks at me and raises an eyebrow.

"Oh, I think it is," she says firmly. "And what are you going to do with all these suits now? Such a waste. We'll take them to a charity shop where they can do some good."

"What, all of them?" I exclaim. "I love some of them. You know, sentimental value. And anyway, I want to be buried in this one." I pull out the dark blue Armani. "It's my favourite and I feel so good when I'm wearing it." She grimaces at that.

"All right, you can keep that one but the others should go."

"No, I'm keeping this one… and this one…" I insist, picking others I like best.

"And some of these shoes?" she sighs. "You've got more than me." I'm finding it hard to get rid of the last links to my old life, but I do see her point: twenty pairs of shoes is a bit excessive. Once we get dressed it takes over an hour for me to make up my mind what I can let go of, but finally I complete it and at my feet there are several stuffed bin bags.

"Now what?" I ask her and she laughs.

"Now we take them to the local charity shops. I know several within ten minutes of here – in fact, I know all the good ones in central London. You can buy some lovely things in charity shops, especially old period clothes from the `thirties and `forties. A lot of them are so beautiful and well-made, not like today's mass-produced rubbish." I don't think I've been in a charity shop since I first came to London and I had no money, so I suppose it is fitting that I give something back now.

After another cup of coffee, Tara says, "Right then, let's go."

"Do we have to?" I ask, hoping to persuade her to stay in and cuddle up on the sofa. She looks at me sternly.

"Yes, we do. We'll take two bags with us and drop them off on the way to Oxford Street."

I groan as I haven't been there for years. It isn't my kind of place and the idea of traipsing around shops is not my idea of fun either, but she isn't going to change her mind so I have to grin and bear it. We get our coats on and make our way out into the chilly but bright November day. She takes my hand and leads me down side streets I have never bothered to explore and soon we come to the first charity shop where Tara pushes the door open and delivers the first bag. A few minutes later the second bag has gone too and we are on our way to the Underground that will deliver us to the West End. As the escalators bring us back to the surface, the cold air filters in making me shiver. I've been feeling the cold far more than I used to lately, something to do with losing over a stone in weight. Tara takes my gloved hand in hers and smiles at me.

"Be brave," she teases. "Right, where to start? Ah, I know. Come on." She pulls me after her as she sets off in a determined fashion towards the front doors of a store I have never heard of before. I know this isn't for me as she starts inside.

"I'm not going in there," I tell her. She stops in surprise and turns to me.

"Why not?"

"Because I'm not seventeen," I reply, pointing to the people already in there, the flashing lights and the pounding music. She blinks once and then a smile slowly creeps across her face.

"Hmm, maybe this isn't quite right for you."

She grabs my hand again and leads me to a large, warm department store where there is no loud music and no teenagers anywhere in sight. We wander around but my heart isn't really in this and it doesn't take long for Tara to work this out. This expedition isn't going to work if she leaves it to me to find something so she sighs and says, "This is hopeless. I'll find you something." She dives into one department where I am not impressed with the racks of the ugliest trousers I have ever seen that look like they've been worn for a year or two already. I might not be wearing my suits any more but I refuse to look scruffy, especially at these prices. We walk on through Ben Someone's area, then Jaspar's and John's and Tom's until eventually I do see some items I might possibly like.

"Have you actually found something?" Tara asks with heavy sarcasm. "You'd better try them on first. I'm guessing you don't want to have to come back and change them."

I groan as changing rooms are another pet hate of mine, a throwback to school days and the horrendous experience of changing for sports in front of others. I was small for my age and often covered in bruises from my father's fists, and the embarrassment has never gone away. But it has to be done. Seeing my reflection in the well-lit mirror, I'm quite shocked at how gaunt I look, especially with my pronounced cheekbones and jaw line. Still, my colour is good, I don't look obviously sick and my eyes are clear. I sigh as I feel my life is only just beginning whereas in reality it is coming to an end. I found love and happiness with Tara but I've left it too late.

"Life sucks," I say to my reflection and a voice outside the curtain answers.

"Is there a problem, sir?"

I open the curtain a little to the eager, young and pimply assistant and hand him the trousers I'd chosen, asking him to find me a smaller size. Twenty minutes later I emerge with three pairs of casual trousers, some polo shirts – no designs or logos – and a couple of jumpers. I follow the young man back to the counter where Tara is smiling in triumph. As I hand over my credit card, my stomach rumbles quite alarmingly and a glance at my watch tells me it is well past lunchtime.

"They do have a restaurant here, don't they?" I ask her.

"Yes, and it's quite nice and reasonably priced."

"That's good, I'm broke now," I tell her. She laughs and loops her arm through mine as we head to the escalator.

"I'll buy you lunch, seeing you've been such a good boy."

We are lucky to find a table in the restaurant as it's very busy, but another couple leaves just as we arrive and Tara grabs their seats before anyone else has a chance to.

"You stay here while I get us some food," she says and I'm more than happy to comply as I suddenly feel very tired. I sink back into my chair and do a bit of people watching, although I'm aware that a headache is beginning. I just wish I had more energy but it gets depleted very quickly. In no time at all I look up to see Tara struggling towards me with a loaded tray so I help her with it and we settle down to enjoy our late lunch. I can't seem to eat meat anymore as I just can't digest it, so I've chosen the one vegetarian option on the menu, a cheese omelette and chips, which isn't bad at all but there's far too much and I can only manage about half of it before I am defeated. Tara looks at what I have left and I feel she wants to say something but then changes her mind.

All I want to do is look at her but maybe my intensity is making her uncomfortable.

"What is it, James?"

"Nothing really, except I'm so happy you're in my life now." She smiles and takes my hand.

"I'm happy with you too, James, whatever the future brings." But as I try to think of a witty reply, the pain shoots across my head and hits me between the eyes.

"Aaah…" I exclaim, holding my head in my hands.

"James, what is it?" she whispers, conscious of the people around us. The pain has now gone just as quickly as it arrived and I look across to her concerned face.

"It's all right, it's gone again, but I have a feeling it'll be back."

"Then let's get home before it does," she says and I don't argue. The thought of collapsing on a street or in a shop is awful. It would be mortifying and the worst part of this illness is the sudden weakness and unpredictability of it all. We make it home by taxi and I am happy to sink into my chair and close my eyes, safe inside my own home again.

When I awake, something makes me glance over to my 'phone and see the red light flashing to tell me I have a message. I wonder if I have the energy to walk over and play it. But now that I have seen the light

I have to know who has called me so I pull myself up slowly and take the five steps over to the `phone and press the play button. A female voice I don't recognise begins to speak.

"James, this is Sarah, Carol's sister. I've talked to Angela and she says she will see you if you want to meet. She lives at a place called Carnival near Penisarcwn in Powys. There is a `phone there but it's a communal one. So if you're serious about talking to her, I think you'll have to travel there to do it… Okay, that's all."

Tara had come up behind me and listened in. "How do you feel about that?"

"I'm not sure… surprised and a little nervous. I wish I could speak to her on the `phone first instead of face to face. But if I have to go to Wales, then that's what I'll do. I need to do this."

"You can do it. And you're right, you do need to say sorry."

"Karma cleansing?"

"Yes." She pauses, then asks, "What sort of place do you think Carnival is?"

"I don't know," I shrug, "I haven't heard from her since she left work and disappeared. I know it sounds heartless but it was a great relief when she left. I guess because she wasn't around to make me feel guilty anymore." In trying to justify my actions I must sound even more callous and it's a wonder Tara can bear to be near me. I look at her expecting to see disgust on her face but instead she is looking at me compassionately.

"Well, James, it was not your finest hour but at least you feel bad about it. And you are no worse than the rest of us – we all have a dark side."

She leaves me to make some tea while I look back on my cowardly behaviour towards Angela and inwardly cringe. She didn't deserve to be treated like that as she hadn't done anything wrong in wanting marriage and a family. The fly in the ointment was me because I couldn't see myself in that role and I wasn't sure what kind of father I would make anyway as my only role model was hardly up to scratch. As talk of the wedding became more intense, so was my desire to run away. In the end I found the courage to call it off but I shudder now as I remember the scene when I told her and the look of total shock on her face. It had obviously never crossed her mind that I wasn't ready for this. At first I think she thought I was joking but then she realised I was serious; she was completely unprepared for that. For a second she was silent and then she hit the roof and I was bombarded with a torrent of abuse the like of which I had never known – and the backlash from her friends and family went on for what seemed like an eternity. That was when I jumped at the chance to go into partnership with Jeremy, a new start away from the office where everyone knew our business. Now, six years later, could I face her?

"Here you are," Tara says as she hands me a mug of tea. We settle back quietly to drink it; with her, I don't feel the need to fill the silence with meaningless small talk. At length she asks, "Would you like some healing, James?" She knows full well that I never say no to that and for the next thirty-five minutes I am transported into another world, free of pain and heartache.

Twenty-Five

Five days have passed and I am still wrestling with indecision about whether to go and see Angela. I get up from my computer and put the kettle on, more for something to do because to be honest I'm bored even though I've been retired less than two weeks. I look at the list I had written a while ago of the things I would try when I retired and realise that many of them are now impossible because of my condition. I can't get travel insurance and any dangerous sports like parachuting require a doctor's certificate and I don't think mine would give me one. As I walk back to my desk with my tea the telephone rings.

"It's me," Tara says.

"Hello, Skip. Lovely to hear your voice."

"You too, so how are you feeling today? Up for a trip to the country?" she enquires. I look at the blue sky and weak winter sunshine outside.

"I most certainly am. Where are we going?"

"Hampshire, if you'll drive?" Her voice has a smile in it. "I'll explain when I see you. I'm coming over to yours now so I hope to be there in half an hour."

"Alright, see you soon," I tell her, a little mystified. She arrives right on schedule and we walk to the car holding hands. I have that stupid smile on my face again but I don't care. There is just one downside though and I can't help sighing heavily.

"What's up?" she asks.

"I just wish we had longer together," I tell her.

"So do I James, so do I." Her eyes glisten with unshed tears that I know she doesn't want me to see, so I look away and lead her into the underground garage where my car lives. She smiles then and looks inside at the cream leather seats of the Lexus.

"Nice," she says as she slips inside.

"Well, keep your fingers crossed she'll start," I tell her as I turn the key. I hold my breath as the engine turns over and fires first time. "Right then, to Hampshire... Ah, where exactly are we going in Hampshire?"

"Kingsclere. Do you know it?"

"Oh yes, you're talking to a racing brat. Where there are racing yards then I know them. Although it's been a good few years since I've been to Kingsclere."

As usual the traffic in central London is horrendous and I need all my wits about me to get us to the M4 safely but once there it's a straight run to Junction 13. I'm thankful for the fine, dry weather as I do find driving quite exhausting now if I have to concentrate too hard. But my eyes are good today and the motorway traffic relatively light so I settle into an almost empty inside lane and resume our conversation.

"So tell me, what are we going to do in Kingsclere?"

"Horses," she says with a smile.

I return her smile knowing that one of my wishes is about to come true. Ever since I learned of her animal healing I have wanted to see her in action, especially with horses, an animal I have always adored. Now a tingle of anticipation runs through me. I have always felt a deep connection to horses, as if I understand what they are thinking. Is it empathy or something else? I don't know but it is real and in my teens I was able to calm horses that no-one else could get near. I just feel their energies somehow. In not much more than an hour we have passed Newbury and are on the A339 to Kingsclere. I remember one racing yard there but I am out of touch with the ins and outs of that world now that I live in London, though I still go racing whenever I can.

"Are we going to racing stables?" I ask.

"Yes, we have two patients." She hands me a piece of paper with the address of the yard. "Then, after lunch, a friend of a friend is having trouble with a horse she has just bought and she's only a few miles up the road so I agreed to see it too."

"Right, well, you can sit back and relax – I know where that is." She snuggles down in the passenger seat with a contented smile on her face. I drive on until I find the sign to Kingsclere. Up ahead is a roundabout that wasn't there the last time I came here; there's a new road system now but before long I find myself by the church and I know where I am. It doesn't take long before we're pulling into the yard and I park in a marked space and turn off the engine.

"This is it."

"Good, well, I suppose we had better go and meet our patients."

I can't wait. We walk through to the main yard and find a girl sweeping it who directs us to the office, although the word is rather grand for the small wooden hut.

Tara looks in and says she's been asked to have a look at two horses and the man there grunts in an unfriendly way as he gets up and indicates that we should follow him.

"Don't worry," Tara whispers to me. "I get this treatment a lot from trainers who think their owners are wasting their money on a con artist like me. But if the healing works and the horse starts winning again they're quite happy to take the credit for it." She sighs. "It's just the way it is, for now anyway, but attitudes are changing."

"Still, as long as the horse gets better it's worth it," I tell her. The man walking ahead of us suddenly stops outside an anonymous, green stable door and we look inside to find a grey horse standing at the back of the stable with its head down, looking very forlorn.

"'Ere's one, name's Harry," the man says, then he points down the row. "Two door down is the other'un, George." He grunts and walks away, not intending to hang around in the cold with idiots like us. Tara opens the box door and I follow her inside. Harry doesn't even lift his head to see who we are, which is very unusual as horses are nosey beasts.

"What wrong with him?" I ask her.

"According to the vet, nothing's wrong with him," she says.

"Well, maybe they should change vets because even I can tell he's not right."

"You're right," she smiles back, "so let's see if we can help him."

She moves slowly towards him, talking softly and gently and I watch him twitch an ear in her direction then turn his head a fraction to get a better look at her. His eyes are dull and incredibly sad. Tara stops and puts out her hand for him to sniff, which he does, then she moves a step closer and tickles his nose. He whinnies a quiet, half-hearted welcome.

"It's all right, Harry, we're here to try and help you feel better," she tells him, and suddenly I'm sure he knows this. His eyes look at her hopefully and I smile, seeing there is still life in him. I have often heard people say that horses don't have expressions but they're wrong; they may not have as many as we do but they do express their feelings clearly in their faces and body language. Harry is a case in point – just by looking at him you can tell he's in pain and fed up with life whatever the vet says.

I continue to watch Tara as she strokes his face and asks his permission to give him healing. Animals might not understand the words but they do understand the intention behind them, she's told me, and he'll let her know if it's not all right to continue. I stay silent and then notice him edging closer to her and I see her smile; that's what she was looking for, that he has just given her permission to continue.

"Have you noticed anything, James?" she asks me.

"Yes, he wants you to heal him."

"Good, I think you're a natural."

I feel a warmth inside from her comment as I turn my attention back to Harry and gradually become aware that there is a fuzzy glow forming around both of them. Is this an aura? Tara has told me about this but I have never had much luck seeing one when we have tried together, so now I scrunch up my eyes and focus on this glow and see it getting bigger and brighter. At first it is gold in colour then slowly it changes and more and more colours materialise until it contains all the colours of the rainbow. Inside an outer ring I begin to see blotches of duller colours, then around his head there is an orangey-red patch and along his spine is a green and purple line.

I seem to drift into this aura and begin getting impressions or visions. I cannot decide what they are exactly but I seem to be seeing him in a field where he is happy and living with some sheep. One in particular he likes, or I think so. It's a bit like watching a very disjointed movie. I see him being manhandled into a stable but he is very afraid of being in it on his own and tries to jump out. Next he's in the stable but this time he is happy as his friend the sheep is with him. In the next scene he's in a horsebox on his own and being brought here, but he's afraid of being in this box alone and missing his friend, which is why he won't eat or settle. This is all very clear to me and I understand completely.

"Okay, boy, I'll tell them for you," I hear myself say, opening my eyes to find Tara looking at me and smiling.

"So what did you find out?" she asks. I feel my face going red but I tell her the visions and hope she'll not laugh at me. She doesn't.

"I'm impressed, James, and I agree. Although he has some back pain too which I'll try to fix now." She then moves her hands along his spine and stops just where I saw the purple patch. I watch as her fingers move backwards and forwards, feeling the area, and then she places both hands on his spine and deftly pushes it down and sideways. There's a loud crack and Harry shudders but that's all he does. I look at Tara in amazement.

"What the hell was that?"

"A disc slightly out of place. That would only get worse," she says. I notice that Harry looks more comfortable already since he's stretching out his neck and chewing, all signs of relaxation in a horse. His head is no longer on the ground and his eyes are brighter and more alert; he looks at Tara who is stroking his neck and reaches out his nose to her as if to say 'Thank you'.

"You're welcome," she laughs as she rubs his face. It looks like Harry knows she has helped him, even if some humans will need a bit more convincing, and I hope that when she reports her findings to the owner he will get some company to cheer Harry up too. He is now tucking into his hay net as if he's starving. As we close the stable door behind us, she ask me again about seeing the aura.

"It was like he was showing me why he is unhappy," I suggest. "What did it feel like to you?"

"Feel like…? Well, it's different every time but with Harry I could feel cold spots where the problem was. But as I've told you before, I only do what I am told to do. You remember me telling you how my healing guide likes to do things? Well, he said there was an injury to his spine. It was out just a little bit but enough to affect him so I had to put it back."

"I heard the crack."

"Yes, that was a bit dramatic, wasn't it? It's not usually like that but it worked. Now his energy can flow properly again. I'll find out if he had sheep for company before and see if they can get him another friend so he isn't scared anymore."

Twenty-Six

I have learned a lot about energy, how it can get blocked and released, so now that I've seen an aura too maybe I will be able to use this to help others. I'd like to train as a healer but ... well, life has other plans for me.

"So, do you see the problem like I did?" I asked Tara.

"No, I hear it," she says, laughing at the face I pull. "No, it's true, James. My guide tells me what it is and I follow her instructions. We don't get a hundred per cent results all the time but I trust her completely. Over the years, she hasn't let me down."

"And if I were to have a go, what would I do?" I ask.

"You would let spirit guide you." She sees my sceptical expression and continues, "Okay, James, what I mean by that is you let go of your own judgement of what might be wrong and instead let your hands go where they want to. The biggest obstacle to healing is too much logical thinking. This stuff isn't logical, so to approach it that way is hopeless. Just let your intuition guide you. Every healing is different, which is what I love about the process. It's never boring or repetitive so each time you give healing is like the first time. Let yourself tune in to the patient's energy and they will guide you where you need to go." I nod as that makes sense to me. After having many healing sessions with her, I've seen how different they are for me as the patient.

We walk down to the box of our other patient and look inside to see a huge bay horse who is restless and pacing. As Tara moves to open the door, I ask her if I can go in first and see what I can sense; she hesitates at first but then stands back.

I speak softly to George and he stops his pacing for a moment to glare at me. He seems angry to me, though I might have got that wrong, so I try to see his aura while whispering sweet nothings to him as I try to concentrate. Slowly I begin to see a deep red ring around him, very different to Harry's as this is jagged and worse around the head, especially under his jaw.

"You are right, child, the pain is in his jaw. There's a hairline crack in it," a voice says in my ear. I start in surprise and look around to see if Tara has joined me but she's still standing on the other side of the stable door. She raises her eyebrows at me and is about to speak when the voice says, "No, it isn't her, only you can hear me." I can feel my heart beating a little faster in shock – is this another symptom of the tumour? Am I going mad? Tara's frown deepens as I stand there with my mouth open.

"James, are you all right?"

I nod and try to pull myself together. "Yes, I'm fine," I lie. "I can see a lot of red around his jaw. What do you think?"

"Yes, I agree the problem is there somewhere. But the vet has looked at his teeth and said they seemed alright. Why don't you try to approach him?"

I grimace as I'm not sure he is going to let me. Still, I will have to get a lot closer if I'm going to do anything for him. "Be careful," the woman's voice says, rather unnecessarily. As I move closer I get a better sense of George's pain and I tell him that I'm here to help, speaking softly and keeping my demeanour as unthreatening as possible. In the past I've watched the great horse whisperer Monty Roberts in action and learned about horse psychology, so I know that I mustn't look George in the eye or approach him from the front because these are both provocative actions. Now I move in from the side and keep looking at his neck until finally I touch him. He shudders but doesn't attack me.

"He's worried that you're going to put a bit in his mouth," the voice says. I sigh. It would appear the voice isn't going away. "I will only speak to you when you're healing, dearie," she says again, rather indignantly, and I instantly get a picture of an elderly, motherly woman with grey hair and pebble-style glasses. "Yes, that's me," she confirms, with a smile in her voice.

I continue to stroke George's neck and work my way slowly towards his head, placing my hands on each side of his cheeks and sliding them to rest them on his cheek bones, whispering to him all the while. When I risk closing my eyes I am struck by the heat emanating from his head – he is burning hot as if he is on fire. "Why is he so hot?" I ask silently.

"He has a small infection in his jaw which needs to be drained," comes the answer. "Just do what I tell you, kiddo, and stop thinking so damn much. That's always been your trouble."

"What?" I exclaim, almost out loud. This is the voice of a nagger and I hear her chuckle.

"Come on, kiddo, no time for a debate. George is hurting, so get on with some healing. Think of ice-cold water, see it and then direct it inside Georges head."

"Umm … how the hell do I do that?" I think.

"Oh, come on, James, use your imagination. I know you've got one so get your finger out and use it."

I grimace and do as I am told since I don't seem to have a choice, seeing in my mind two blocks of ice and holding them to George's cheeks. Then I imagine this going into his jaws and cooling the infection, washing out the puss, the heat and the pain. Amazingly, I feel him begin to relax; he shudders and his head drops as he lets go of some of the pain. Next I move my hand as gently as possible to his infected jaw, half expecting him to explode, but he doesn't move an inch. I'm sure he now knows that I'm only trying to help him so I run my fingers gently along the jaw line until I feel a pulsing sensation in it. In my mind's eye I can see a pool of puss, but how do I get rid of it?

"You send it light, is how," the voice says impatiently, as if I should already know this. "Think it, then send a beam of light into the pool to evaporate it."

"Oh, just like that?" I mutter under my breath.

"Just do it," comes her waspish reply.

The only way I can imagine doing this is with a laser gun, so I make my forefinger into a gun and shoot golden light into the heart of the trouble. My beam of light hits the pool and it begins to dry up and slowly evaporate until there is nothing left.

"Good, now you have to pack it so it can't fill up again," she says in my ear. "Before you ask, the most healing colour is green so put green into the hole." I repress the urge to make a wisecrack and get on with doing as I'm told, visualising the first green leaves of springtime since this seems the freshest, purest green that nature produces. I fill up the hole with this until there is no space left. "Yes, that's it, James, he'll be fine now." Only now do I look George in the eye – and he nips my arm.

Tara bursts out laughing. "Oh, that's priceless," she says, wiping a tear from her eye. "Your face."

"Hmm, does that happen a lot? Because if it does I'm quitting while I'm still intact."

"No, James, most patients are grateful but some are not very nice, just like humans. They complain even if you help them." And speaking of not very nice people, the surly assistant comes out of his office and over to us.

"You finished yet?" he demands.

"Yes, all done," Tara tells him. "I'll let the owner know what we found."

We walk back to the car and I drive us to a great thatched pub I used to know for a meal by a roaring log fire. When we sit down to discuss the morning, I begin to tell Tara about the woman's voice telling me what to do for George. "Don't worry, I haven't got another woman … well, I have, but it's not what you think." She listens intently, finishing her lasagne while I fill her in on my strange encounter. "So what do you think? Am I hallucinating?" I ask her, but she grins and shakes her head.

"No James, I think you should feel honoured to have her come to you like this."

"Honoured to have some nagging woman telling me what to do?" I snort.

"Yes, you're honoured. Most of us healers train for years to forge a relationship with our healing guides and the connection can be tentative or often hardly there at all. This leaves us having to do what we think will help and sometimes not making a very good job of it. But you, James, already have a clear and direct link with yours and she has told you exactly what to do. I wish I had such a guide. I don't get instructions like that. I wish I did."

"You don't?" I exclaim in shock. I had assumed she must hear something similar herself.

"No. She must really want you to do some healing, James, or she wouldn't be with you. You helped to heal George today, so it's a gift you need to accept."

"I don't think I did much. I was just following orders," I reply, feeling uncomfortable with her words.

"Yes, but that's all any of us do, really. We have to be there, open and receptive to these instructions and to directing the energy where it needs to go."

I hadn't thought of it like that. If 'the voice' could have healed George without me I suppose she would have; but since she used me I must have been integral to the process. I feel good about that.

"So you now have your guide," Tara continued. "Did you get any impression of what she looks like?" I had forgotten until she asked that in fact I had.

"Yes, I did, for a second or two. I saw a small, plump woman with short, grey hair and bright blue eyes behind round pebble glasses."

"She sounds jolly."

"Jolly she is not. Bossy, but definitely not jolly," I tell her.

"You probably needed persuading, James, that's why she came over as bossy. Once you get to know her better I'll bet she'll turn out to be jolly, you see if she doesn't. I doubt very much you've heard the last from her."

As they drive away, Tara reflects on just how lucky James is to have his guide communicating so clearly with him; it normally takes many years even to get a connection half as good as this, but here he is doing his first healing and receiving things even she hadn't picked up. A wave of jealousy engulfs her, surprisingly intense as she rarely feels negative emotions so strongly anymore. She thought she'd gone past that but her reaction to James' success shows her that there is still work to do. Then she hears a gentle chuckle and knows that Juliette is with her…

"Remember, little one, everyone's path is different even though you are all heading for the same destination. Along this path you have experiences tailored for your own growth and development. James should have been healing a long time ago so he has some catching up to do now, while you've more time to develop. This is how it is. Blessed be."

Tara smiles, lets go of her feelings of jealousy and gives thanks for another chance to learn and to grow.

Twenty-Seven

By the time we leave the pub to go to our next patient I am really tired, just about functioning. I have read a lot about my condition and, although everyone progresses differently, I am now suffering more and more symptoms – which means my time grows ever shorter. What I have to look forward to is either a slow, agonising death or, if I'm a bit luckier, a sudden deterioration; my favourite option is a stroke and a quick end. I still haven't told my mother about my condition either and I can't put that off much longer.

"Where are we heading now?" She pulls out a piece of paper with directions on it.

"We need to go to Tadley. Do you know it?"

"Just up the road," I tell her. We turn out of the car park and once we are through Tadley she reads me the directions. Less than ten minutes later we arrive. I turn down a long drive lined by a double row of lime trees like sentinels and at the end is a small stable yard and a large redbrick house. As we pull up four dogs come rushing out of the tack room, barking their heads off and wagging their tails. A blonde woman comes from the house and yells at the dogs who suddenly stop barking and run to her.

"Hello, you must be Tara?" she asks, looking past me. "Lovely to meet you. Don't worry about the dogs, they don't bite." Sure enough, as I get out the dogs gather around my legs waiting to be petted, so I get down to a good ear-rubbing session while Tara talks to the lady, Bonny. I listen to what they say while being thoroughly licked by the dogs.

"It's my daughter's new polo pony that I'm worried about. We got her about two months ago and she was vetted before we bought her. Come and see for yourself." She leads the way back up the drive to the barn which is divided into two large areas; in one of them are two bay horses standing together, both with hogged manes. Bonny picks up a rope, enters the second area and easily catches the taller pony of the two and brings her through to us before taking her rugs off.

Tara moves in closer as I stand back to watch. I'm not sure what I should do but the first thing I notice is that the aura around her is fragmented and incomplete though I'm not sure what that might mean.

"Mineral deficiency, I'd say," the voice says in my head.

"You're back then?" I reply silently.

"Sure am, kiddo, you can't get rid of me so easily."

"So who are you exactly?" I ask, a little testily.

"Don't get all uppity with me, kiddo. I didn't choose you, believe me, no way. Boy, if I'd gotten a choice you'd certainly not be top of my list. You've wasted so much time when you could have been healing. Instead you chose to sit in a stuffy office in a smelly city and make money." It's funny that I didn't notice her American twang before and now she's clearly annoyed. I turn my attention to watching Tara at Vesta's head, gently rubbing it as she talks softly to her and then beginning to run her hands down the body. The voice interrupts my thoughts again.

"It's a waste of time her doing that," she says. It would appear she is not going to shut up. "Damn right, I'm not. Not until you listen to me."

"Alright, I will," I concede, "but right now I really want to watch what Tara is doing."

"Okay," she gives a reluctant sniff, "but that horse has a mineral deficiency. Ask her where they got it from. James, ask her. It's important."

"Alright, alright, just please stop nagging." So I turn to Bonny and ask her.

"A friend bought her from a guy who brings them over from Argentina. She's ten years old which is getting on for top flight polo but she'll be perfect for my daughter to learn on. We bought Galion from the same man but he's been here a few years now."

"And he is well?" I ask, looking over at the other bay horse

"Oh yes, he's fine, it's Vesta who can't get any weight on. The vet keeps saying she'll pick up but she doesn't. He just says she's fine and charges me a fortune." I smile in sympathy as I've heard people say that being a vet is a licence to print money, but they say that about stockbrokers too.

"Ask her if he did a blood test," the voice demands. I give up and do as I'm told. Bonny nods.

"Yes, but it didn't show any abnormalities."

"Did he look for any mineral deficiencies?"

"I don't think so," Bonny frowns. "Why? Do you think she has a deficiency?"

"Perhaps. But let's wait for Tara to finish."

Tara smiles at me but makes no comment. I suspect she has guessed that I am being nagged to ask these questions. She stops near Vesta's left shoulder and squints, trying to look more closely at the area, and then I notice a bulge in the energy field just where Tara's hands are.

"What's that?" I ask my guide but for a few seconds there is silence. "Oh, come on," I continue, exasperated, "if you're here to help then get on with it."

"Alright, keep your hair on. Alright, yes, there is something amiss there. Hmm, a pinched nerve and she did it recently. Have I been wrong yet?" she demanded.

"I guess not," I agree. "So what can we do about it?"

"Tara knows what to do but she'll need your help to do it." Immediately, Tara stands up and looks at me.

"James, can you give me a hand? Can you hold up her leg while I manipulate her shoulder?"

I approach Vesta and offer her my hand to sniff. She seems calm and I talk to her as I gently run my hand down her shoulder and onto her fetlock. As I apply a bit of pressure, she obediently lifts her leg so I can cup her hoof in my left hand, spreading my legs a little to take the weight. But I don't think I can hold her up for long. Tara moves in quickly and begins to feel around the shoulder blade. From my cramped, bent position I can't see anything but the ground in front of me, although I can feel a pulsing in Vesta's leg that gets stronger. My back is beginning to ache but thankfully Vesta then shudders, sighs heavily and I can feel her relax.

"Okay, James, you can -" I've already let go before she can finish the sentence and slowly straighten up, rubbing my aching back.

"What was that?" Bonny asks.

"A pinched nerve," both Tara and I say together, then we laugh. "She did it recently," I add. "Has she slipped at all?"

"Oh … yes, she did. About four days ago when we were out riding."

"She probably caught the nerve then but it will be as good as new in a few weeks. As for the weight loss …" Tara looks at me and we both say, "It's a mineral deficiency." Tara goes on to recommend some wonderful new mineral supplement on the market that's not the most expensive either. While they put Vesta's rug back on I get a mental image of her grazing with a lot of other horses under the hot sun and suddenly I know what she's showing me.

"I think she's also a bit sad," I offer. "She used to be with a lot of other horses – and she's also missing the sunshine." Tara glances over to me and smiles but Bonny gives me a look like she's not too sure whether I'm mad. Tara rescues me.

"James is intuitive and often picks up on an animal's mental state as well as the physical," she tells Bonny.

"Well, I suppose you're right. She did come from a man who owned over a hundred polo ponies. And it's a lot warmer in Argentina than here." I would agree, as I'm frozen solid and feeling exhausted now. This is the trouble: I can be fine but then all of a sudden my energy drains out and all I want to do is sleep. So I leave them to talk and make my way slowly back to the car where I sink gratefully into the passenger seat and close my eyes.

A jolt bumps my head against the side window and I open my eyes to find that it's dark outside and the car is travelling fast. Disorientated and groggy, I look across to see Tara behind the wheel, looking far from relaxed.

"Aah … where are we?" I ask as I struggle upright with a stiff neck.

"Nearly at Heathrow. How are you feeling now?"

"I'm fine, more or less. How are you finding the car?"

"It's a bit more powerful than I'm used to." She grimaces. "Would you like to take over?" she asks hopefully. I see her desperation and tell her to go off at the next junction so we can switch. She nods and goes back to concentrating on driving and five minutes later she pulls over and we change places. A blast of cold air hits me as I get out of the car and wakes me up. I swear and we both rush around the car and dive back inside the warm interior. She places her hand on my arm.

"Are you really up to driving the rest of the way, James?" she asks, a look of concern on her beautiful face. I smile and nod.

"Sorry I flaked out on you, don't know what came over me."

"No worries. Healing work can take it out of you, even when you're a hundred per cent. Most people think that because you're just standing there you're not doing much, but you are of course."

"Well, it's wiped me out. Still, I have enjoyed today, so thank you for taking me. I think you deserve a take-away."

"Fish and chips, please."

Twenty-Eight

A point of light appears in the darkness far away and I need to find it to get out of this darkness that is pressing down on me. I struggle onwards knowing that I have to get to that speck of light, but the faster I move the further away it seems to go. Fear clutches at my throat as I scream, "Come back! Don't go!" My voice sounds harsh and ragged and I can feel my heart pounding in my chest. I am exhausted but I can't stop because if I don't touch the light then I'll be lost forever, so I push on in desperation until then a flash of blue light like a lightning bolt lights up the darkness and transforms it in an instant. I see that I'm inside a cavern but then another blue light appears and begins to head straight for me. I turn to run but only manage one step before it hits me in the back of the head and a nerve-jangling shock courses through my body. The pain is excruciating and I wake up screaming.

"James? James!"

I can hear Tara's voice but the pain in my head is too overwhelming for me to answer her. I am being fried from the inside out and all my nerves are sparking at once and there is a fire raging inside me. Now cool hands are being cupped around my head and the pain instantly reduces, although the fire is still going strong. I can hear her voice now but I can't make out the words, then slowly the pain lessens and there is a freshness circulating around my body that brings the fire under control.

"Aaah…" I manage to croak as my wits begin to return.

"Lie still," she tells me. I don't think I can do anything else.

I must have fallen asleep again as the next time I open my eyes there is light outside the window. I groan and stretch, feeling at least a hundred and three as all my muscles ache and it takes me two attempts just to sit up. The weakness on my left side is much worse and my tongue feels huge and furry. Then the bedroom door opens a crack and one eye looks at me, making me smile.

"It's all right, I'm still alive… just," I tell her as the door opens. Tara comes in and sits next to me on the bed.

"That's not funny, James," she says and I see tears in her eyes and dark circles under them. "I thought…" She goes quiet for a moment and then adds, "When you woke up earlier you couldn't speak and it was scary." I don't remember this at all.

"Before? I don't remember. Tell me what happened, Tara."

"Well, I managed to help you and you went back to sleep. Then a few hours later you woke up again but you had trouble forming any words – they were garbled but you weren't properly awake. At least, that's what I hoped." I know what she means: I could have had a stroke. "Anyway, you did go back to sleep and that was hours ago."

"So what do you think happened?"

She shakes her head. "I don't know. But if you're up to it maybe we could ask your guides." She moves behind me and supports my head in her lap and we start to lengthen our breathing and enter a meditative state. I soon find that after yesterday's events my guide's voice is never far away.

"Hi, kiddo. What do you want to know?" she says.

"Have I had a stroke?"

"Yep, a little one. But don't panic, your number's not up yet."

"Do you know when I will die, then?"

"No, that's up to you. But I don't think it will be the long, drawn-out affair you're worried about. Look, there's no definite day for your death. Fact is there are several days – and ways – you could die, spread out over your whole lifespan. It really isn't as cut and dried as you think."

Nothing ever is, I'm learning, just like karma. She knows my thoughts.

"Ah yes, karma. There's still more to do, someone you need to see, isn't there, James? Don't leave it any longer. Do it now." I know she means Angela because of all the people I have hurt it is she I need to see the most.

"And if I do that, then will I die?"

"Maybe. Maybe not. Look, karma is not just for this lifetime, it carries on. But you can do something about it, like asking to be forgiven, and rid yourself of a load of it right now. That chance doesn't come along very often. Do yourself a favour." I am just getting my head around what she's said when she continues, "By the way, I'll tell you this – that tumour is changing."

"What? How?"

"Not for me to say. But you'll not lose your speech again for a while so get on with what you have to do. I'm not going to tell you any more. I'm just here to help you heal others and Tara is there to help heal you. Let God decide what happens to you."

With that she is gone and I hear Tara telling me to bring myself back and ground myself again. I open my eyes and smile up at her.

"That was interesting," I tell her. "I had another chat with the voice. She thinks I should go and see Angela now." There's a look of surprise on Tara's face; she obviously wasn't expecting that any more than I was.

"If that's her advice then I think you should take it. It's unfinished business that needs to be cleared."

I know she's right but that still doesn't make it any easier for me. I know, I'm a coward. This isn't going to be pretty. Still, I have to go but I don't want to go alone so I ask Tara if she'll consider coming along. She frowns and my heart sinks as I think she's going to turn me down. Maybe it's asking too much. After all, Angela was once my fiancée. "Ah, forget it. I'll go on -" She smiles and puts her fingertip to my lips.

"Shut up, James," she says. "I'm flattered you've asked me and if you really want me to come I will. I'm curious about her." She blushes at this, then adds, "And I don't think you should go alone – or drive all the way to Wales, either. I may have someone who'd drive us there in your car… for a financial consideration."

I look askew at her, not sure I want anyone else driving my car. "Oh, and who might this be?" I ask.

"Mike, he does odd jobs for me at the clinic. He's trying hard to get his life back on track so I give him work when I can. He's had some problems but is determined to put them behind him."

"A drug addict?"

"No, not any more. He's been clean for nearly three years now but it's hard to get anyone to employ you when you don't have a proper CV or job experience. You can't exactly put down 'drug addict' as a job, can you?"

"I don't suppose you can." I have no experience of drugs; the closest I've ever got is smoking and that's normal tobacco. It has never appealed to me, the same with drinking though having an alcoholic father has something to do with that. I like a glass of wine but that's about all; I never want to get so that I can't find my own way home. I think this is one of the reasons I hate this tumour, taking my control away from me.

I look out of the car window two days later and I feel dread in my stomach. Is this a good idea? Part of me knows I have to do this and the cowardly part is screaming at me not to. But it's too late now. I'm on the way to Wales, no turning back.

I try to think of something else and focus on the back of Mike's head. He isn't at all as I imagined he would be. I suppose we all have stereotypes of drug addicts in our minds and I thought he'd look sickly but he doesn't; in fact he's a tall man in his twenties with brown hair and bright, intelligent brown eyes who shook my hand firmly this morning. He went into raptures when he saw the car and couldn't wait to get behind the wheel. He is proving to be a good and careful driver too. Tara squeezes my arm.

"What do you think of Mike now?" she whispers, well aware of my concerns about him.

"Do I need to say that you're right again?" I whisper back. She giggles and nods.

"Yes, you do."

I suppose that life could easily have happened to me if I'd failed to get a job when I arrived in London or had help with getting a place to stay. It's only now, looking back, I realise how fortunate I was and how easily I could have ended up living on the streets. And I've been thinking a lot lately about the choices I've made in this life and how some of them look decidable questionable now. Sure, I made a lot of money. But until I met Tara I lived a pretty lonely and unfulfilled life. Having someone who loves me has opened up so many new and exciting possibilities – except for this bloody brain tumour.

"What are you thinking?" she asks me.

"Oh, just wondering how to get rid of this tumour so I can be with you longer."

She tries to smile but it doesn't really come off.

"I wish for that too," she replies. Oh well, maybe next time around.

It takes us three and a half hours to get to Penisarcwn and we have trouble finding the remote farm. I had rung the number and talked to someone called Maggie who seemed to know who I was and told me that Angela was willing to see me. But her directions are proving to be little more than useless. We drive around until Tara's sharp eyes spot a small sign on a gate that says 'Carnival Farm'. I still don't have any idea what this place is.

The Angela I knew was tall and willowy, always immaculately dressed with her brown hair cut short in a gamine style that set off her oval face and high cheekbones. She was more striking than beautiful and the gaze from her hazel eyes was commanding; she was every inch the modern businesswoman and the whole idea of confronting her now is making me very nervous. I certainly don't remember her being a country girl – she had a love of shopping, nightclubs and good restaurants. What the hell is she doing here where the nearest shop is ten miles away?

Mike turns the car into a long, rutted driveway and finally a very large, old stone-built manor house comes into view. It probably once belonged to quite an important family but its grandeur has long since faded. We pull up in front of stone entrance steps that have lost their railings and a large front door that could do with more than a lick of paint.

"Big place," Tara observes. "It must have at least ten bedrooms." She smiles and touches my nose with her finger tip. "Are you thinking like a property developer, James?" she asks me. I do tend to look at houses in a different way to most people.

"I'll refrain from asking them how much it cost," I reply.

Mike turns off the engine and turns round to ask us how long we'll be. I pull a face and shrug. "Your guess is as good as mine," I tell him. We could be out again in minutes after I've said my piece and she has given me an earful. Who knows? But I just have to do this. I look at the house, grey and foreboding, and would like very much to run away; but I've been doing that for six years already.

"Are you coming in with me?" I ask Tara.

"Of course I am. Whatever happens, I'm there for you." And I suddenly feel a lot braver with her by my side. Mike grins and pulls out a newspaper.

Twenty-Nine

An icy wind seems to cut through me as I grab the huge brass door knocker and bang it against the oak door. Tara takes my hand and gives it an encouraging squeeze, then finally we hear the sound of footsteps getting closer and the rattle of a bolt being drawn back. The door slowly opens a crack and a small woman peers out at us.

"Yes?"

"I am James Wylie. I've come to see Angela. She is expecting me."

The woman frowns and looks at us as if she has no idea who I am talking about. "Do you mean Angel?" she asks. "There's no-one called Angela here but there is an Angel." For some reason she must have changed her name but this seems close enough; if I want to see her I have to get pass this gorgon.

"Yes, Angel then," I agree.

"Oh well, you'd better come in out of the cold then. I think she is in the kitchen."

We follow her inside and find ourselves in a large, square hallway with black and white tiles on the floor and a huge, rather ugly black staircase which rises up over us. Down the rather gloomy corridor there's a closed door at the end, but it opens onto a brighter, warmer world where the smell of baking makes my mouth water. This is the heart of the house with a happy feel to it; there are several adults and children here plus a lot of laughter. But then the room falls silent as we are noticed standing in the doorway.

A plump woman with wild, long dark hair looks over at us and my heart misses a beat. It's Angela. I feel my mouth drop open in shock because she looks nothing like the girl I was engaged to. Back then she was a pale, skinny and rather solemn creature but this version is tanned and healthy-looking, with a lot of curves to her figure. There's flour on her cheek and an apron around her waist. Her eyes widen as she recognises me.

"James!" she exclaims. The silence in the room makes me think that everyone here knows all about me and I'm not welcome here. I'm sure the temperature has dropped several degrees.

"Hello, Angela … er, Angel. How are you?" I mutter as I can't think what else to say.

"I'm very well, James, thank you. Very well. Come and sit down and have a cookie." She holds out a plate of still warm chocolate chip biscuits as all around us people get up and usher children out of the room until there is just Angela, Tara and me left. "I'll put the kettle on," she says, "not that it's often off around here." I begin to realise that she is as nervous about this meeting as I am and this knowledge, strangely, calms me a bit. Tara smiles encouragingly to me and we take seats around the large oak kitchen table in the centre of the room. Angela looks at Tara and I realise I haven't introduced her, so I do and they smile tentatively at each other.

"Um … sorry," I babble on, "you look so different now. I don't think I would have recognised you in the street."

"It's the hair," she says, then laughs. "And I'm not that skinny, uptight and scared person I was when you last saw me." She notices my surprise. "You never knew that?"

"What were you scared of?" I ask, shaking my head.

"Being found out," she replies. "I was playing a role – the city businesswoman, you know, strong and independent and ballsy. Trouble is, that isn't me, not really. At heart I'm a country girl who loves to bake cookies and raise animals and grow vegetables." I feel my eyebrows rise up in surprise as I never knew this about her. She laughs again. "I've really shocked you, haven't I, James?" That's an understatement.

"Yes, you have. I never would have guessed."

"Then I must be a better actor than I thought," she sighs. "When you broke off the engagement, I was so sure you'd seen though me. I thought that was why you dumped me." I feel my cheeks going red and my palms sweat as I shake my head. I take a long drink of the tea she has made and then start on a cookie to hide my confusion. Tara's foot touches mine under the table and all at once I feel more calm again.

"No, I never knew your secret. I broke off the engagement because I was a shallow, selfish bastard who felt trapped. So I panicked. I'm here now to say I'm so sorry for hurting you, Angela."

"It's Angel now," she smiles. "And James, it's fine, it really is," she continues, looking deep into my eyes. "Oh, I'm not saying it didn't hurt at the time and it wasn't humiliating and embarrassing, especially as we worked in the same place. I felt everyone was laughing at me behind my back. But in the end you did me a huge favour."

"I did?"

"Yes. It made me take a good hard look at my life and decide what I really wanted to do with the rest of it. I knew I'd never be myself in the City. I'm very happy now. I don't think I would be if I hadn't moved on." She goes on to describe how she fled London to stay with an aunt in Devon living on a farm she'd loved as a child, to have the peace and quiet she needed to sort things out. The aunt told her about Carnival so she visited – and stayed.

"So what exactly is this place?" I have to ask.

"It's home now," she says softly with a smile. "It's also an eco-community and a working farm, but it's so much more than that too."

"It's a very spiritual place," Tara says. Her voice surprises me as she hasn't said a word since we entered the house. Angela smiles at her.

"Yes, you're right, it is. It has a heartbeat that is so old and deep… I can't explain it in words."

"Anything spiritual is very hard to express. We find that a lot, don't we, James?"

Angela frowns at me but perhaps she's beginning to see that I have changed too. I suppose she's noticed the casual clothes I'm wearing and probably how thin I am now, yet there is so much more change that can't be seen so easily.

"Spiritual? You, James?" she asks and Tara grins at her.

"Yes, James has quite a talent for healing."

"Oh, don't exaggerate," I object. "It's only been two horses so far." Angela's face is a picture as both her eyebrows have disappeared under her unruly hair and her mouth has dropped open.

"James, healing? Really?"

"Yes, I've gone through a few life-changing months myself," I tell her.

"Then it's your turn to tell me," she says, leaning forward.

I'm reluctant to start, because my new beginning is sort of the end, a tragedy but not a total disaster. I decide that maybe it's best just to say it as it is. She gasps and puts her hand over her mouth when I tell her about the tumour. I go on to describe how the news made me sit up and look at my life – and what I needed to do with what's left since I didn't like what I saw when I looked closely at it. On the other hand, of course, I've struck lucky by finding two therapists who have opened my eyes to a world I never knew existed before, though Tara's more than that. I take her hand and kiss it and her eyes well up with tears, a sad smile on her face. Angela looks on and I catch a fleeting look of sympathy, not so much for me but for Tara. I carry on to describe exploring karma.

"Really, I'm surprised you even know what it is," Angela commented dryly.

"Yes, I've been in a different world. And I've been a bastard for way too long but now I am trying to make amends."

"And that's why you wanted to see me?"

"To say 'sorry', yes – and before you say anything about this not being a completely selfless act, I know, and I ask you to forgive me for that, too."

"Okay, I just might," she says, wrinkling up her nose and smiling.

"I do regret how I treated you, honestly. It was callous and totally selfish. I just wasn't ready to commit to anyone and I was terrified of the responsibility. The thought of having children scared me to death, too. I'd be a useless parent and I was afraid I might turn out like my father and hit them." I shudder at the thought.

"Your father hit you? I never knew that. In fact, I knew very little about your family. The only one you ever mentioned was your mother but I never met her or even spoke to her on the `phone. Isn't it strange that I never asked you about your past?"

"No," I shake my head, "not really. I'm good at avoiding things I don't want to discuss." Tara nods in agreement. "Maybe that's why I just agreed to the engagement too, even though I was so unsure. I think I was hoping for a nice long engagement so I could get used to it but suddenly the date was booked and the countdown had begun. I should have told everyone to back off but I felt like I was being steamrollered into it and I panicked."

Her eyes are fixed in the middle distance, to another time and another life. After a while she agrees, "Yes, I know what you mean. My family really did get their teeth into it, didn't they, especially Mum. But I thought you loved me so it would all be alright in the end." I reach out and take her hand.

"I did love you – in my own shallow way. Please don't think I didn't. But I had never felt real love before, not from my family or from any other woman I'd dated. So I had no idea what love was or how I should feel. I missed you when you weren't around and I liked being with you, but that would never have been enough. Still, I behaved badly and I'm not surprised you had to get as far away from me as possible. I don't deserve your forgiveness but I still had to come to apologise."

"I'm glad you did, James, and I forgave you years ago." She gets up and takes our cups to the sink, turning the kettle on again as I rock back in my chair in surprise.

"You did?"

"Yes, though I did it for myself really. I didn't want to be a bitter because that eats you up inside. Anyway, I'm a much happier person now and that's down to you in a way, because I wouldn't have come here if we'd got married. And then I wouldn't have met Ryan."

"Ryan? Are you married now?"

"Yes I am, to a wonderful Irishman. We're very happy. It was three years ago and love at first sight." She pauses. "I never believed that was possible but it happened and now I couldn't be happier. Of course, he has always known about you. In fact, he'd like to meet you."

"Oh!" I exclaim, wondering how big Ryan is and whether he would hit a dying man. I look towards Tara and she squeezes my hand. "I'd love that," I say as enthusiastically as I can, though from both women's faces it's clear I haven't succeeded. Angela laughs and gets up.

"I promise he won't hurt you. James. He's as grateful to you as I am." It takes me a second to work that one out. "And I do believe you have changed. You must be someone very special, Tara, to have had this effect."

Tara smiles but shakes her head. "No, I can't take the credit. I just opened a few closed doors and James is the one who has put in the hard work. There's still more to do."

"I'm a work in progress," I tell them.

Angela grins and pours us all more tea, taking down an extra cup before going to the door. "Stay here, then, and I'll get them."

Suddenly I have butterflies doing cartwheels in my stomach and I don't know why, but something big is about to happen.

"This is going to be good," says the voice in my head.

"What?" I exclaim out loud. Tara jumps in surprise and looks at me. I tell her about the voice and her eyebrows rise. But she doesn't get time to comment because the kitchen door is opening again. We both turn towards it and the first person to appear is a young boy with black hair and blue eyes. I gasp as I look at him: I could be looking at myself, aged about five. Angela follows him into the room and behind her comes a ginger-haired man. This must be Ryan but I barely acknowledge his presence because I can't take my eyes off the boy.

"James," says Angela, "this is Jamie. He's your son."

Thirty

Tara gasps and squeezes my arm but I am unable to do anything as I'm frozen with shock. Angela nudges the boy towards me and he comes to my side. As our eyes meet something profound happens inside us; I know his mind and it's like our souls recognise each other. We have been together in many lifetimes, part of the same soul group. He returns my smile and then I open my arms and hug my son. There is a glow inside my chest, like my heart has finally opened completely and a huge weight lifted from my shoulders. I look at Angela and see tears in her eyes too as I let go of Jamie.

"Hello, son," I manage to say.

"Hi, Daddy," he replies with a smile. I nearly lose all composure at this and gulp down my tears, almost overwhelmed by the love I feel for this tiny person. I can't find the words to express it but it doesn't matter because I know he feels it too. Without any prompting he climbs onto my lap and somehow it feels right for him to be there. Finally I drag my gaze away from him and turn to Angela.

"Why didn't you tell me?" I ask her and there's sadness on her face.

"I don't know really. I didn't find out until after I'd left London – just thought I was late because of the stress, never thought I could be pregnant. But I was feeling tired all the time so my aunt took me to the doctor, who took one look at me and said 'Congratulations, you're pregnant'. I nearly fainted with the shock. Well, we had broken up so I had to make some decisions immediately. There was no way I could live without my baby and luckily my aunt was over the moon and insisted

I stayed on with her. She was a tower of strength, with me all the way through it all. Becoming a mother was quite a shock."

"I bet," Tara agrees. Now, Angela still hasn't really said why she hadn't told me about Jamie, but Tara gives my hand a squeeze again as if she knows this and wants me to let it go.

Angela goes on to describe coming to Carnival when the boy was about nine months old and meeting Ryan a year later when he came to help repair the nearby mill. She looks across at him and I do the same, finally seeing him properly for the first time. He is shorter and stockier than I am, with short, ginger hair and a round, ordinary but pleasant face with pale blue and friendly eyes.

"Love at first sight," he says, moving round the table and giving her a hug.

"This place seems to do that to people," Tara says.

"Aye, you're right. It might look forbidding on a grey day like today but in the summer it's Heaven," Ryan tells her. I'm not sure about that but I can see the attraction of living in a spiritual community. So many of us live alone, separate and lonely without a place we truly feel we belong to. Living in a community must be like having a large, extended family around you – except that you can choose the people to be in it rather than being born into it.

Never in my wildest dreams when I got up this morning would I have imagined that I'd be meeting my son. He is leaning against me now with his eyes closed and I can't get over how much he looks like me. I trust that Ryan loves him as his own because a boy needs a father's love, something I never had; I know that some of my emotional problems come from never having had a father who cared a damn about his children. It saddens me to think I won't be around to help and support him. I've already missed his first five years and this may well be the one and only time we'll meet. Having his small head pressed against my body feels, well, wonderful. I stroke his head and his eyes open and we exchange grins. Angela's voice breaks in.

"Jamie, why don't you take James on a tour of the house?"

He nods, jumps down from my lap and takes my hand. It feels so small and fragile in mine. I get up and glance at Tara who is looking a little anxious, so I smile reassuringly to show her I'm fine. I'm not sure if I am though as it's been quite a day and not over yet. I have very little experience with young children, so how am I going to cope with one of my own? We leave the kitchen and return to the foot of the massive staircase.

"I'll show you my room," he says. He points up the stairs. I take a deep breath as we begin to climb and by the time we get to the top I'm out of breath and feeling old. On the landing there are four doors that look like normal house front doors; I'm intrigued with the layout of the place from a property developer's point of view.

"Are these separate homes, Jamie?"

"Yes, we live here." He points to a blue door. "Kerry and Tim live there, the red door. The Smalls live in that one, the green one. And the Joneses lives in the other one." The last door is yellow. He leads me proudly to the blue door and we go in, where Jamie disappears into his own room. I hesitate at first, feeling like I'm intruding, but he comes back out and smiles up at me so I step inside his small bedroom. My eye doesn't linger on the furniture, instead it is taken by the large brass and wooden telescope that stands next to the window, almost as big as Jamie. The posters covering the walls are images from the Hubble telescope, beautiful pictures of nebulae and galaxies with ethereal colours and shapes. As a boy I had also spent many hours looking at the stars, though through my father's binoculars, trying to identify the different constellations.

"Wow, this is a beauty," I say as I run my hand along the telescope, feeling how smooth it is. Jamie smiles proudly.

"It was my grandfather's. He gave it to me for my birthday." I nod, remembering Angela's father as a bit of a scholar.

"You're a lucky young man to have such a beautiful thing. I had to make do with my Dad's old binoculars."

We move slowly together along one of the walls and Jamie explains the various space images. He's really knowledgeable for such a young man and clearly passionate about his hobby. And I don't know if it's looking into the universe that does it, but there's a peaceful and spiritual feeling developing between us. Something has to be said.

"You are my Daddy, aren't you?" he asks at last, solemnly.

"Yes, Jamie, I am …" Then I pause before asking, "How do you feel about that?"

It's a question I'm also asking myself so what do I expect from a five year old? But he looks up at me and grins.

"I'm happy you've come. I knew you would. Mammy has pictures of you and told me you're my Daddy. And she named me after you." He pauses, then says, "I love you."

I nod dumbly, feeling stunned, though I can feel my heart leap with joy and tears beginning to come into my eyes. The love I feel for him is total and as strong as the love I have for Tara, but also very different. For so long my life has been devoid of all love and now it's overflowing, which is very strange. This is very emotional but I don't want to cry in front of him. And how on Earth can I tell him that I am dying?

We have only just met and maybe I won't see him again. I know my time is short. Today is a good one for me but there are fewer of them, even with all the healing Tara is giving me, and I know I am losing the battle.

"Jamie, I wish I had come years ago so we could have got to know each other," I begin. He nods at me, his large eyes looking straight into mine, so I take a deep breath and continue. "I came here today to see your Mammy and to say 'Sorry' to her because I was mean to her before you were born. Do you understand?"

"I'm naughty sometimes," he says simply and I have to smile at how matter-of-fact he is.

"The other reason I have come now is … that I'm not very well." He frowns and takes hold of my hand and this time I can't stop the tears coming. One runs down my cheek.

"But you will get better. I know," he insists. I look down at his young, innocent face and see wisdom in it like I have never seen before. A shiver runs though me under the intensity of his gaze and the certainty in his eyes; it is as if he can see my soul and knows everything about me. And for a brief moment I believe him. But then logic kicks in and that spark of hope is extinguished.

"No, Jamie the illness I've got is very bad and it'll take a miracle for me to beat it."

"Then I will get you one," he says, just like that.

"I wish you could. But only God can give out miracles."

He thinks hard then says, "I'll ask Him for one for you, Daddy."

I gulp down my tears as his innocence touches me deeply. "Thank you, Jamie," I just about manage to say, gulping back tears. "Maybe if you ask He will give me one. I don't want to be sick because I want to see you grow up. You're going to be a fine young man so I'll try my hardest to get better, I promise you."

There seems to be a steely strength in him that I wish I possessed. He may only be five but his soul is ancient and very strong. His hand is burning in mine now and there is an energy pulsing between us. My head starts to swim and for a few seconds I see a vision of a battlefield; instantly I know that I was an English soldier at Agincourt and fighting beside me was my best friend William, a tall blond man whose soul now lives in Jamie. I open my eyes to find Jamie smiling at me and I know that he has also seen what I have just witnessed.

"You saved me once before, didn't you?" I ask him.

He just nods again and I shiver as this is so weird. I am his father but I feel like the child in this relationship because his soul is so much older and wiser than mine. He has skills I can't begin to comprehend but somehow I do know that he will be a great healer and teacher – just what our troubled world needs. I so wish I could be around to see it.

"You're a wonderful boy and you're going to do great things, Jamie. Don't let anyone ever tell you different. Okay?"

"Okay, Daddy," he grins cheerfully.

"Good, then let's go back downstairs and see if there are any more cookies, shall we?"

"Okay."

So James is a father and somehow she isn't as surprised about that as he obviously is. In a recent meditation she had been shown a boy, the image of Jamie, and knew he was coming into her life. He really does look like a young James and she's so pleased that they have met before it's too late.

In a way, she envies Angel a little as she would have loved to have a child with James; but unless there's a miracle that will not happen. A thought sudden comes into her mind: 'Be careful what you wish for'. No, wishing it would come true won't make it happen. She knows this from past experience. But at least James has a child and she knows he will bring him great joy.

In the kitchen we find Ryan, Angela and Tara have moved on from tea to a bottle of something and I notice a camera on the table that hadn't been there before.

"I thought we should take some photos to celebrate Jamie meeting his dad," Angela says brightly, but her eyes look a little red to me as if she's been crying. They've probably been discussing my condition.

"Great idea," I agree, "but my thinking is a bit muddy lately." Then I frown because I didn't mean to say that, I meant 'muddled'. It seems that I'm not only slurring words, I'm getting them mixed up as well. What's next, total gibberish? What a joy that will be. I also wonder how much longer I'll be able to keep writing this account – but I have to, it might just help someone else when I'm gone. And it will be a way for my son to get to know more about me too. I look around, embarrassed, but only Tara appears to have noticed my gaff.

"Come and sit on this bench, James. And Jamie, you sit next to him," Ryan instructs us as he picks up the camera and follows us across the room to the wooden bench. I normally avoid having my picture taken as I never like the results, but this time I am more than happy to oblige. So I do as I'm told and put my arm around Jamie who looks up at me with a cheeky grin and there's a flash as the camera goes off.

"Why don't you join us?" I suggest to Angela and she smiles and sits next to Jamie. Once again the flash goes off and we are captured for posterity. Now I look across at Tara as I'd really like one with her in it too; Angela notices my gaze and waves Tara over to take her place in the line-up. But this time the flash hurts my eyes and for an instant the world tilts sideways and I have to take a deep breath, waiting for the dizziness to pass. A small hand touches my face and I feel a tingling all around my head; it is quite strong and seems to be helping because the world is now coming back on an even keel.

"James, are you alright?" I hear Tara's voice, a bit distant. Then slowly I open my eyes to see Jamie standing in front of me, his hands on each side of my head, and it is his energy that I can feel running though me. Our eyes meet and once again I see the old soul staring back at me as he grins and takes his hands away.

"Thank you, son," I say softly and he nods. Tara is looking at me with concern and I have to admit that I do feel incredibly tired now. It's been a long day and I need to rest soon – but I don't want to leave my son.

"James, be sensible," she says, sensing my feelings. "It has been a busy day for you with a few surprises along the way." She grins as she looks at Angela and Jamie. "And you have to look after yourself. So it's time for you to go home and get some rest."

"Yes, Tara's right," says Angela. "Don't worry, we're coming up to London to see the Christmas lights in a couple of weeks so we can all met up again then."

I suspect they have already arranged this in my absence but I am overjoyed because I'll get to see my son again. I give Jamie a big hug; he smells wonderful and I don't want to let him go, but I must so I release him and look him in the eye.

"Have you ever been to London, Jamie?" He shakes his head. "Oh, well you're going to love it and the shop windows are beautiful at Christmas. It's like Wonderland." His eyes grow big and round.

"Like Disney?"

"Yes, but even better," I reply.

"Wow!" he says, eyes gleaming, and everyone laughs.

Thirty-One

It actually takes me several days to recover from the strain that the trip to Wales took on me but by Friday I am feeling strong enough to do what I have to do. So I ring Craig's office and make an appointment to change my Will next Wednesday morning. After I've put the `phone down I sit at my dining table to work out exactly what I want to change since I now have a son to consider and include in my Will. And then there's Tara. She has done so much for me and given me unconditional love, which is a precious gift that no-one has ever given me before. I wish I could repay her with a lifetime of love and happiness; but that is impossible so I shall have to settle for something I can give her – simple money. I know how much she'd love to go to South Dakota and train with Ray Trees, so I can make that dream come true at least. She deserves so much more than just money but I can't provide it.

I also have to tell Mam about my illness. I really can't put it off any longer but the thought of driving all the way down to Lambourn is just not on. I suppose I could ring Mike and see if he'd like a bit more driving work … or I could just `phone her. I know, that's the coward's way out, but I need to do this soon. I guess there is no time like the present so I sigh and pick up the receiver again.

"Hello?" she says softly. I am convinced she's a little frightened by the telephone.

"Hello, Mam, it's James."

"Oh, son, it's lovely to hear your voice. I was going to ring you this weekend and tell you how happy I am with the redecorating. It looks

so posh now and I just love showing everyone what I've had done."
The sale has gone through quickly and I've arranged for some modernisation. I smile as I can just imagine the scene, Mam escorting her
old cronies around like a tour guide in a stately home, pointing out all
the new mod cons that she has at her disposal now that the bathroom
and kitchen have emerged out of the Dark Ages. I did make a fair bit
by selling her hideous 1970s furniture on eBay and that helped offset
some of the costs. Tara was horrified when she found out what I was
doing, but when the offers came rolling in she had to admit it was
worth the effort. Watching the bids on the computer reminded me of
the auctions I used to go to.

"Well, I'm glad you're happy with it. Is it all finished now?"

"Oh yes, Pat did the last bit on Tuesday. Are you coming to see it,
Jimmy?"

I now realise that I can't tell her I'm dying over the `phone. There
is also the news that I am a father and I can only show her the photographs that Angela emailed me in person. It also occurs to me that this
might be the last time I see her, so I swallow what I was going to say.

"Yes, Mam, I'd like that," I say instead. "Are you doing anything
this weekend?"

"No, son. Come on Sunday and I'll see if Trish and Terry can come
over too. I'll make lunch," she says and I cringe.

"Great," I reply ironically but she doesn't get that, she only hears
what she wants to hear. If I'd just told her on the `phone, I wouldn't
have to see my awful siblings. It's not a meeting I want to have at all.
Moreover, Mam has never been much of a cook. In fact, I am a lot
better than her and I don't think I can face one of her over-cooked
meals in my present state of health. "Ah … Mam, I'd like to treat you
to a nice meal out so you don't have to bother with cooking. I'll book
a table somewhere for us, okay?"

She objects, of course, that eating out is expensive but I manage to
persuade her eventually, wondering what I've got myself into. All I have
to do now is persuade Tara to come with me but I'm sure I won't have
to do much persuading as she is curious about my family, especially
my siblings. I find a nice restaurant near Lambourn which has just had

a cancellation so can fit us in, which is a bit of luck – although Tara would say it was meant to be.

Sunday comes around all too fast and I find myself once again snuggled up in the back seat of the Lexus with Tara as Mike heads for the M4. She starts to quiz me about my family.

"I don't really know how to describe my brother and sister," I shrug. "I don't know them very well myself. I left home as soon as I could and I've not been back much since. I don't have much in common with them at all; in fact, it's a wonder we came out of the same parents. I don't even look like them: they both have Mam's colouring and Dad's small stature, whereas I'm taller and dark."

"And you're the youngest?"

"Yep, the baby. I think that made it hard on Mam when I left, though she never tried to stop me. I think she knew I had to get away from Dad."

"So why you and not the others?"

"Maybe I just had more ambition then they did. Or perhaps they didn't mind being known as Paddy the Drunk's son. It is a very small town where everyone knows your business and gossip is the main sport."

She kisses my cheek and we lapse into a comfortable silence that gives me time to think more about my past. I may have become someone in the City and made a fortune but I am now sure that this really wasn't what I came down to Earth to do this time around. Somehow I got side-tracked into a career that I proved to be good at but which ultimately left me unfulfilled. Only in the last few months have I begun to know my true self and my vocation. It saddens me to think that I have so little time left to use these gifts for the good of others. Since visiting the racing yard I have worked alongside Tara as much as possible, learning and practising and it fills me with so much joy. How different my life would have been if I had found my path years ago; it almost feels as if I've been cheated, finding it now that I'm dying. Tara nudges me.

"What's the matter?" she asks, sensitive as ever, but I don't want to dwell on this so decide to lie when I answer her.

"I was wondering when I should tell Mam my bits of news … you know, do I do it as soon as we arrive and probably ruin the day or do it when we're leaving. What do you think?"

"I think if you tell her you're dying and then just leave, it would be cruel because she'll have questions once she gets over the shock. And it seems wrong to be giving her a grandson and then taking away her son. There probably isn't a good time so let's just play it by ear. I'm sure you'll know when the time is right."

"There's Terry and Trish too, they'll have to know though I don't see what it has to do with them."

"They're your family," she objects.

"I know, but otherwise we're strangers. If we weren't related, we wouldn't even be friends."

"But don't you think they'll be upset by the news?"

"No, I don't," I snort. "The only thing those two will think about is whether I'll leave them anything in my Will. They'll not get a bean. I know that if I did leave them money they'd only waste it – so it's going where it will do some good." Tara seems shocked by my attitude and a bit disapproving.

When we arrive, I invite Mike in to meet my mother but he says he'll be fine with his book and a flask of coffee in the car. I think he finds meeting new people difficult. I open the door for Tara and we turn to walk up the front path just as the door opens and Mam looks out, waving. I shiver, not looking forward to this, but there's no escaping it now. Then a second cup of tea and a tour of the improvements later, we sit comfortably in the front room and I have never seen Mam so happy. Tara smiles at her, then looks across at me and raises her eyebrows; I fear Mam has now run out of her news and is about to turn her attention to us. I have warned Tara of her obsession with getting me married off and producing even more grandchildren for her to cuddle.

"Now, my dear," she begins, "when did you and Jimmy meet?"

"Oh, it was early September."

"Really?" she exclaims, looking at me for an explanation.

"Tara is a dear friend and also…" I pause, wondering if this is the right time, and Tara nods at me to continue, "…my therapist."

"What do you mean, Jimmy? Are you ill?"

"Not exactly, Mam." I pause and try to smile. "I'm dying. I have a brain tumour." She gasps and her hands shoot up to her mouth, a look of disbelief and fear on her face as if I'm speaking a foreign language. I take her cold hands and give them a squeeze. She stares at me with unfocused eyes.

"How long?"

I'm not sure if she means how long I've got or how long I've known so I tell her both. "Well, I had some tests in the summer but they didn't know for sure until August. I didn't want to upset you before, Mam." She turns her head and looks me in the eye.

"Can't they take it out, Jimmy?"

"No, Mam, it's in an area they just can't get at." Tears have started to roll down her face now and I feel sick inside at being the cause of them. Tara hands me a tissue for her and she takes it with a nod.

"What am I going to do without you, Jimmy?" she says. "A parent shouldn't have to bury their child. It's not right. Or fair."

"No, Mam, it's not fair." I smile to take the sting out of my words and she leans forward to pat my hand.

"If you pray hard enough to the Virgin Mary, I'm sure she'll save you. But you still don't believe, do you?"

"Well, I have a different way. And I do get support from Tara and lots of other people."

"Yes, I can see that," she says, smiling at Tara. Then, like she always has done when she doesn't want to talk about something unpleasant, she simply changes the subject. "How is your business going, Jimmy, and how is Jenny?"

I realise that I hadn't even told her that I'd given up work so I bring her up to date with everything that's happened and reassure her that I'd had enough of that life anyway. Then Tara takes out the packet of photographs from her handbag and passes them to me; I guess she thinks that now is the time for some good news. I take a deep breath before continuing.

"Actually, we went to visit Angela the other day." Mam's mouth drops open in surprise. "She lives in Wales now."

"Oh, does she? I don't know why you ever broke it off with her. She was such a nice girl, Jimmy," she says accusingly and rather insensitively.

"That's water under the bridge, Mam. Anyway, she's happily married now." Her face falls at that news and I realise that she has been hoping I was going to say that we were getting back together. She hasn't recognised how important Tara is to me yet. "While we were there," I continue, "I got a lovely surprise." I take out my favourite photograph of me and Jamie and hand it to her, waiting for her reaction with a smile on my face.

"Jimmy… he is the image of you. Is he…?"

"Yes, he's my son, your grandson."

"Oh, Jimmy, he's beautiful." She beams at me and then asks, "What's his name?"

"Jamie, and he's five years old."

"She named him after you?"

"Yes, she did. And she has told him all about me too." I hand her the other pictures and see the surprise on her face as at last she recognises Angela.

"Oh my, she looks so different now. All that hair!" When she gets to the one of Tara, Jamie and me she says, "You look like a family."

I groan inwardly – she has to go and ruin it with her stubbornness that everyone should conform to the perfect family unit. I feel my irritation rising but manage to push it down; it really isn't worth fighting about since neither of us are going to change our views. Instead, I get out the piece of paper I had written Angela's address and 'phone number on, so that she knows where her grandchild lives when I am gone.

"Here, this is where Jamie is in case you want to contact him." She frowns, taking a few seconds to understand what I am implying, and then her eyes fill up with tears again.

"Oh, Jimmy, you're going to miss so much."

I know that, and I've already missed his first five years. Only now do I realise that I'm a little bitter about that; but at least I've got to meet him now and I can't wait until the 10th of December when they come to London so we can meet again. I have already booked tickets for the London Eye so he can get a bird's eye view over the capital. I tell my mother to keep the prints as I have another set and she holds them to her chest, a sad smile on her face.

"Thank you, Jimmy, I'll always treasure them."

I nod and try to suppress the urge to cry. Tara takes my hand and starts telling Mam about the farm and the community Jamie is living in, which gives me time to reign in my emotions. Just lately it has been all too easy to break down and start crying for no good reason. And I used to be renowned for my hard heart and ruthlessness.

Thirty-Two

The meal at the pub is good but there is much too much and my serving could have fed three people easily. Once back at Mam's we await the arrival of my siblings: what a joy this is going to be. A sharp knock cuts the silence that has descended on us and I exchange glances with Tara as Mam goes to open the door. I recognise the sharp tones of my sister Trish, then their voices lower and I guess Mam must be telling her about my tumour. I'm sure my dragon of a sister will be irritated with me because I'm sick; somehow she never has had any patience with me, maybe because I was often left in her care while Mam went to work and Dad was drunk. They do say that middle children are often resentful at being overlooked, neither the eldest nor youngest. I am not sure this is really the case, she's just not a nice person and she took her anger out on me.

Their footsteps approach the door and I am holding my breath as my sister walks in. But when I look her up and down I am shocked by her appearance and would not have recognised her. I remember her as small and thin, like Mam, with a trendy wardrobe and long, reddish-blonde hair and large earrings but standing in front of me now is an overweight woman with short, muddy-brown hair, wearing charity shop clothes.

"Hello Trish, how are you?" I manage. She sniffs – that bad habit, I do remember.

"Better than you by the sound of it."

"I told her, Jimmy," says Mam, looking sheepish.

"Yes, well, that's okay," I tell her. "She has to know."

Trish glances over at Tara but doesn't say hello, so her manners haven't improved either over the years. I fear this is going to be an awkward reunion and I'd love to take Tara's hand for support, but I don't want to alert Trish to how important she is to me.

With Tara there is no pretence, no need to be other than whom I am, warts and all, and I am so grateful for her uncomplicated love and support. But Trish wouldn't understand this as she was always a master manipulator. She once said to me that men were only good for two things, money and sex, as she left me alone to go on a date with an older man who took her to an upmarket restaurant which she then bragged about to her friends. She used him to get what she wanted then dumped him, which is how she treated all men. I was thirteen at the time and I've always remembered her words; perhaps it's not so strange that I did the same to the women who crossed my path.

The silence in the room lengthens as we all size each other up and try to think of something to say. I look over at Tara and roll my eyes and she smiles, then the door knocker makes me jump again and Mam gets up to answer it. It must be Terry now. Being eight years older than me, he never really had much interaction with me and we never played together or talked much. He should have been my hero, someone I could look up to, but he was too much like Dad, with no ambition or direction. Unlike Trish, I'd recognise Terry anywhere: he is short and thin with a tanned, weather-beaten face from working on the downs in all conditions. I get up and take his outstretched hand, looking him in the eyes that still have a twinkle.

"Hello, Jimmy," he says, his Berkshire accent strong.

"Hi. How are you and the family, Terry?" I ask, more out of politeness than actual interest.

"Oh, we're jogging along," he replies with a smile. Trish sniffs again.

"Then you're doing better than him." Terry frowns and looks around for an explanation. I open my mouth but she beats me to it. "He's come here to tell us he's dying. Nice of him, don't you think?" Sarcasm is dripping off her words but Terry's face drops and the colour drains out of it.

"No!" he exclaims, grabbing my arm, and I look at him in shock as he looks genuinely upset – which, frankly, is a hell of a surprise to me. "Jimmy, is this true?"

"I'm afraid so, well, that's what the doctors tell me. I have an inoperable brain tumour."

He winces and now I remember his terror of doctors and hospitals. Once when he was around nineteen he had to have an emergency appendix operation and as he was being taken away in the ambulance you could hear him screaming for them to stop and let him out. They had to sedate him just to get him to the hospital.

"Can't they do anything?" he asks and I shake my head. "So... how long have...?" He doesn't finish the sentence but he doesn't need to as I suspect they all want to know the answer.

"Not long," I tell them and Mam bursts into tears and rushes out of the room with Trish on her heels, throwing me a disapproving glare. Terry chuckles and then stops short.

"Sorry, I'm not laughing at you. It's Trish." He shakes his head. "She don't change, do she? Ah, I've often asked Tom why he married her. Says he loves her."

"He must," I reply with a shrug.

He then turns to Tara and says, "I'm sorry, m'love, I haven't introduced meself."

"That's all right."

"No, it's not. It's rude and I apologise. I'm Terry," he says as he wipes his hands down his trousers before offering it. She laughs and takes it.

"I know. And I'm Tara."

"Pleased to meet you, Tara." They exchange smiles and I'm going to have to explain why she is here with me. We had discussed earlier what to tell them and agreed to say that we are 'good friends'; but for some reason I want to tell Terry what she means to me. As Mam and Trisha are out of earshot I decide to risk it.

"Tara is my therapist... but also much more than that," I say. His eyebrows rise a little at that and a small smile appears on his face.

"Good for you," he says. "Do Mam and Trish know?" I shake my head. "Oh, I see." And I know he understands completely as he turns to Tara and says, "Well, I wish you well with me little brother. He were always a law unto 'imself. You look after 'im for us."

"I will, don't worry," she says as the door opens and the others return. Trish sniffs.

"So what happens now?" she asks me and I frown at her, unsure what she means. "You know, are you going into one of them hospices?" I gasp and feel like she has punched me in the stomach.

"God no, I'll die at home, thanks very much. I don't need any help doing it." Mam glares at Trish and this is enough to shut her up.

I've had enough of this inquisition now and I just don't have the will to fight; all I want to do is go home with Tara so I look at her and know she understands. She gets up and takes my arm as if to emphasise my invalidity and Mam and Terry get to their feet too. I shake Terry's hand again and turn to my mother.

"Sorry, Mam, but we have to go now. I have to rest and take my medication. It's been good to see you, Terry."

"Yeah, Jimmy, you too." He is a bit choked up so I turn to Trish.

"Bye, Trish."

"So long, Jimmy," she sniffs.

With that said, we make our way out to the car and Mike opens the doors for us. I turn and give Mam a hug and a kiss on the cheek but she is unable to speak to me. Instead, she turns to Tara and hugs her too.

"Look after my Jimmy for me?" she whispers.

The emotional strain of the trip home has affected me more than I had anticipated and I feel my strength ebbing away almost daily. Mam now rings me every day and Terry has started to ring me too. I must say I'm surprised by his reaction to my illness and feel sad that we have never taken the time to get to know one another. Perhaps we could have ended up as friends as well as brothers. Not so with Trish, whom I'm quite glad not to have to meet again. She has also rung me once, not to enquire about my health but to find out what I am going to do with my money! Really, does she have no shame? Sure, I have a ruthless streak too although I doubt I'd ever have stooped so low as to ask a dying man if I would get some of his money. It did cheer me up to think of her face when she hears my Will. I sometimes wonder how much karma that act has earned me but I've long given up hoping to be karma neutral by the time I kick the bucket; changing the habits of a lifetime isn't easy. On the other hand, I had a `phone call from Rodney the other day, thanking me for all the new business I'd sent his way, which was nice of him. He's even looking for bigger premises and has taken on another broker to cope with all the work. When I next meditated, I asked my guide Freizal if I had now cleared the karma I had with Rodney and she said yes. She added that this was also the case with Angela. Hurrah!

But the depressing thing is that I am now suffering more bad days than good ones and even with healing every day I can feel my life slipping away from me like the sand in an hourglass. It's strange, I thought I'd be frightened by this but for some reason I'm not. I just seem to know now that it will be fine and that there is something better on 'the other side', where the pain I am suffering now will no longer exist. At times this pain is unbearable and I actively look forward to escaping from it; I have found that there is something worse than death and it's all too real.

I'm so much more aware now, too, of how much suffering there is in the world and Tara and I talk about it a lot. I find it very hard to hear of good people having their lives torn apart by illness or by the evil of others, while some truly nasty people breeze through life and seem to get away with it. Tara laughs at my righteous anger and reminds me that no-one gets away with anything.

"Karma – remember?" she tells me. Of course she is right and I have to remind myself that I am only responsible for my own karma and not to take on anyone else's.

Craig has finally completed the changes I wanted to my Will. Jamie will have a million pound trust fund, so he will never have to worry about money when he's older and can concentrate on finding his true life purpose. Tara will also have a nice surprise when the Will is read.

Today is December the 10th and Jamie is coming to London. I am
praying for a good day so that he doesn't remember me as a sick and
weak man. I've woken to find a cold but bright morning in the capital
which will be perfect for our trip on the London Eye. The views from
the top will be superb. We are due to meet them at 11.30 so I lie back
in bed and try to assess how I am feeling. I know from bitter experience
that I can start out feeling quite strong but all of a sudden my strength
can desert me and I collapse in an undignified heap. I really don't have
any control over this. I turn and look at Tara's beautiful face next to me
as she slowly opens her eyes.

"Good morning, gorgeous," I say and she smiles.

"How are you feeling today, handsome?" she asks.

"Okay for now."

"Well, we have plenty of time for some healing before we have to go."

"Great, then I better get myself into gear and get up."

Thirty-Three

I search the crowds of people around us for Jamie and shiver in the bitter cold, the weak winter sun not having much effect, and I move from foot to foot trying to keep warm. It also releases some of my anxiety as stress is likely to bring on my symptoms.

"Calm down, their train was probably late – you know how it is," Tara smiles.

"Yes, but what if they've had an accident or they're not coming?"

"Then I'm sure they would let us know. Angela does have your number. I know how you feel and I promise it will be a day for him to remember." She squeezes my arm. I am so lucky to have someone who understands that this will probably be the last time I see him. "There they are!" Tara says suddenly and points to the knot of people coming towards us.

Jamie spots us first and runs to meet us. I open my arms to catch him and give him a hug, breathing in his smell and trying to imprint it on my mind before I have to let him go. I'd love to hold him like this all day.

"Are we late, Dad?" he asks, his blue eyes shining brightly.

"No son, you're right on time," I tell him, trying desperately to keep tears from my eyes as just hearing him call me 'Dad' almost makes me lose all control. As usual, Tara comes to my rescue and takes over to give me time to pull myself together.

"Did you enjoy the train journey, Jamie?" she asks him. He turns to her and nods.

"Oh yes, it was cool."

Angela and Ryan reach us and soon it's time to join the queue for the Eye. I hold out my hand to Jamie and a warm glow fills me when he takes it. There are already quite a few people waiting even on this cold winter's day and from the look of them most are foreign students. The queue starts to move forward and before long we are ushered inside our glass capsule, ready to begin our slow journey. I start pointing out landmarks like St Paul's and Buckingham Palace to him and Jamie bounces up and down on his toes in infectious excitement. As we rise up over the glittering River Thames he gasps at the beauty of the Palace of Westminster, the shining sun making the stone look almost like gold, and we all stare at it in reverent silence.

"Cool," Jamie whispers and I have to agree.

"Yes, it's cool."

Our trip is over all too soon and we are ushered out again into the cold. We hurry to the Tube station and Jamie sits on my lap on the train, all wide-eyed and interested in everything. It is a day of firsts for him and I am so glad I can be part of it. Then we head for a themed restaurant that I think Jamie will enjoy as it is designed for kids. We enter and his eyes grow wider as he recognises characters from children's books and TV shows and he grabs my hand and starts talking very fast, pointing out the ones he likes best for me. Angela, Ryan and Tara sit at our table smiling as I get dragged around the restaurant by this over-excited five year old who is determined to tell me everyone's story. I don't mind one bit and I nod a lot as he looks from one character on the walls to another; it seems I'm not required to do anything but listen, which is fine by me as I have never heard of any of them. Finally he is satisfied and we can join the others. Angela decides it's time to reign him in.

"Now, Jamie, settle down and have something to eat."

I sit back and watch my son happily getting ketchup all over his face and hands as he eats his vegeburger, while I pick at my food – nothing tastes very good these days. After lunch we start to walk along streets looking at the Christmas windows and the street lights but the displays seem rather minimalist and commercial.

"They always used to be magical and beautiful," I observe to Tara, "but now…"

"Well, Mandy told me that Harrods' windows are really lovely this year."

"Right, let's go up to Knightsbridge, then."

We take a taxi this time so that I don't get too tired but Jamie still looks like he is having fun, his face glued to the window. It is beginning to get darker outside now which does make the street decorations look better, much more as I remember things used to be. I guess that over the years everyone loses their enthusiasm and the joy of this time of year under the pressure of buying presents and paying for it all; as we age, reality sets in and with it cynicism. Tara squeezes my arm.

"How are you feeling?" she asks me.

"Old," I tell her with a smile.

When we arrive, Jamie is so full of life and wants to skip down the road ahead of us and, because of the crowds, there is an anxiety in me that I have never felt before. It is amazing how many new feelings this little person has introduced into my life and I am so relieved when Angela runs after him and brings him back. But his pleasure at all the sights around him makes me happy and lifts my spirits too. He wants to look at all the shop's windows so it takes us a while and by the time we get to the last one I am frozen to the bone again and need sustenance. There's a coffee shop across the road.

"Anyone ready for a coffee and a cake?" I ask and we all hurry over to the oasis of warmth. We pile in like explorers from the North Pole and manage to get a table where a pretty blonde waitress comes over to take our order of coffees, orange juice and an assortment of cakes.

Slowly I begin to feel some warmth creeping back into my extremities and it makes me feel a little sleepy. It has been quite an exhausting day for me and I have missed my usual nap after lunch, but I'm pleased that I've managed to keep going. Very soon Jamie will be leaving to get the train back to Wales and it saddens me to think that we probably won't meet again in this lifetime. If what Tara says is true, we will always be connected by an unbroken tie that binds all of us in this soul group… but I'd still prefer the chance to be his Dad this time around.

It is strange to think that only six months ago I hadn't even thought about life after death, yet now I am really beginning to understand that we never die. The body, yes, but the spirit… or whatever… never does. And finally I feel content with who I am; although I'd like more time to experience these new feelings, I know I have learned a few valuable lessons this time around. A small, warm hand takes mine and brings me back into the coffee shop to find Jamie looking up at me with a puzzled look on his face.

"What kind of illness have you got, Dad?" he asks me. The chatter around our table suddenly stops and everyone looks at me. Angela nods slightly, to tell me it's all right.

"It's not so good, Jamie. I have a tumour." He frowns and I could kick myself – how would a five year old know what a tumour is? "That's something that grows inside you where it shouldn't and it does a lot of damage," I try to explain.

"But it can come out, can't it?" he asks. He looks at his mother who shakes her head.

"No, love. It's not like Max's tonsils, this is worse. Your Dad can't have it taken out because the doctors can't get to it."

He opens his mouth as if to ask another question but pauses and then says instead, "Rupert says you don't have to go yet. There's more work for you to do if you want to." I feel my mouth drop open in surprise and I look at Angela for an explanation of this extraordinary statement. She smiles back at me.

"Rupert is Jamie's imaginary friend."

"Oh!" I exclaim and look at Tara who is smiling. I nod and smile too as we know all about 'imaginary friends'. This is probably Jamie's guide who comes to him as a playmate so as not to frighten him, so I squeeze his hand.

"Will you thank Rupert for me and tell him I'll remember what he said." He nods and gives me a look that confirms he knows very well who Rupert really is.

All too soon it is time for them to go or they will miss their train home so we leave the warm café, hail a taxi and I take the opportunity to have Jamie sit on my knee again. Once we reach the station I give him a final hug and watch him head off down the platform between Angela and Ryan. They all turn around and wave as they reach their carriage and I watch my tiny son disappear. It feels like my heart is breaking and all the tears I have been holding in all day now begin to run down my face. Tara puts her arms around me and kisses my cheek.

"He will be fine," she whispers. "He is a special child and lucky enough to live with people who will help him become all he is meant to be." I know she is right but it still hurts; I wipe away my tears and try to compose myself as a few people around us are looking. "After all," she continues, "maybe Rupert will turn out to be right. Miracles do happen. I've seen them with my own eyes."

We sit is silence during the journey home and I keep thinking about what Rupert said. 'Do I have a choice?' I wonder.

Thirty-Four

I am frustrated by how long it takes me to recover from our day out but it was worth it. Soon it will be Christmas and Tara and I are going to buy Jamie a Christmas present today. There are now only ten days to go so we're cutting it a bit fine. I also need to buy something for Mam although as usual I haven't a clue what to get; but this year I have someone to steer me in the right direction of what she would like.

I hope Tara likes the present I have for her. Jeremy has an old school friend who is now a well-known jewellery designer so Jeremy took me to his studio where I ordered a bracelet for her. She loves Art Nouveau and I designed a frieze of our names intertwined with flowers that represent undying love. I say that I designed it… maybe that's a bit of a stretch: I told Tony what I wanted and he drew up some designs for me to choose from. It is made of white and yellow gold with small diamonds, emeralds and rubies in the flowers and I think it's beautiful – the most romantic gift I have ever given. Probably the last one as well. The sound of her key in my front door brings me back to the present.

"James, are you ready? The taxi's waiting."

"Yes, all set, credit card in hand," I tell her. She laughs and gives me a kiss.

"Good, then let's hit the shops."

We start with Mam's present and I discover that Tara is a detective as well as a healer when she tells me the perfume my Mam loves but cannot afford.

"Really?" I exclaim, as this is news to me. "How did you find that out?"

"That's my secret," she tells me with a smile. I leave it to her to find the right perfume and then we move on to Hamleys, probably the most famous toy shop in the world. It is certainly huge and I'm at a loss to know where to start; perhaps I should have rung Angela to get some ideas of what he'd like before setting out on this expedition. We stand by the escalator looking at the floor listing, trying to figure out where to start. I turn to Tara who appears just as puzzled as me.

"Well, do you have any ideas?"

"No," she shakes her head. "I never realised this place had so many departments."

"Right, then, pick a floor."

"How about three?" She grins. "My lucky number."

"A good enough reason," I agree and take her hand as we fight our way through the crowds. But when we get to the third floor we can see at a glance that these toys are not suitable for a five year old. I mop my brow free of sweat. It is hot and stuffy in here and I hate crowds anyway and can feel myself getting panicky inside. I need to get out of here as soon as possible. Tara grabs a passing salesman and asks where we would find toys for fives.

"One floor down," he replies, barely stopping as he rushes off with his arms full of teddy bears. We retrace our steps but the sheer volume of people forces us apart and somehow I get pushed into the upward line; before I can do anything about it I am heading to the fourth floor. I manage to see Tara heading the right way and gesticulate to her that I'll meet her down there; this place is rapidly becoming my idea of Hell. However, on reaching the top I immediately spy something that I know Jamie will like. There's a display of globes, not just the Earth but other celestial ones too, and thankfully there aren't so many people around here and I can get close enough to have a good look at them. I remember Jamie's room with his star maps and telescope and I am sure he'd love these.

"Can I help you, sir?" a voice asks me and I turn to find a salesman, about thirty, dressed in a smart suit and somehow managing to look impeccable amid all the bustle. I point out a celestial globe that shows the night sky. "Ah, yes, sir. These are new in. There is a microchip inside so when you push this button here…" he demonstrates and the constellation of Orion lights up, "…you can illuminate different constellations, to learn which stars belong where. It also comes with an illuminated star map book that can be used outdoors and a Hubble telescope calendar for next year." He has sold it to me.

"That sounds perfect. Does it need batteries?"

"Either mains or batteries, sir," he replies.

"Good, I'll take it. Can you gift-wrap it for me?"

As I wait at the counter where three assistants are busy wrapping presents, there's a gentle hand on my arm and I turn to find Tara smiling at me.

"There you are," she says.

"Sorry, my love, I got distracted. But I have found the perfect gift for Jamie – look."

"Oh yes, he'll love it."

I open my mouth to speak but a flash, like that of a camera, hits me in the eyes and blinds me with its intensity. I stagger to remain upright as another light explodes in my face, this one accompanied by the pain of a dagger striking me above the temple. It is so intense and sudden that I only have time to gasp before it hits again and I am engulfed in a terrible, hot stabbing pain that is unbearable. Far away somewhere I hear a scream but I don't know whether it's me, then my legs fold up under me and I tumble to the floor where I am swallowed up in a misty netherworld.

Everyone can hear the scream of pain, even over the hubbub in the shop. Her heart almost stops as she kneels at his side.

"He has a brain tumour. Call an ambulance," she says calmly to the salesman as she takes James' hand.

"I've already done it," says the young man with a reassuring tone, kneeling next to her. "But I don't know if it's safe to move him from here." She thinks quickly and realises how long it would take the paramedics to get him out if they have to get up to this floor. If he can be taken downstairs he would get the help he needs a lot faster.

"We need to carry him down to where the ambulance will arrive, right now," she orders.

To her relief the man nods calmly and waves to someone who comes over to see what's needed. She looks up to see a huge security guard with the look of an ex-soldier, who takes in the situation at a glance. She tells him what's needed and with just a nod of agreement he bends down and picks James up as if he were a child, carrying him to the service lift which gets them to the ground floor in seconds.

Their journey to hospital is one of panic and fear for her and later she only remembers fragments of it, just the agonising wait to see if he'll survive. She hopes never to have to live through such a terrible nightmare again.

All I can see around me is a white mist. I don't understand – only a moment ago I was in the toy shop, so where has it gone? Somewhere in the distance I can hear a voice and I strain my ears as it slowly becomes clearer. It's Tara and she's shouting, "Help him, please!" I try to call out to her but I don't think she can hear me as there's no answer. I'm confused. I look around this misty place and I haven't a clue where I am or what is going on and wherever this is I don't like it.

"Is anyone here? Can anyone help me?" I ask in a whisper, not sure who or what might reply. There's no response but instead a tiny pinprick of golden light appears ahead of me and as I watch it begins to grow bigger and bigger until it is as large as a tunnel. A tunnel? "Oh, my God. THE tunnel. I must be dead."

Everything makes sense now. For so many reasons, I really don't want to go now because I have found a real purpose at last and people I love. But I also know that if this is my time then there is nothing I can do about it. I try to look along it but it is too bright, all I can see is light, and now I feel myself moving forward against my will as if I am being sucked into a vortex.

"No, wait please. I want…" I begin to protest, but then a feeling of bliss envelops me and all of a sudden whatever I was going to say doesn't matter at all. Around me is such love and warmth that everything else is irrelevant. I remember it now, this feeling. It is home. It is the place of eternal spirit, where I am safe and unconditionally loved. I know I have been here many times before, this world of spirit… or nirvana… or Heaven… and nothing in my physical life comes close to this experience except perhaps my feelings for Tara and Jamie. This is the only thing that means anything; all the rest is illusion. Then as I continue along the tunnel I feel a presence around me and know I am not alone.

"I have always been with you," a familiar voice says.

"Freizal?" I ask.

"Yes, I am here. I am never far away."

"Where are you? I can't see you."

"Nor I you, but it doesn't matter. We are linked by energy. Your eyes are down there." Instinctively, I look down and get a shock. Far away I can see myself, or what looks like me, being hurriedly wheeled along a corridor on a hospital trolley with a lot of people around my body working on it. I see tubes in my arm and someone is pushing on my chest.

"Is that me?"

"No, not really, it is just the vehicle you used for James Wylie's life. But it's not you." I look again at the hospital scene but for some reason it doesn't upset me.

"I do feel regret," I tell her. "But why don't I feel sad?"

"Aaah, regret. Well, now is a good time to express it. But be quick about it." Her words confuse me and she laughs. "Let me explain. In the spirit worlds we are mostly unaware of the passing of time but when someone returns from the physical world there can be a brief window of opportunity for them to make some important decisions. You have this opportunity now."

"Decisions? I don't understand."

"Yes, you do," she replies.

There's another flash of blinding light and I feel as if I am moving backwards until the light fades and I find myself at a meeting with Freizal who is agreeing to be my gatekeeper, or guide. I have just chosen my life's lessons, the things I need to experience and learn, and there are a lot of other choices too such as my parents and friends, those who will help me achieve my goals and those who will challenge me. My so-called enemies will be other members of my soul group who have agreed to teach me the hardest lessons; in life I shall probably perceive them as 'bad people' but in reality they are my greatest friends who love me the most.

I can see the whole picture so clearly now. It is like a huge spider's web with each of us connected to one another, helping each other and learning from each other. When we incarnate we shall appear to be separate people but in reality we are all one being, like single drops of dew on the spider's web, individual and yet connected to each and every other dewdrop on the web. We each have our place on this web and however much we might struggle against it and fight our destiny, we cannot leave the web. That is impossible as we are part of it. We are one inside of the One who created us all.

It is so clear to me now. I realise that I intended to be a healer but then fought against this instinct, which brought unhappiness on myself. I see that I chose to have a child and lose him. But I also know that these decisions made before birth are not set in stone and can be altered by free will. Life is not meant to be easy, but we make a lot of our problems for ourselves. So my biggest regret is that I didn't remember all this earlier. I could have saved myself a lot of grief.

"I did try to reach you, many times," Freizal says.

"I know that now. I just wasn't ready to listen. I wish I had." There are so many possibilities, so much left unexplored and unfinished. "I wish I could go back and do some more." There is a short silence.

"You may be able to."

"What?" I exclaim, "But I'm dead, aren't I?"

"Not quite. You are in a place of recognising."

"A what?"

"Listen, you don't have long to decide what you want to do, stay in spirit or return to your body."

"I want to go back," I reply immediately.

"Yes, you are so impatient," she sighs reproachfully. "It's one of the lessons you still need to work on. But... there are consequences if you do decide to go back." I don't like the sound of that but for once I keep quiet and let her continue. "Your body has suffered because of your choices. The stress of resisting your true calling contributed to the tumour for one thing. That is still there and cannot be removed completely – but you have been working hard towards returning to your path and you've accepted healing too. So it has reduced and should not be too much of a problem – if you continue in the right way."

I am stunned. "So what happened today?"

"The tumour can be reduced by you making new choices and by our healing, but the pressure needed to be released. So if you do decide to return, things won't be easy or quick. It will take time and effort. But you will have the ability to heal."

She pauses again and I get a mental picture of myself learning how to walk and talk again. It isn't pretty. Still, it is another opportunity to learn and to grow spiritually – and it will certainly teach me a lot about patience and perseverance even though I know I will have a lot of help. It's ironic – I have always been a bit squeamish about disabilities and the disabled and I will be one of them if I go back.

I'm sure that I do want to go back and, just as I open my mouth to tell Freizal, the mist lifts around me and I find myself in a garden. It is no ordinary garden, however; this is perfection with no dead or dying plants, only colour and beauty.

"Where am I now?"

"You are in the healing garden," she tells me. I think that showing me the peace and beauty of this place is some kind of test, but it doesn't work.

"I want to go back and take my chances," I say quietly. "After all, I still have some karma to work on, don't I?"

"Oh yes," she chuckles, "though not as much as you once had. You're on the right path ... at last. My, you really have tried my patience at times. You might even have heard me weeping in quiet moments. Do you realise that being a guide to someone who neither knows nor cares that you exist is the most frustrating job in the universe?"

"Can't you interfere a bit if you see them making a big mistake?"

"Heavens, no! You have free will, it's your gift."

"Or curse," I mutter. So many opportunities wasted. So many mistakes.

"Indeed," she says. "This is what it means to be human. Well, James, your window of opportunity will be closing soon. Do you really want to be human? You could return to the spirit world now and have no pain – or return to Earth and those you love, having to regain your speech and learn to walk again. Remember that those who love you will also be affected by your difficulties. No-one lives in isolation. Consider what these people who love you want for you – to live with the problems life brings or to return to spirit and not be in pain. Is it better that you are with them than not?"

I hadn't thought of that. Can I put Jamie and Tara through it? It seems that even when you're nearly dead you still have hard decisions to make. I remember talking to Tara about this. She said that this life is a chance to take on the lessons we have to learn but if we don't then we'll reincarnate at another time to learn them. There's no right or wrong choice.

Thirty-Five

The white mist returns and through it I can just see my body in a bed with a lot of tubes and wires attached and monitors bleeping next to me. I get the feeling that the doctors are considering turning off the machines that are keeping me alive. From this distance, all those vanities we have about our bodies seem utterly irrelevant and silly as I realise that this body isn't me; but if I go back it will be my vehicle and will need a heck of a lot of work to get it up and running again.

"I'm going back," I tell Freizal.

"Good for you. Try to remember that I'm here to help you – all you have to do is ask."

Then I feel myself falling, slowly at first and then faster and faster until I seem to be in freefall. "Aaah…" I cry inwardly. I have never liked theme park rides. I close my eyes as I near my body and wait for a crash; but it never comes and instead I just feel a shock and became aware of my body again as if I'm putting on a heavy, damp overcoat. I have made my choice and now I must make the most of it. A door opens and I can hear voices nearby but when I try to open my eyes they seem to be stuck shut. Someone is checking the monitor beside me and I hear him grunt with surprise.

"These readings are… well…" He stops for a moment then says, "They're amazing."

"What do you mean?" I can hear Tara exclaim.

"Look, I don't know what has happened here but I'm going to order another scan to get a better idea."

"Are you saying he's coming back?" Tara asks.

"Well… if what I see on the monitor is borne out by the scan, then… yes, somehow."

I feel her take my hand and say, "That's my boy, James."

I glare down at my leg and feel so frustrated. I keep telling it to move but the bugger just won't respond. I have been back for a month now and it hasn't been much fun; but I knew that before I came back so I try to calm down. It seems that the drugs I've been taking have limited the damage and are helping in my recovery, but it is still a struggle. Every little movement that I used to take for granted is now a major challenge as I am, apparently, in the process of retraining my brain. Firstly, I have to think of the move I want to make, then I have to visualise it and upload all this information into the right part of my brain, press the metaphorical Send button and hope the message gets from my brain to my limb. It is exhausting and so far not altogether successful as some bits of me work better than others. My right arm and leg are still quite strong and work fairly easily but the left side is considerably weaker, the leg more so than the arm. My vision has returned, after some initial concern, and my hearing is fine; but I just can't get words to sound like anything recognisable yet. I am told it will improve, with work, and how much is up to me and my willpower. I have daily sessions with a speech therapist and she thinks I'm making progress, although I'm not sure anyone else would agree.

The brain scan I had when I returned to my vehicle showed only a tiny residue of what was once a large tumour. Of course, at first the doctors said I must have been misdiagnosed but Tara wasn't going to let them get away with that. She made them review my records and all the previous scans I have had; there it was as large as, well, life. Now they can't deny it had existed.

The surgeon next to my bed now has scratched his head and has ended up saying that the bleed I suffered at Hamleys must have ruptured the tumour and when he made the hole in my skull to release the blood part of the tumour must have come out as well. Yeah, right, as if we believe that. I know the truth of why it has shrunk, as Freizal said it would. Tara is sitting beside me and seething so I squeeze her hand and give her the best smile I can. The tension leaves her as we both realise that we'll never get them to believe in miracles.

> She laughs as James fidgets nervously and clumsily tries to brush his hair while they wait for Jamie and Angel to arrive. He is only making it worse so she takes the brush and does it for him, and it's as if she sees her younger brother again from all those years ago for a moment. But this time he is not dead and she has contributed to saving him.
>
> She looks down at him and smiles, so happy that he is alive. And even though he has a long way to go to get back to near normal, they will do it together. She knows he'll get there in the end.
>
> As for the future, they will go into it hand in hand; and now, hopefully, they are both much closer to being karma neutral.

I am waiting impatiently for a very important visitor. Now that I don't have lots of tubes sticking out of me, Jamie has been given permission to come and see me. I missed Christmas of course but Tara made sure he got the gift I had chosen for him; I wonder if he liked it but I can't ask him so I have to hope he'll tell me anyway. Although I'm thrilled he is coming, I am also worried in case he finds me a bit scary: all the muscles on the left side of my face have weakened, giving me a lopsided look and a droopy eye. I do my facial exercises three times a day and they are helping but I still look different to when he saw me last. At least I don't dribble too much anymore and I can make a half-decent smile which hopefully will be good enough for him.

Another look at the clock. Where are they? I know it's a long way from Wales but still… and I can almost hear Freizal whisper that patience is a virtue and I'm sure I hear the faint sound of laughter. I do get an enormous amount of comfort from knowing she is nearby and that I can call on her any time for moral support and the occasional kick up the backside when I need it.

I also know that she will never let me down, which I can't say about everyone, particularly my family. Well, maybe that's a little unfair because I'm only referring to one member of my family. As Mam can't drive and Terry has lost his licence, Mam asked Trish to drive her up to see me in hospital but Trish refused, saying she had 'a pressing appointment' – more pressing, apparently, than taking her mother to visit her dying son. Unbelievable? In the end Terry paid a friend to drive them here to see me and Tara gave them the keys to my flat so they could stay for a few days until they knew for sure if I was going to live or die. I've been told that I was on the brink for three days, though it only seemed like moments to me. It just goes to show how different time is in the spirit worlds to here; perhaps that's why when a guide says that something will happen it could be years before it comes to pass. Tara is often frustrated by this so when I can talk properly I shall have to tell her all about my near-death experience.

I look at the clock again and just then the door flies open and in comes Tara with Jamie in tow behind. He looks at me somewhat nervously from behind her legs and I guess he's been warned that I don't look quite the same as last time, so I try out my modified smile and hope for the best. He looks at me with those big blue eyes and slowly a smile spreads across his face and he comes out from behind Tara and runs to me. When I hold out my good hand he doesn't hesitate in taking it and jumps up to sit beside me on the bed. The love I feel for him almost overwhelms me.

I try to say, "I love you," but it comes out more like, "I wu boo." Instead of being scared, he actually seems to understand me.

"I love you too, Daddy," he says and I can feel a tear running down my face. It annoys me because I don't want to cry, I am incredibly happy, so to deflect his attention I try to speak again.

"Persnt?" I say and again somehow he gets it.

"I love it, it's cool. I have it in my room and I look at it every night. Thank you, Daddy."

"Gud," I manage to say and it doesn't sound too mangled. He leans back to rest against me and this is blissful; there's no need to talk as we seem to understand each other perfectly well anyway. Tara had left us alone for a while but soon comes back with drinks and biscuits. He smiles at her and takes a chocolate one and I see the relief on her face.

"Well, Jamie," she says, "tell us about your Christmas." I sit back to listen to everything. His face lights up as he talks, telling us that the people in the community don't approve of buying presents as such and only exchange small handmade gifts. Once I'd have laughed at such a notion but not anymore; maybe they have the right idea. If I have learned anything from my recent experience it's that material possessions don't count for much. My only thoughts had been of Jamie and Tara and the love I have for them.

He goes on to tell us about the wonderful Christmas dinner they had all shared and how he had helped to make the pudding way back in October. His face shines with pleasure and I feel happy and sad at the same time. I wish I still had his innocence and his joy in simple things, and I so hope he doesn't lose this gift too early like I did. Life doesn't have to be a struggle but we often make it one, so I have decided to simplify my life as much as possible. And when I can talk again I am going to ask Tara to marry me – as soon as I'm able to walk her down the aisle.

As I happily watch Jamie, I begin to notice a faint golden light around him. I frown and squint and it is still there. It's his aura. This is so ironic because I have been desperately hoping to see auras for months and, now that I can, I can't tell anyone. As I watch, it becomes even brighter and more magnificent around my wonderful son but all too soon Angela and Ryan arrive to take Jamie away.

"Jamie will be in to see you again tomorrow," Angela says. I frown in surprise and look at Tara, who laughs at me.

"I knew you weren't listening before. I did ask you if it was all right for them to stay at your apartment for a few days."

"Thas gurt," I smile.

"We'll look after it, I promise," says Angela with a grin, and she kisses me on the cheek. That is such a shock that even if I could speak I'd have been speechless.

Thirty-Six

I lie back and do some thinking. Now that I have a second chance at life, what am I going to do with it? My enforced silence, however frustrating, has given me the chance to do some planning, to go inside myself and gain strength and solace. I have decided to knuckle down and concentrate on my healing gifts and spiritual development. It is wonderful to be able to have daily conversations with Freizal although these have, I think, caused my nurses some concern because I appear to be staring into nothing for prolonged periods; but this is how I have been sorting out who I want to be.

It will be very different to James Wylie, stockbroker. It hasn't been a particularly pleasant task to trawl through my past, seeing where I deviated from my path and understanding how I got to where I am now. Even one year ago I could not have conceived of the change that has taken place in me and in all areas of my life. I look back at that other life and I am amazed at how poor it was. Oh, I had a lot of money but not a lot else; and even though I still have a lot of challenges ahead, I would never go back to that life for all the money in the world.

I have been working with Freizal on my past lives and learning about the karma I have brought through with me; this is both fascinating and a little scary. Over the centuries, it seems, my father and I have incarnated many times together as part of the same soul group and we have a lot of karma to clear between us. I have been able to start trying to forgive him and I'm still working on it, not just for him but for myself as well. Sometimes it is easier to forgive someone else than it is to forgive oneself and I still have some way to go on both counts. I have come to realise that being forced to stop and look at oneself with no distractions is a great gift.

Freizal has told me a saying about that. I can't remember it exactly but it goes something like, 'The past is gone, the future hasn't come, but now is the present.' I confess that I didn't understand her point at first until she told me to concentrate on the word 'present' and asked me what it means to me. I thought for a while and suddenly it hit me.

"A gift!"

"Yes, the present moment is a gift. Every new minute is the present and is the gift that the Creator has given to everyone. But so few people recognise it – moaning and wailing with regrets and anxieties instead of just enjoying their special gift."

So I am going to enjoy every moment and give thanks for it. I also know that I have been given another kind of gift, that of healing, and as with any ability I must work at improving it. Since I have been with Tara I have met quite a few so-called 'enlightened' people who seem to believe that they don't have to do anything to develop their skills – it just happens like magic. If only! We have all been given some kind of gift, I think, but we still have to put some effort in.

Life is now progressing at a much slower pace for me than before, but every day I push myself to get stronger. Having money does help, of course, and I have employed a private speech therapist who comes five days a week. Katrina also comes twice a week to give me reflexology treatment and Tara gives me healing every day as well as encouraging – or should that be bullying? – me with the exercises that the physiotherapist has prescribed. I know that my body is recovering faster with all of this and I am regaining control over my limbs much better than my doctors anticipated. With a bit of willpower, I believe I shall make a full recovery.

After six weeks in hospital I am being discharged since they can't do any more for me; but as my apartment is up a flight of stairs which is well beyond my present capabilities I am moving into Tara's place which is on the ground floor. The hospital has provided a walking frame and crutches so I can practise at home and a private physiotherapist will also come regularly. I can't say that I'll miss the hospital; it has a nervous energy that makes it very hard for me to relax. Now I find myself waiting as patiently as I can for my doctor to give me the all-clear so that I can leave. Finally the door opens and he appears.

"So, James, are you ready to leave us?" he asks.

"I am," I reply quite intelligibly, which pleases me greatly.

"Well, I have reviewed your latest charts," he continues, "and although there is still a long way to go I see that you have all your therapists lined up to continue your treatment." I watch him sign the paper and I let out a silent cheer to be on my way out of here; it feels like a great weight has been lifted off my shoulders. Once I'm at Tara's place, I know I'll get better much faster. She arrives fifteen minutes later with some clothes for me and a question.

"Are you finally getting out of here, James?"

"You trib add stob me," I reply. She can more or less understand me now.

"Good, then let's get you dressed." I let her help me into my clothes. It's hard being so dependent but I am beginning to accept help with at least a little grace and gratitude, instead of the old resentment and anger. It's another lesson on the learning curve of life.

I don't know what the future has in store for me but I know it will be a lot better than my past, now that I have love and a wonderful son – and maybe one day a child with Tara too? There is my spiritual development and healing to work on and there's enough money in the bank not to have to worry. I smile happily as Tara guides my arm into the shirt.

"What was that smile for, James?"

"Am sho appy. Lyf's gud."

She brightens and gives me one of her hundred-watt smiles that warms me to the core as she kisses my forehead.

"Yes, my love, it is. And now we have a future together, it can only get better."

She helps me to my feet, gives me the walking frame and together we make our way slowly out of the hospital. I take a deep breath of the beautiful fresh air as I make a new start in life. I'll let you know how it turns out.

If you have enjoyed this book...

Local Legend is committed to publishing the very best spiritual writing, both fiction and non-fiction. You might also enjoy:

DAY TRIPS TO HEAVEN

T J Hobbs (ISBN 978-1-907203-99-2)

The author's debut novel is a brilliant description of life in the spiritual worlds and of the guidance available to all of us on Earth as we struggle to be the best we can. Ethan is learning to be a guide but having a hard time of it, with too many questions and too much self-doubt. But he has potential, so is given a special dispensation to bring a few deserving souls for a preview of the afterlife, to help them with crucial decisions they have to make in their lives. The book is full of gentle humour, compassion and spiritual knowledge, and it asks important questions of us all.

A UNIVERSAL GUIDE TO HAPPINESS

Joanne Gregory (ISBN 978-1-910027-06-6)

Joanne is an internationally acclaimed clairaudient medium with a celebrity contact list. Growing up, she ignored her evident psychic abilities, fearful of standing out from others, and even later, despite witnessing miracles daily, her life was difficult. But then she began to learn the difference between the psychic and the spiritual, and her life turned round.

This is her spiritual reference handbook – a guide to living happily and successfully in harmony with the energy that created our universe. It is the knowledge and wisdom distilled from a lifetime's experience of working with spirit.

THE QUIRKY MEDIUM

Alison Wynne-Ryder (ISBN 978-1-907203-47-3)

Alison is the co-host of the TV show *Rescue Mediums*, in which she puts herself in real danger to free homes of lost and often malicious spirits. Yet she is a most reluctant medium, afraid of ghosts! This is her amazing and often very funny autobiography, taking us 'back stage' of the television production as well as describing how she came to discover the psychic gifts that have brought her an international following.

Winner of the Silver Medal in the national Wishing Shelf Book Awards.

SIMPLY SPIRITUAL

Jacqui Rogers (ISBN 978-1-907203-75-6)

The 'spookies' started contacting Jacqui when she was a child and never gave up until, at last, she developed her psychic talents and became the successful international medium she is now. This is a powerful and moving account of her difficult life and her triumph over adversity, with many great stories of her spiritual readings. The book was a Finalist in The People's Book Prize national awards.

AURA CHILD

A I Kaymen (ISBN 978-1-907203-71-8)

One of the most astonishing books ever written, telling the true story of a genuine Indigo child. Genevieve grew up in a normal London family but from an early age realised that she had very special spiritual and psychic gifts. She saw the energy fields around living things, read people's thoughts and even found herself slipping through time, able to converse with the spirits of those who had lived in her neighbourhood. This is an uplifting and inspiring book for what it tells us about the nature of our minds.

A SINGLE PETAL

Oliver Eade (ISBN 978-1-907203-42-8)

Winner of the national Local Legend Spiritual Writing Competition, this page-turner is a novel of murder, politics and passion set in ancient China. Yet its themes of loyalty, commitment and deep personal love are every bit as relevant for us today as they were in past times. The author is an expert on Chinese culture and history, and his debut adult novel deserves to become a classic.

5P1R1T R3V3L4T10N5

Nigel Peace (ISBN 978-1-907203-14-5)

With descriptions of more than a hundred proven prophetic dreams and many more everyday synchronicities, the author shows us that, without doubt, we can know the future and that everyone can receive genuine spiritual guidance for our lives' challenges. World-renowned biologist Dr Rupert Sheldrake has endorsed this book as "...vivid and fascinating... pioneering research..." and it was national runner-up in The People's Book Prize awards.

RAINBOW CHILD

S L Coyne (ISBN 978-1-907203-92-3)

Beautifully written in language that is alternately lyrical and childlike, this is the story of young Rebekah and the people she discovers as her family settles in a new town far from their familiar home. As dark family secrets begin to unravel, her life takes many turns both delightful and terrifying as the story builds to a tragic and breathless climax that just keeps on going. This book shows us how we look at others who are 'different'. Through the eyes of Rebekah, writing equally with passion and humour, we see the truth of human nature...

CELESTIAL AMBULANCE

Ann Matkins (ISBN 978-1-907203-45-9)

A brave and delightful comedy novel. Having died of cancer, Ben wakes up in the afterlife looking forward to a good rest, only to find that everyone is expected to get a job! He becomes the driver of an ambulance (with a mind of her own), rescuing the spirits of others who have died suddenly and delivering them safely home. This book is as thought-provoking as it is entertaining.

TAP ONCE FOR YES

Jacquie Parton (ISBN 978-1-907203-62-6)

This extraordinary book offers powerful evidence of human survival after death. When Jacquie's son Andrew suddenly committed suicide, she was devastated. But she was determined to find out whether his spirit lived on, and began to receive incredible yet undeniable messages from him … Several others also then described deliberate attempts at spirit contact. This is a story of astonishing love and courage, as Jacquie fought her own grief and others' doubts in order to prove to the world that her son still lives.

These titles are all available as paperbacks and eBooks.
Further details and extracts of these and many
other beautiful books may be seen at
www.local-legend.co.uk

www.ingramcontent.com/pod-product-compliance
Lightning Source LLC
Chambersburg PA
CBHW071130200626
46817CB00018B/2641